E I

No.

MW00944336

Elysium

Cover Art by K.M. Smith
twitter.com/medinaquirin

For Adrian, who was there when the nightmares started

ONE

"Evey, the backyard is on fire."

I look up from where I'm straddling the tub and find Casper perched on my bathroom sink. She doesn't look at all apologetic for sneaking up on me but stares back expectantly until I finally say, "It does that sometimes."

"Your wolves are upset," Casper says, like they've ever been anything but. "They've been pacing by your door for an hour now."

"Bull," I say, not because I doubt my angry welcome party but because I haven't been in here that long. Casper lost sense of time when she died, though, and each passing day pulls the concept of it further away from her. She still tries because she's new enough to being dead that "forever" is terrifying, but the fight will go out of her eventually. I'm hoping she moves out of Elysium before that bubble bursts. "Tell them to get lost."

She sends me a withering look. "You know they can't see me."

"They'll feel it if you stick your fingers in their spines. Can I shower now?"

She leans forward and splays a pale hand against my dark skin. "Can you?"

"In private, in case I had to clarify that part."

"Prude," she says, but slides off the edge of the sink. "Fine, I'll go watch Alexandra sleep."

"She's not sleeping," I point out, but Casper's already slipping through the wall to the next bedroom over.

I give her up as a lost cause and cut the water on, but my thoughts stick with her warning. Of course the backyard is on fire. It's burned every February 3rd since my arrival.

My arrival. The words are venom, eating through my throat and burning my tongue, but it's an old poison I know well. There's a fifth of Jack in the medicine cabinet where mouthwash should be, and I bring it into the shower with me.

Elysium's rooms are all soundproof—a blessing, considering what some of my tenants eat—so no one else can hear my off-key rendition of "Happy Birthday". I take a swig of Jack after each line, one-part toast and

1

one-part an attempt to fill the gaping hole in my chest. For a moment I'm tempted to call tonight off and get sloshed in private, but the thought of spending the night in this hellhole when I could be anywhere else makes me ill. I take one last swallow for luck and put the bottle back where it belongs on my way to getting dressed.

Most nights I just show up for work in jeans and whichever shirt looks cleanest, but today I make a marginal effort to look decent. It's too cold out for a skirt cut this short, but I look good in it and I need that emotional boost today. I slather lotion on my legs as far as I can reach, rub the excess into my arms, and collect a pair of sandals from the closet on the way out.

Casper wasn't lying; Marilyn and Hogan are waiting for me in the hallway. If they were wolfed out I imagine their fur would be all out of sorts, but somehow they manage to convey that same furious anxiety in human form. I barely spare them a look on my way to the stairwell, so Marilyn launches away from the wall to stand in my way.

"The yard is burning," she says.

I try to remember that she wasn't here last year, but that doesn't keep the *Duh* tone from creeping into my, "Well, yeah." She stares at me like she's expecting more, like perhaps a real explanation, but I'm not in the mood. I motion for her to get out of my way. I know from experience that I can't move her. For someone so tiny she weighs a metric ton. Consequence of carrying two bodies around at all times, perhaps. "The neighbors can't see it and it's not going to burn the house down. Just leave it alone. It'll be gone by midnight."

"You're supposed—"

"—to be at work in fifteen minutes," I cut her off. "I'll tell Falkor and Smerg to keep an eye on it. Happy?"

She bares her teeth at me. Nerves have taken the human shape out of her jaw. My stomach flops a little at how alien her mouth looks, but I've been at Elysium too long to show fear. My position as Elysium's linchpin and landlady means no one under this roof is allowed to hurt me, but there's no rule against making my life a living hell. The trick to surviving as the only human in a preternatural asylum is to pretend at all times that I'm the bigger monster, and I've had years to perfect the act. I raise my hand, slow and easy, and point down at the floor.

"Heel."

It takes everything in me to not flinch when she snaps at my throat. Luckily I'm distracted by Hogan's fierce, "*Sarah.*" It's been months since I heard Marilyn's real name; I slap a nickname on all of my tenants the day they arrive and refuse to acknowledge that they were anyone else. It's a

2

habit carried over from childhood, this obsession with renaming the people in my life. My mother said it was my way of establishing control in situations. These days it's more a petty way of keeping my oft-monstrous tenants at arm's reach. Not even Casper the ghost is immune.

Marilyn, named after Marilyn Monroe due to her classy looks, shoots Hogan a fierce look. She'll understand later why he's siding against her, but right now she's as angry at him as she is at me. I couldn't care less, because a two against one vote means she steps out of my way without further argument. I leave them to deal with each other and head downstairs to call a cab. Normally I'd bike there, but I learned the hard way that miniskirts and bicycles don't mix.

Jinx is a bit of a dive, a street or two down from the heart of Augusta, Georgia, but it's as much my home as Elysium is. It's not the first bar I stumbled into when I was trying to adjust to my husband's violent betrayal, but it was the first one that didn't think to card me.

I spent the better part of a year crying on a corner bar stool before Dallas said I could pay off my sky-high tab by covering a couple shifts. In the kitchen, he was quick to amend when he found out how young I was. It's not the kind of career I thought I'd fall into, but tending to Elysium's monsters isn't something I would have ever wanted, either.

There's a sign taped up on the front door when I make it there, well-worn from years of use: "We will be closed for repairs on February 3rd." I don't know if Dallas gives me this day out of kindness or if he's just glad to get one guaranteed night off from work each year. Frankly, I don't care.

I let myself in and find a placard waiting against the wall inside. "Closed – Please come back tomorrow" it says, and I arrange it on the sidewalk right outside the door. I don't bother to lock the door behind me, though, and instead go to set up the bar.

It'll be a low-key night, since only our oldest regulars know that we're not completely closed tonight and less than half of them will think tonight's everything's-a-quarter sale is worth intruding on my private pity party. I gather a till from the back office, crack open a roll of quarters, and stuff a handful of coins into the jukebox in the corner.

I know the number for *Sunday Morning* from memory, and I punch it in until the machine finally tells me I'm out of change. Like always, the first notes are poignant enough to cut my chest open, and I stand at the jukebox for a moment as a violin and piano sing a sad duet to the empty bar. Why I wanted such a mournful tune to be my wedding song, I still don't know. Maybe past-me knew what was coming and was trying to send me a warning.

3

Such thoughts are enough to drive me back behind the counter, and I fill a Collins glass with whiskey from the well. A couple gulps are enough to quench the fire in my soul and I set to work prepping the rest of the bar. It doesn't take long, and I'm nearly done when Officers Rodriguez and Miles bring the winter chill in with them.

Miles props the door open with a shoe so he can rearrange the placard out front, but Rodriguez doesn't wait on his partner. He winds his way around empty tables to the bar and trades me a quarter for a shot. I've had just enough to drink that smiling comes easy, and I carry his quarter to the jukebox. Rodriguez is ready to make the same trade by the time I get back, and he adds an extra quarter so I can drink with them.

We raise a silent toast to my daughter and knock our shots back as one. They trade me quarter rolls as advances on the rest of their drinks, and I pass a bottle over in response. They take their glasses and booze to one of the small tables in the corner, and I carry my monetary prize straight to the jukebox. A26, I type in, over and over until my fingertip hurts. *Sunday Morning, Sunday Morning, Sunday Morning.*

It's been years since any of our regulars asked how I lost Ciara. According to Betty the popular theory is a car accident, since I've admitted to losing my newborn daughter and my husband on the same day. She shared the gossip hoping I'd correct her, but Adam's betrayal, Ciara's death, and my subsequent unholy union with Georgia's ley line are tragedies I still can't talk about. My customers don't believe in magic, after all, and Betty, despite being my only likable tenant, views mortal pain as a source of fleeting entertainment. It's kind of a pity she's got that ruthless streak in her. Of everyone who's come and gone in my life I think she's in the best position to understand how much I hate Elysium.

I use "Elysium" to refer to the house I rule, but the name is taken from the scraps of Augusta's jumpgate. Earth is striped with ley lines that preternatural Society and magical humans can tap into, and wherever the power is strong enough to leak from the ground one can find a gate. A jumpgate is pretty much what it sounds like: a portal connecting A to B around the world. Society uses them to bypass the increasing scrutiny of an oblivious mundane world. It's a pretty limited system, since there are only forty-nine registered gates and Elysium barely counts anymore, but so long as Society submits to GLOBE's secrecy rules it's the best thing they've got to work with.

The only ones forbidden to access the gates are vampires, consequence of an ancient grudge between them and the gatekeepers. Rumor has it they got into an all-out war over the ley lines twenty years

4

ago, but the details are a little bit muddled. Mom said nothing about it while I was growing up and I knew better than to bring it up with the one man who could've explained it to me.

Quite honestly, I couldn't give a rat's ass what it was about. What's more interesting to me is the outcome: the vampires lost, the gatekeepers retained control, and Elysium granted Betty asylum anyway. It shouldn't have, but it carved a room out for her right beside mine before I'd even realized what she was. The gatekeepers spent a week contesting it, but Elysium refused to sacrifice her. It's the only time they've ever lost a challenge. Now they can't even enter any room she's in, which is pretty much the reason I started liking her in the first place. Only downside of the arrangement is now she's as stuck as I am. The gatekeepers are waiting her out, intent on killing her as soon as Elysium rescinds its protection.

I'm jerked from the dark spiral of my thoughts when the bell above the door jingles. I'm not surprised to see another pair of cops coming inside. Most of our regulars are firefighters and policemen, thanks to the discounts Dallas likes to spoil them with. His father was a highway patrolman, so when Dallas finally got this bar up and running he made sure to win over the local law enforcement as quickly as he could. Smart move for a black man in the South, but it took years before I felt comfortable around them. House rules say my monsters can't hurt me, but humans aren't bound by Society laws.

Jinx only gets another six customers before sundown, and I know when it's full dark out because Betty finally breezes through the front door. Betty—actual name Alexandra and the current object of Casper's incorporeal desires—is wearing even less than I am tonight, and I don't miss the way every gaze tracks her endless legs across the room. I consider pointing out that it's forty degrees outside, but Betty doesn't care about petty things like the cold. She's been undead for a couple centuries. "Warmth" is just a word now, too long forgotten to even be a memory.

She shoos me out from behind the counter with long fingers and longer nails and takes in my outfit with a hooded gaze. "You've gained weight. You should probably invest in a bigger skirt."

"You should probably invest in a cup of *No one asked you*," I shoot back. Her slow smirk says she's unimpressed by my comeback, so I give her a good look at both middle fingers. "Casper says you look fabulous tonight, by the way. She also says you snore."

That's enough to take the smile off her face. How the undead can be so prejudiced against the actual dead, I don't know, but it's nice knowing even vampires can get the creeps. "How many times must I tell you to keep your ghost out of my room?"

"She's not my ghost," I remind Betty. "She goes where she wants."

"She goes where you are," Betty returns, "same as they all do."

Which is kind of true, so all I do is shrug at her. I didn't inherit any of Mom's powers except the ability to see the dead. That wasn't enough to garner a second look back in Orlando, but here in Augusta I'm one of maybe three true psychics and I'm the only one bound to a ley line. Casper says I blink like a vacancy sign, which explains why every ghost along the Savannah River has stopped by to see me at some point over the last sixteen years. She also says the broken gate is a screaming void against her nonexistent nerves. I assume that's why she's the only ghost who's ever stuck around to keep me company. Casper's as curious about Elysium as she is scared of it, and she doesn't want to leave until she figures out what's causing that pull.

Betty waves me off again, so I leave the argument unfinished and carry a bottle to the other side of the counter. Betty can handle our meager crowd tonight without any help from me, so I'm free to drown my sorrows on the stool I once considered carving my name into.

I've only just gotten settled when Jude Pantini shows up, predictable as always. If Betty sees the look I send her, she doesn't deign to acknowledge it. She greets Jude with the slow smile all of our customers have tried to tip out of her and has a drink waiting for him by the time he gets comfortable three stools down from me. Root beer, I know, because Jude only comes to Jinx these days so he can flirt with Betty. She's been surprisingly good with him since finding out he was attending the local AA meetings, never once coaxing him over the edge or sneaking anything into his soda.

I want to ask her if she actually cares, but it's probably better not to know. All that matters is that she keeps her hands off his wrists. Horror stories still ascribe to vampires chomping on one's neck, but apparently wrists are the way to go these days. Betty says it's easier to pass the death off as suicide that way, not that anyone around here would believe Jude capable of killing himself. The sheriff's son is a devout Baptist with more friends than anyone could know what to do with. I'm hoping Betty will remember this when temptation inevitably strikes.

I watch their fingers meet on passed glasses, study the way Betty almost looks alive and interested as she leans in to murmur at Jude's ear, and for a few moments I hate them both for looking so happy. I chug the rest of my drink in a vain attempt to sear away the pain in my chest and feel my stomach roil in response.

6

I try to remember the last time I ate. I've gotten used to Dallas sliding me a plate while I'm on shift, but our kitchen is closed tonight. I know the fridge is stocked, though, so I launch off my stool and half-stumble toward the back door. It swings open when I knock my shoulder into it and I treat the contents of the fridge to a long and serious look. My need for grilled cheese wars with my desire to not have to clean the griddle. There's a fifty-fifty chance I can bribe Betty into cleaning up behind me, so I reach for the butter.

I've just touched it when there's a thump I feel more than hear, and I only have a second to be startled. The heat right on its heels is fierce enough to boil my blood and melt my skin from my bones, and I can't even hear myself screaming over the static hissing in my ears.

I'm an overripe fruit bursting from too much pressure. My life sloshes away from me faster than I can stop it. A thousand miles beneath the pain is the slap of my hands against the ground, the vicious bite of sharp fingernails into my arms, and a woman's voice trying to pull me back from the edge. But Betty's magic has never worked on me, and there's nothing I can do but ride this wave to my own agonizing death.

As quickly as it came, it's gone, leaving the memory like a bruise on every inch of my skin. I gasp for breath, choke on the first one I manage, and try to twist onto my side as I cough. Betty lets go of me so I can move, and I flop uselessly onto my stomach. There's heat on my cheeks, and I drag a shaking hand through it. I expect to find blood on my fingers, but that slick moisture is all tears. I manage a rattling breath and clench my hands into bloodless fists.

"Evelyn," Betty says, enunciating each syllable like they're individual words. "Are you here with us?"

The "us" is deliberate, but it's hard for me to look past her. Our customers followed Betty through the swinging door to help any way they could, and now they're a white-faced and wide-eyed crowd around us. Betty is crouched near my hip, expression tight and lips pulled to a hard line, and she doesn't follow my watery gaze. She waits until I look back at her, and she only nods at whatever she sees on my face. Now she looks up, and she stares at each of our customers in turn.

"Thank you, but it's nothing," she says, and although her power can't touch me I can still hear it in the strong tones of her voice. "I'll be out in a moment to get everyone some free refills."

They go without question, the way sheep don't question a wolf, and I know if Betty tells them to forget this they won't even remember my meltdown. Betty waits until the door swings closed behind the last of them, then takes my arm and helps sit me up. I slump back against the counter and stare at her. The chill at my back is only partially from the memory of that torrential pain. I close the fridge and let my hand flop to the ground at my side.

"Elysium," I say. "Something's wrong with Elysium. I have to—"

I make a valiant attempt to get up, but my legs aren't cooperating. Betty rises soundlessly to her feet and hauls me upright. The kitchen gives a sickening swirl around me and I feel the night's drinks leap from my stomach to my throat. I swallow hard twice and squeeze her shoulder in warning. Betty's worked here long enough to understand what's wrong, and she unsubtly leans out of my path.

I wait until the waves have subsided before nodding. The kitchen door bangs off my hip as she leads me to the front. *Sunday Morning* is still crooning through the speakers, but I can barely make it out through the buzzing in my ears.

"Darling," she says. For a foolish moment I think she's mocking me, but a few seconds later Jude is beside us. He slides an arm around my shoulders and takes my weight from Betty. "She's had a bit much to drink and didn't bring her bike with her. You'll give her a lift home, won't you?"

"Of course," he says in a tone that says he'd bring her the moon if she asked in that voice.

Jude helps me across the room and out into a chilly night. He came here straight from work, so his patrol car is parked only a couple spaces down from the door. I slump in the passenger seat and stare out the window while he drives me back to Elysium.

It's not the first time I've bummed a ride from a cop, or Jude in particular, but he skips the small talk tonight. It doesn't occur to him to ask about the screaming, since Betty already said it was nothing, and he doesn't want to press me into unwanted conversation on my anniversary. I'm grateful for the silence, because I ache too much to be good company.

My house is a short ride up the road, two miles southwest and a couple right turns from Jinx's spot against the Savannah River. Jude's dropped me off often enough that he knows how to get there, and even though he knows I'll turn him down again he offers to walk me to the door.

I know he's going to wait for me to get inside before he leaves, so I dig out my keys on the walk to the porch and ignore my so-called guardians where they're perched on pedestals to either side of the front door. Jude can't see them since he doesn't have a lick of magic in him, but it's generally best to not draw police attention to unexplainable things.

I get the lock on the third try and feel the familiar tremble of

8

Elysium's magic over my skin as I step into the doorway. I turn there to wave at Jude. He waves back and pulls away from the curb. He's barely out of sight before the translucent dragons assigned to protect the house start hissing and spitting their displeasure. They're not really dragons, more like draconian faeries, but the misnomer makes them feel important. It helps that I told them Falkor and Smerg were terrifying beasts of legends.

"What happened?" I ask.

Falkor ignores my quiet demand. "Who was it, who was it she lets into our yard?"

"You've seen the police before," I say, "and he didn't come into the yard. He didn't even get out of the car." I press careful hands to the door frame to either side of me and close my eyes. Elysium's magic is a balm against that lingering bone-deep ache. I was wrong. Whatever happened tonight is connected to the lines, but not to mine except by proxy. I suck in a slow breath to steady my nerves and try again. "What happened to the ley lines?"

Smerg is busy gnawing at a perpetual itch on his shoulder, so Falkor answers. "Chronos falls, falls, falls. Begins again, or never ends? How boring, yes, how boring. We thought they might sleep forever."

"Wait," I say, over the stutter of my heart against my ribs. Chronos is the jumpgate outside of Salt Lake City and the sixth largest in the continental US. I know Falkor can only mean one thing, but disbelief drives me to demand, "What do you mean Chronos falls?"

They toss their heads, jaws gaped in silent laughter. How these two could find it funny is beyond me, but they're not exactly living here by choice, either. The faeries might not be real dragons, but they're just as possessive as the beasts they resemble. I was a gift from the gatekeepers, which makes me the gold in their treasure hoard. So long as I'm the most valuable thing they own, Falkor and Smerg will guard Elysium to their deaths. My being stuck here means they're stuck here as well, and they hate me as much as they love me.

"How did we lose another gate?" I demand.

"We, we, we," Smerg echoes. "She forgets, she forgets she is human."

"But she is precious to us," Falkor chimes in, "so we will keep her."

"Forever and ever," Smerg agrees.

"Ever and ever and ever," Falkor says, and they toss their heads in silent laughter again.

They're done being useful, so I go inside and slam the door behind me. All of the lights are off downstairs, but it takes no time at all for the wood sprites to show up. They're a stream of glowing glitter flying down the floorboards toward me, and they clump around my shoes in a silent but fluttery greeting. They've been part of the house as long as I have, and their inability to speak makes them the most tolerable creatures under my roof.

They wait with me while I stand at the front door to thaw. Elysium's heating system is spectacular, so it only takes me a minute to forget about the chill outside. In another hour or two it'll be just this side of too warm to be comfortable, but for now it feels great. I cluck a warning when I'm ready to go, and the sprites precede me to the stairs in dizzying swirls.

Casper meets me at my bedroom door, arms folded across her chest.

"Betty says go to hell," I tell her in lieu of hello.

"Vicereine Alexandra," Casper corrects me, a little dreamily.

I frown at her. "How do you know she has a title?"

Casper's look is pitying. "It's how she answers her phone. What's the point of being a ghost if you can't spy on people? Rude," she says, sliding through the door I just tried to close between us. "The yard is still on fire, if you were wondering."

"I wasn't wondering."

I kick my shoes off to one side and wriggle out of my skirt. Betty was right; the blasted thing is almost too tight to get over my hips. I think I lose a couple of layers of skin in the process, so maybe that will help the next time I want to wear it. I expect Casper to make a smart comment about me getting undressed in front of her, but when I glance her way she's crouched by the door, watching the wood sprites dance in the grain. I take advantage of her distraction to shed my shirt as well. My fingers skim the jagged scars across my abdomen and I snatch up my nightgown as quickly as I can.

"Who was he?" she asks, apropos of nothing.

I wait until I'm dressed to ask, "Who was who? The policeman?"

"The boy in the cellar," she says.

I've met a lot of ghosts in my life, and while they all get a little odd the longer they cling to the mortal realm, I've never actually seen one go mad. Maybe that's where poltergeist legends come from? I'm not sure; my mother had all of her visiting spirits under control. For one moment I consider calling her for advice, but the reality sinks in a heartbeat later and puts a knot in my throat. I haven't spoken to Mom since I left home. She warned me that leaving with Adam meant goodbye, but I hadn't thought she meant it. I found out the hard way when I called home after his death. Her line was disconnected, and every letter I sent was returned with a *Wrong Address* stamp.

10

"Evey?" Casper asks.

I blink away the heat in my eyes. "There is no cellar."

"Fallout shelter, then," Casper says, with a hint of impatience. "Who was he?"

"Can you lose it another day?" I ask. "I'm really, really not in the mood for this tonight."

She stares at me like she's waiting for me to stop being obnoxious. I stare back, willing her to get the hint and leave me alone. She's the first to crack, and a frown tugs at the corner of her mouth.

"You have no idea what I'm talking about, do you?" she asks, but she doesn't wait for me to confirm it. She jerks a thumb over her shoulder, and she's close enough to the door that her hand goes through the wood. "Elysium had a brownout or something while you were gone, and your living room buzzed like hell while it was going on. I was looking to see if some bees got in and it turns out there's a part of the floor I can go through. You've got a dead boy in your basement. Wanna see?"

"Do I look like the kind of person who likes looking at dead people?"

Casper points at herself. "Ghost, hello."

"Never said I liked looking at you," I say, but after a glance at my bed I start her way.

Sleeping was a hobby of mine until I moved into Elysium. These days sleep feels like dying, like plummeting down an endless hole with nothing around to break my fall. Panic that I'll never make it back out of that abyss is what finally wakes me up, and although my clock always promises time has passed I never feel fully rested.

"I can't believe you're making me look at bones on my anniversary."

"He's not bones," Casper says a little primly. She doesn't move, so I'm forced to walk through her to get out of my room. "He's very well preserved. Like jam."

"You put one more mental image like that in my head and I'm going to ignore you for a week."

"You'll understand when you see him."

"Yeah, that's real encouraging."

I motion for her to take the lead and follow her to the living room. I get the lights while she walks in circles in the middle of the room. I get dizzy on her fifth pass and am about to say something when she drops a few feet with a startled yip. I edge closer, ignoring her smug prattling, and crouch to stare at the floor. It takes some serious squinting but at last I make out a faint outline in the wood. There's definitely a square seam in the floorboards, mostly hidden by the grain of the wood around it, but it's

11

so thin there's no way I can get a grip on the edge. Nothing larger than my fingernails can fit in the crack.

"This isn't a door," I tell Casper. "It wasn't meant to be opened."

"So they just buried him down here, like that story," Casper says. She snaps her fingers silently as she thinks, and it's obvious by the tension in her shoulders that she's more bothered by her failing memory than she is the coffin she stumbled across. She was a high school English teacher when she was still alive, so she's always trying to get me to read things from her syllabus. Her expression clears as she remembers, and she points at me with a grin. "The Cask of Amontillado."

"This is why today's kids have issues," I say. "You make them read creepy stories."

"It's Edgar Allan Poe," she protests.

"Whatever. Look, there's no opening this thing. I'll just—" I forget what I'm saying when a floorboard dips under my fingers. I pause, then press again harder, and it's like pressing a lever. The cellar door groans upward an inch or two. I expect the stench of rot and stale air, but the breeze that washes over my face is cool. "The hell?"

Casper claps a couple times in delight and turns away. She bobs downward out of view, and it takes me a moment to realize she's descending stairs. I'm starting to rethink this whole thing, but I've done just enough work that there's no point in turning back now. I hook my hand under the door and pull, and it pops free of its tight frame at last. I set it off to one side, hope to god my tenants don't wake up and decide to bury me alive, and slide off the ledge. It isn't far down, just enough that I know it'll be awkward climbing back out, but I still manage to jar my ankle a bit on the landing.

Casper is waiting further down the stairs, barely visible in the gloom. I look around for a lightswitch and, finding none, put a hand to the concrete wall as I start toward her. The dim light from the living room only travels so far, and everything beyond that point is lost to inky shadows. I slow down as we cross into darkness, not wanting to trip on the stairs. I can't even see my nose down here.

I put my other hand out for a little bit of extra balance. Wood has given way to stone, and the further down we go the colder it gets until I feel like I'm standing in someone's fridge. My fingers go numb from the icy stone, but I don't dare let go to warm them up. I'm too afraid I won't be able to find the walls again.

"How far down does this go?" I demand, because I swear we have to be three stories underground by now. My voice echoes off the stairwell for

12

a second before it is swallowed up by the shadows. Casper doesn't answer, and I veer between irritation and a flutter of nerves. "Casper, I said—"

My next step lands me on something lumpy and wet that gives out under my weight and bursts between my toes. I yelp, flail backward, and fall hard on my rear on the stairs. I give my foot a couple frantic shakes, trying to dislodge whatever it was I stepped on, and in my head I'm picturing a dead body that somehow reminded Casper of jam. My stomach gives a violent twist and I feel bile lick at the back of my throat. I breathe through clenched teeth in a desperate attempt to avoid throwing up everywhere and hate Casper very much for dragging me into this.

"Oh my god, oh my god, oh my god."

"Evey," Casper says, loud and sharp like she's been saying it for a minute now. "Calm down."

"Why did you let me step on him?" I shriek at her.

"What?" she asks, startled. "No, Evey. That's not—oh, you can't see down here, can you?"

A second later she starts glowing with a pale gray light that is positively painful after being blind for so long. I send a wild look from my foot to the floor as the room comes into view. What I stepped on wasn't a body, but a clump of red *something*. A second later my mind makes the connection, because whatever it really is, it does kind of look like someone spilled raspberry jam here. Jam doesn't have roots, but dark tendrils curl out from the lump and disappear into the stone floor. Whatever it is, there's a lot of it. As I take in the room I count at least twenty piles.

In the center of the room is a table, and on the table is a body. Casper starts toward it as soon as she knows I'm all right. I hoist myself up a few more steps so I can scrub my foot against the rounded edge of one. I'm not quite brave enough to poke my fingers between my toes to dislodge those clinging blobs, so I drag that foot along the ground as I follow after Casper.

The closer I get, the easier it is to forget the strange mess I stepped in, because the air around the table is practically vibrating with energy. It sends prickles up my neck and down my spine and I can feel every hair on my arms standing on end.

The boy on the table is indeed well preserved. I assume he's human, except I didn't think humans came in that shade of gray, like charcoal burned just long enough that it's about to crumble to ash. His hair is a short and jagged mess around his skull, red as fresh blood and rose petals. He's fully dressed, shoes and all. The all-black ensemble only serves to make his skin appear darker. It seems impossible that he could be dead and still look this perfect, frozen environment notwithstanding. He looks like he

13

stretched out maybe an hour ago for a quick nap. But his neck is a block of ice under my fingers, and I can't find a pulse.

"Weird, right?" Casper asks. "You sure you don't remember someone burying him down here?"

"Elysium warns me every time someone stops by the house whether I'm home or not," I say. "I would've known if someone brought him by, which means he's been here longer than I have. I don't know who owned the place before—before I moved in." Casper glances at me, frowning a little at that verbal stumble, but I don't give her time to ask. "I could ask the police if they have records anywhere, but even if we figured out who he was, would it matter?"

Casper's response is very quiet: "Being remembered matters."

A tap against my fingertips kills my rebuttal in my throat. I stare at the boy stretched out between us and my hand where it still rests on his skin. Casper either doesn't notice my distraction or is too caught up in her own personal tragedies to care. A minute drags by in utter silence, and then another, and then that tap comes again.

Not a tap. A heartbeat.

I can barely breathe. "Casper, he's not dead."

That jars her from her misery, and she looks from me to the boy. "What?"

My thoughts go unbidden to the dragons' strange greeting: *We thought they might sleep forever.* Although I know this is crazy to even consider I also know I'm right. It just feels right, in that dark part of me that's never questioned why there are ghosts and monsters in the world. I drag my eyes up from the boy to stare at Casper.

"He's not dead," I say again. "He's sleeping."

TWO

Casper walks slow circles around the table, arms folded over her chest as she considers the sleeping boy. Now and then she passes through me, blurring my vision for a second, but she doesn't seem to notice and I don't care enough to protest her inconsideration. I'm more distracted by the problem before me. This boy that looks human—that can't be human, not with a heart that beats once every two minutes—is oblivious to our intense scrutiny.

"Wake him up," Casper says, for the fourth or fifth time since she started pacing.

"No," I say yet again. "I want to know what he is before we even think about waking him."

"So his name doesn't matter, but that does."

"Remember who you're talking to, Casper." I emphasize her nickname and ignore the face she makes. "I wouldn't use his name even if I knew it. But what he is matters, especially tonight. That brownout you saw was a gate collapsing in the west. I think he had something to do with it. Not him specifically," I say when Casper flicks a sharp look my way, "but someone like him. The dragons said something about how 'they' were sleeping forever. I gather the two things are connected."

"You think someone woke a friend of his," Casper guesses. She gives him a critical once-over. "Sleeping Beauty doesn't look like he could bring a gate down."

"We're not calling him Sleeping Beauty."

"Point: missed," Casper says.

I know that's not what she was getting at, but I don't want to tell her that gates are more fragile than any of us thought. I don't want to tell her I was there when Elysium broke, or that my husband was the one to annihilate it and he didn't look like the sort who could pull it off, either. Instead I focus on the easier problem of giving our unwanted guest a name. Sleeping Beauty is too long to seriously consider, but I know she had another name. Aurora? Briar Rose? I look again to his shock of red hair. Rose, I decide, will have to do for now.

"Wake him up," Casper insists when I am silent too long.

15

"Let me get some answers first."

"Boring," Casper protests, but she follows me back to the stairs.

It's a longer trek up than I'm expecting, and my thighs are burning by the time I hoist myself out of the hole into the living room. Casper scrambles out of the way while I close the trap door behind us. Once it's sealed it's easy to lose track of the seam again. I run a hand along the floor, looking for that crack, fearing for a moment that we've lost our one chance to wake the sleeping boy buried beneath our feet. The lever still works, though, so I leave Rose to his tomb and head into the kitchen.

A few tugs on a beaded string open the blinds covering the back door. The backyard is still burning, if one could call that blackish-red glow a real fire. I'm not so sure myself, since the glass door is still cold under my hands and my rickety fence is still standing, but I'm not willing to go outside and test my theory.

Far as I can tell, the fire's a consequence of what happened sixteen years ago today. I'd say it's Elysium's way of mourning its current status, same as mine is to throw Ciara a birthday party, but I've never figured out how sentient Elysium's magic is. It can choose its tenants and it decided to protect Betty from the gatekeepers, but it's never answered any of my demands.

It's strange timing that Chronos would fall the same day Elysium did. My head calls it coincidence, but my heart just aches. I press my hand to my nightgown, trying to feel my scars through thick cotton. Sixteen years ago tonight the gatekeepers dug their talons into me and turned me inside-out on this floor. I still remember what it felt like; I still remember the slosh of shredding organs and ripped flesh hitting the floor.

Elysium is the only reason I survived. It was puking magic all over Augusta in the wake of Adam's stunt, looking for an anchor to stabilize it, and it followed the gatekeepers to me. For some reason it decided I was strong enough to rebuild around, and there was enough of my blood in the floorboards that it dragged the house in as well. Now the three of us are irrevocably fused together, and none of us are the same.

Elysium the jumpgate can only send, not receive, maybe because its original location was a half-mile southeast of here. Elysium the house is quasi-sentient, and it can choose its own tenants and rearrange itself to accommodate our fluctuating numbers and individual needs. Then there's me, who can't go five miles from Elysium's front porch. It's akin to walking into a brick wall, and any cab I've hired to take me past that point breaks down at the five-mile mark.

"Can you stop it?" Casper asks at my elbow.

16

It takes a moment to realize she means the fire. "It'll stop itself."

I leave the blinds open and head to the fridge. It takes some rummaging to find food that's actually mine. The wolves use up the lion's share of fridge space, since their metabolisms run so much faster than a normal human's. My Wyrn tenant only needs a little bit of room for his tubs of meal worms, and that's only in the winter. In the summer he catches his own food, and I stopped being grossed out when I realized he was clearing most of the screaming cicada from around the house.

Betty grazes on Augusta's unwitting inhabitants, as do the remaining two tenants when they think they can get away with it. The rest of the time they're forced to pick up their meals from Society's version of a food shelter: a farm where humans and livestock are specifically raised to be meals. For years I thought it was just a story. Betty disabused me of that notion when she gave me a list of every such farm in the continental US. The closest one is in Athens, almost two hours west of here.

I still want grilled cheese, but I don't have any bread, so I end up popping a freezer meal in the microwave. As I'm reaching for the keypad to set a cook timer, I notice the glowing numbers of the clock. My microwave thinks it's half-past ten, but it can't be. I know I was home by eight. I twist to stare at the clock over the kitchen doorway. It confirms what the microwave says.

I round on Casper. "How long were we in the basement?"

"In and out," Casper says, but I'm already brushing aside her answer as useless. She's the last person I should ask about the passage of time. I look at the clocks again, waiting for this to start making sense. Casper follows my gaze from one to the other as she tries to figure out what's wrong. The numbers I'm staring at mean nothing to her, though.

"Have you ever heard of ley lines warping time?" I ask her.

"You're really asking me that?" Casper asks, a little pityingly. "I used to think Ouija was the end-all be-all of supernatural things."

"It doesn't make sense," I say. I leave my dinner in the microwave as I head for the door. "Come on. I'm going back down there to test this and I need you to come with me. I don't know where my flashlight is, so you're the next best thing."

"Nice to feel useful."

I ignore her sarcasm in favor of hunting down the near-invisible trapdoor in my living room. It doesn't matter that I was crouched beside it just a few minutes ago; finding it again is harder than it should be. I'm about to send Casper on laps until she falls through the floor when the doorbell rings. I hesitate, warring with my need for answers, then launch to

17

my feet and walk through Casper on my way to the front hall.

"Find it!" I throw over my shoulder.

"Please?" Casper singsongs after me.

I ignore her in favor of greeting my guest. Elysium can detect preternatural power in those who show up on my doorstep, and it relays that recognition with a two-tone chord that's jarringly different from the simple bell played for humans. I appreciate knowing before I open the door if I'm dealing with a monster or a solicitor, and because of that warning system I'm expecting to find something nasty on my porch. When I throw the door open, though, I'm facing a scrawny human not much taller than I am.

I hesitate for a second too long in my surprise, and the man makes an imperious gesture at me. "I am here for Vicereine Alexandra by order of Duchess Olivia of the Atlanta Nest. You will present her to me at once."

"You don't smell like a vampire," I say, and I can see him take offense at that supposed insult to his masters. Vampires have a distinct smell, if not an entirely unpleasant one. Like bread on the verge of molding, if I had to put a name to it. I give him that rude smile my mother used to smack off my face and continue with, "That means you're just livestock. You want to try asking a little nicer this time?"

"The Nest does not ask humans anything," he says, like a walking vampire snack outranks the rest of us normal people. "You will do as we require without argument."

"I am Elysium," I correct him, "and you will ask me nicely or I will send you on your way."

It's a bluff, because I've never had a say in who can or can't take refuge at Elysium, but I'm hedging my bets on this man not knowing such a thing. I'm hoping he doesn't call it, because I want to know why Olivia was thoughtless enough to send someone here.

This man might be human now, feeding his masters and biding his time until he's judged worthy to join their immortal ranks, but he's got enough of the Nest's taint in him for Elysium to read him as preternatural. I don't know if Elysium's already sent a warning out to the gatekeepers or if it'll only do so if he requests refuge here. I have to assume we don't have a lot of time to waste, and I need to know if he rushed all the way here from Atlanta because Chronos fell. I refuse to believe the two aren't related.

"I'm waiting," I say, when the silence has dragged on a little too long.

He looks at me like I'm the gum on the bottom of his expensive shoes and grinds out, "May I come in and speak to Vicereine Alexandra?"

"Better," I say, and move aside.

Elysium's magic trembles under my skin as the man steps through the doorway. I look past him at the dragons, waiting to see what they make of this, but Falkor and Smerg don't care for Society politics and don't share the gatekeepers' hatred for vampires. They'll only stir themselves if this man proves to be a threat to me somehow. I close the door on their watchful eyes and lead my uninvited guest further into the house. Casper is halfway through the floor, which means she was able to find the stairwell again, and she watches with interest as I cross the room.

I take him to the kitchen and point at the landline. He looks from it to me and back again, and I finally explain, "She's at work right now, and no, I'm not telling you where we work. I don't need the Nest scoping out my customers like they're a potential a food source. You can call her from here and tell her what you need to say. Number's on a sticky pad next to the phone."

He looks irritated by the deception, but he's not in any real position to argue. I leave the room as if I'm giving him privacy but prop myself up against the living room wall just outside the doorway. Casper hoists herself out of the floor and comes over to join me. I put a finger to my lips before she can ask the obvious questions. She considers that a moment, then shrugs and goes through the wall to spy on him from a closer position.

It takes forever to get through to Betty. Since Jinx is technically closed tonight, she's not obligated to answer the phone. We don't have an answering machine, though, so the phone will ring until someone picks it up. Normal customers give up after ten or twelve rings and try again a few minutes later. This guy's got enough riding on things to stick it out, though, and after a small eternity he's finally connected. His ingratiating tone has me rolling my eyes at the empty living room, but I lean closer to the doorway to hear him better.

"Vicereine, I apologize for disturbing you tonight. I am Thomas Weather, here at the behest of the Atlanta Nest. Duchess Olivia was unable to reach you on your cell and sent me to see you in person. Yes. Yes, my Lady. We are aware, but recent developments require your attention and expertise, and we hope you will forgive us the intrusion into your solitude. We would not violate your contract without due cause." He lowers his voice before continuing with, "Chronos has been challenged and won. Yes, my Lady. Current estimate is five Lymanczyc casualties."

"Lymanczyc" rolls easier off his tongue than it ever has off mine; it is the gatekeepers' true species and a complicated mess of consonants I've given up on ever getting right. I don't have time to envy his perfect pronunciation, though, because the rest of the sentence matters a thousand times more. I didn't think the gatekeepers were mortal. That five died tonight sends a bolt of adrenaline through my drunken veins. My glee evaporates with the next words out of his mouth:

"We have reason to believe it was Notte."

It's like swallowing tacks, a vicious prickle followed by an all-consuming heat that nearly takes me off my feet. It's been over ten years since anyone's spoken Adam Notte's name in this house. Back in the early days it was whispered like a curse, my tenants' rage nearly as terrible as my own. I hated him for betraying me and killing my daughter, whereas they knew him as the man who'd destroyed Elysium. I learned real quick not to tell anyone my married name, and they learned faster not to say it under this roof. The gatekeepers coded an alarm into this house, and "Notte" calls them here faster than anything else can. No one survives their retaliation.

It doesn't matter that Thomas isn't here seeking refuge or that he has questionable ties to Betty; his chances of surviving the night have just flat-lined. I dart into the kitchen, knowing I'm too late to save him but needing him to take back his words before the gatekeepers arrive.

"You're lying!" I shriek.

He nearly jumps out of his skin but recovers enough to send me a fierce look. Instead of responding to me, he speaks to Betty in a tight voice. "Apologies, my Lady. Your housekeeper listens where she should not and—yes, of course you can hear her," he says, backtracking like only the best servants can. I stalk across the room toward him when he turns his back on me once more. "The Salt Lake Nest claims to have two eye witnesses under their protection, so Duchess Olivia put your name forth to oversee the process. And Cinder says—"

I snatch the phone out of his hand and slam it down on the counter. "Answer me!"

I don't see him swing, but I definitely feel the pop of his fist against my cheek. I stumble under the weight of it and take one of the table chairs down with me when I fall. That hurts more than his punch did, but at least the pain gives me something to hang onto while my head is spinning.

Elysium's magic snarls across my skin, reacting immediately to the threat against me, and the pressure in my chest is the house preparing to expel him by force. I can hear Falkor and Smerg screaming through the ringing in my ears.

"Wait," I say, but it's too late. We are no longer alone.

Two of the gatekeepers are standing between us now. I've endured sixteen years of them coming and going as they please but I still can't keep from recoiling at their silent and abrupt arrival. The gatekeepers outrank everyone in Society due to their connections to the ley line gates, but no one is ever happy to see them. They are pretty much the bane of my ongoing existence.

This side of drunk the only thing I can compare them to would be snow owls, save the gatekeepers are halfway to nine feet tall and ten times creepier. From their featureless faces down to the crooks of their legs they have perfectly smooth white hides, and I have no idea where their arms go when they don't need them. I'm more familiar with their talons, and like always my abdomen aches with the bastards this close.

The gatekeepers haven't traveled here in pairs since Elysium stabilized. I know they aren't breaking tradition on my behalf. This is because someone attacked them where it hurts most, damaging one of their precious gates and killing their kind. It doesn't validate all of what Thomas said, not really, but I reach for him anyway.

"Tell me you're lying," I say, because I have to have that answer before they kill him.

He doesn't seem to hear me. He's staring at the gatekeepers like one might a pack of rabid wolves, equal parts fear and disgust. I've never seen anyone look at them this way. Not even Betty goes out of her way to antagonize them, and she's got Elysium on her side.

LEAVE US, the gatekeepers say, their voices an awful chorus echoing in my skull.

I'm desperate enough to ignore that demand. "Tell me he wasn't there!"

One of the gatekeepers turns to me, and my scars go white-hot in warning. I wind my arms around my middle like I can somehow smother that fire, but the gatekeeper's voice is nails in my brain: **YOU WILL LEAVE US NOW**.

It clacks its talons against the linoleum in warning, and panicked self-preservation wipes out all thoughts of Adam. I lurch to my feet and run as best I can out of there. The sprites chase me as I stumble up the stairs. My bedroom unlocks for me at the first brush of my hand against the knob, and the sprites and I escape inside. I slam the door behind me and lean against it. There my legs give out and I slide slowly to the ground.

Casper bursts through me a second later. She stumbles toward my bed, making an awful sound in the back of her throat, and catches at my footboard to steady herself. "Evey," she chokes out, and although I know she can't get physically ill anymore she sounds on the verge of puking. "They're tearing him apart down there. Why are they—why would they—?

21

You didn't even try to stop them! You just left him to die!"

"I couldn't have saved him." I rub at my chest in an attempt to ease the hollow ache beneath my ribs. It doesn't help, so I hug my knees to my chest and smash my cheek against one of them. "He said something he shouldn't have, and there's no going back from that. Don't repeat it, okay? I know you're already dead, but I don't want to find out the hard way if Elysium has a workaround for someone like you."

"But what is it?" Casper demands.

"*It* is a *he*, and he's the one who broke Elysium. But he's been dead for years."

"You sure about that?" Casper asks. She points a finger in the general direction of our kitchen and says, "He seemed to think otherwise, and that reaction from the gatekeepers is a little extreme for a guy who's been dead for what, twelve years?"

"Sixteen," I say. "He's dead, Casper."

She stares at me, waiting for more, but I can't give her the truth. I can't tell her that Adam was my husband. I can't tell her that we eloped when I was eight months pregnant or that Adam brought me here to Elysium instead of to a church. I thought maybe the house was a surprise for me, that this was where he wanted us to start our new family. Instead he dug his magic deep beneath the ground, seized the ley line, and pulled it so hard he shattered Elysium's gate. I'll never forget the sound it made, or the way the gate magic felt as it rolled wild into the night.

But more than that I can't forget Adam dropping the line and rounding on me with heavy hands. He beat me into labor, forcing Ciara into the world a month before she was due and using magic to pull her free faster than my body wanted to let her go.

I had two seconds to see her face before the shockwave from Elysium reached us, and there was nothing I could do but watch as they evaporated under the weight of too much magic. The gatekeepers found me screaming on the floor a few minutes later and, having no one else around to punish for the loss of their gate, turned on me.

"I was there when it happened," I say at last, because Casper has moved to sit at my side. "I know what I saw."

I know what I saw, but Thomas sounded so sure and claimed they had two witnesses to back it up. Panic is an unsteady murmur in my veins, threatening to boil over at any second, so I close my eyes against the room and focus on breathing.

Casper gives me space for a few minutes before asking, "Now what?"

"Now we wait for Betty," I say. "I need to know the truth."

"You really think she'll know?"

"Chronos fell tonight, and the Atlanta Nest sent a man straight here," I point out. "Here, to a gate, where they know the Nest isn't welcome, just because Betty turns her cell phone off when she's at work. They were that desperate to reach her. You heard him say it: she has expertise they need right now. They want her to go to Utah and check out the wreckage."

"You think she knows this guy?"

"Knew," I correct Casper shortly. "He's dead."

"You're taking this pretty personally, you know."

"Remember that he destroyed my life by destroying Elysium," I snap back. "Now let me think."

Adam is dead. He has to be dead, because I saw it happen, because I can't believe he might have gotten away with what he did to me. I won't believe he left me for dead and never once in sixteen years came back for me.

But beneath that roiling knot of uneasiness and bitter rage is a sick and desperate what-if. If Adam survived such terrible odds, could Ciara have somehow lived through that explosion too? She'd been in his arms, sheltered by his body, so if the magic wasn't enough to break him somehow, then maybe—

This is a dangerous road to send myself on. This kind of speculation might be the straw that finally breaks me. I can feel it in the way my throat is pulled too tight, in the queasy roil of my stomach.

I tell myself that Betty will know everything, because if I don't believe that I really will go mad. It's a hard lie to sell, though, considering how long she's been on her own. Autonomous vampires like Betty are a rare thing these days. Immortality is too expensive to face alone, and the constant advances in technology means it's increasingly difficult for the undead to avoid raising red flags over time. Allies in Society are good for alibis and references, and the Nests take tithes from all members and associated livestock, but it's still not easy to fly under the radar.

Betty thinks easy is boring and claimed that was her excuse for leaving the Madtown Nest in San Francisco almost twenty years ago. Until today I assumed she was lying and that she hadn't had a choice, because who in her right mind would walk away from the most influential Society hub in the US? Now I know I'm wrong, because Thomas and Casper have both referred to her as Vicereine. I've got a half-dozen holes in my knowledge of vampire hierarchy but I know that title is a good ways up the food chain. She couldn't have retained it if she'd been expelled from Madtown. She used to be someone important, and she obviously still has

23

connections.

Elysium's magic hums against my skin, signaling Betty's return. I have to be imagining it, because the bar is supposed to be open for several more hours, but the subsequent flare of a gate opening kicks me out of my shock. I scramble to my feet and throw open my door. There's no way I can get from here to the front door in time to stop Betty from stepping through her summoned gate, so I settle for screaming down the hall.

"Wait!"

But my skin pulls too tight for a few sharp seconds, and then the magic is gone. So is Betty.

I stand in the hallway until Casper finally comes looking for me.

"She'll come back," Casper says.

But she won't come back tonight—she can't. A jump is nearly instantaneous, but there's no telling how long it'll take her to deal with the Chronos mess. Even if she just needs a couple minutes to glance the scene over without somehow getting spotted and killed by the gatekeepers, Elysium is outbound only. She'll have to return via a different gate and trek back here like a human would. There aren't enough hours before sunrise for her to make that kind of round trip. I could explain all this to Casper, but then she'd just want to know why I can't wait for my explanation.

"Fuck you," I say instead.

I storm back into my bedroom and slam the door behind me, and for once Casper is smart enough to not follow me inside.

I spend half of the following day leaving voicemail messages on Betty's cell phone, demanding she call me as soon as the sun sets, and the other half sitting in the middle of my bed feeling sorry for myself. I try reading just to take my mind off things, but I keep tracing the same lines over and over without retaining anything.

I don't care about any of this. I don't care about anything. I sure as hell don't want to have to go to work tonight and face my customers. I'm tempted to call out sick, but Betty and I are all Dallas has in terms of staffing. I can't leave him high and dry after everything he's done for me.

At three I finally drag myself out of bed and get ready for the day. I expect Casper to show up when the shower cuts on, but she's conspicuously absent, and I even manage to get dressed in peace. I tell myself that work will be the distraction I've been needing all day. Around the fourth or fifth time I start believing it, and then I open my bedroom door and the day goes right down the toilet.

The stench of death hits me like a sledgehammer and has me bolting for the trashcan at my bedside. I've barely stopped gagging before a door slams down the hall. Heavy strides come to an abrupt stop right outside my room and my doorframe creaks under an angry fist. I spit a couple more times in a vain attempt to clear the sour taste of sickness and look over my shoulder. Marilyn has a sweatshirt wrapped around the lower half of her face to try and block out the smell. I try to follow her example with my bath towel, but it's not as effective as I want it to be.

"Now you wake up," she snarls, the accusation barely audible through her makeshift mask. "We've been trying to wake you for hours."

I've been awake since eleven; I've just been hiding in here to wallow in my misery. "You know the doors are proofed," I tell her. I dig a shirt out of the pile in my laundry basket and make a second mask atop the first. I can still smell death, so thick and awful it's a physical weight on my tongue. The thought sends a shudder through my gut and I swallow hard against my weakening gag reflex. "You also know I keep late mornings because I work nights. You could have just taken care of it yourselves instead of waiting on me."

"Your kind," Marilyn says. "Your house. Your problem."

"He's technically not human," I start to explain, but she doesn't stick around to hear me out.

I stare at my doorway for an endless minute, looking for a way out of this nightmare and coming up empty. I don't want to go downstairs and face the mess the gatekeepers left for me. I'm weak in the knees just thinking about it, because if it smells this bad I know it's going to look even worse. I go through a mental checklist of all my tenants, hoping there's one I can somehow con into dealing with this for me, and come up empty.

At last I have no choice but to steel my nerves and inch down the hall. From the top of the stairwell I can tell this is going to be a major undertaking. The urge to cry is as fierce as it is fleeting, and I crush my impromptu mask so hard against my face my nose goes numb.

The gatekeepers weren't gentle. The last time I saw Thomas, he was standing at the kitchen counter near my phone. Now he's scattered from there to my den, with a trail of limbs down the hallway between. I take the stairs down on wooden legs, stopping on the last step to stare at the hand sitting palm-up just inches from my shoes.

Looking in the kitchen is a mistake. His lower jaw is wedged under my fridge and the rest of his head got caught against a table leg. The disaster the gatekeeper made of his torso has me clutching at my own scarred abdomen. I lean against the railing when the world crackles black.

25

"I'm okay, I'm okay, I'm okay." It's my voice, I think, but it doesn't sound like me.

This isn't the first dead body I've had to clear out of Elysium, but it's definitely the worst scene yet, and the too-warm air has done his body no favors. I don't even know where to begin. It's not like I can sweep up an arm. The thought draws a hysterical giggle until I realize one of the arms is missing. So is part of a leg and a good bit of the man's guts. I make an unsteady lap of the downstairs rooms, unwilling to draw the obvious conclusion. I have to face facts by the time I reach the stairwell again.

Marilyn and Hogan are keeping their distance from this stench, and the Wyrn eats only insects. Betty needs blood, not flesh, and she booked it out of here last night. The remaining two tenants, though, are a couple of carnivorous monsters who loathe humans. One of them snacked on the man's remains while I was sleeping last night. Sasquatch, I think, and for a moment I can almost see her on her hands and knees with her jaws buried in the man's shredded chest. I take a step back, shaking my head to clear that horrible image, and step barefoot on the man's left hand.

It gives a little under my heel and that's more than I can take. I race for the front door, yank it open, and stagger halfway down the sidewalk. I rip my towel and shirt from my face so I can breathe, and I gulp in fresh air until my chest aches. I only manage a few more gasps before my empty stomach turns inside out, and I brace my hands against my knees as I dry-heave.

Falkor and Smerg kick up a fuss behind me, spitting and hissing their disapproval, and then one of them gives a passable impression of my gagging. I flip them off with an unsteady finger and sit down on the sidewalk.

It doesn't take long for Falkor to abandon his post. A rough snout pushes against my cheekbone and he inhales deep enough to suck up some of my hair. He snorts it back out and gives a violent shake of his head. I swipe sticky locks off my cheek with a shoulder and give him a dirty look. He gnashes his fangs at me in response.

"She smells, she does. More than usual, for sure."

I'm a heartbeat from telling him what I really think of him when inspiration strikes. "How much do you love me?"

"Oh, she is precious," Falkor says, with not an ounce of affection. "She knows she is, she knows. We wonders why she asks such an obvious question?"

"The gatekeepers left something here that hurts me," I tell Falkor. "Get rid of it."

He shifts from side to side as he considers. "She knows we does not go into the house!"

"You don't," I agree, "but you can, can't you? Won't you help me?"

Falkor lolls his head to one side to study his counterpart. Smerg says nothing, more interested in the perpetual itch in his left shoulder, but abruptly Falkor spins away from me and waddle-gallops like a ferret up the sidewalk.

I half-expect him to reclaim his perch, because he has to know the gatekeepers would never leave anything truly dangerous here with me, but after a brief pause on the porch he heads into the house. Smerg drops off his pedestal and follows after him.

I stay put until they come racing back a couple minutes later. They cavort in the yard a bit before abruptly untangling and retreating to their pedestals.

"Is it gone?" I ask when they've settled down.

"She lies to us, we think," Falkor says, "but we does not lie to her. She is ours always and always."

It's a long way to say "yes", but I'll take it. Relief is intense enough to make me go limp, and I give in to the urge to lie down. A minute's all I give myself, because I do have neighbors and I don't want them asking me why I'm sprawled on my sidewalk like a loon. I collect my shirt and towel on my way to the door but give up on remaking my mask when I reach the porch. From out here I can smell only heat and sulfur. This smell is no kinder to my stomach, but it's a definite improvement.

"Thank you," I say, and close the door on my dragons.

There's nothing left of the body. Instead there are charred holes in the living room carpet and scorch marks several feet long streaking down the hallway. The table is a wreck, since the dragons burned away two legs when they went after the man's head. I know the house will fix itself before long, but the sprites are pulsating madly in a corner of the living room.

"Everyone accounted for?" I ask them. They give an agitated dance and scrunch closer together. "You'll be all right."

I head upstairs, chuck my towel and shirt aside, and collect my keys from my dresser. The smallest key is for the chain on my bike, and I don't bother to lock Elysium's front door behind me. My bicycle is where I left it two days ago, locked against the gate leading to the backyard. I loop its chain around a handle and set off for downtown. It's an easy ride to Jinx, and with a half-hour out from opening there's only one car in the parking lot.

My key works on either door, but I go in through the kitchen whenever Dallas beats me to work. He's already setting his kitchen to rights, bobbing along to the music coming from the overhead speakers. It's loud enough that we'd have to shout our greetings at each other, so I settle for waving. He points out the till where he's already pulled it from the safe. I lug it up front with me and busy myself setting up the bar. When Dallas calls an okay I flip the outdoor sign to OPEN, and we knock a shot back to start our shift.

It takes twenty minutes for the first couple to show up, and after that it's a slow but steady trickle of customers. This time of day the majority of our orders are for early dinners. I carry plates back and forth from Dallas's window to their tables, top off their sodas, and shake up the occasional cocktail.

Most of the time I watch the clock, waiting for nightfall. Betty's supposed to work tonight, and Dallas hasn't said anything about her calling out sick. That doesn't mean she can't fake a last minute emergency, but I'm desperate enough to feel hopeful. Every time the door opens I stop what I'm doing to look, and every time I look I'm disappointed.

At a quarter to six, I look up to find a stranger in the doorway. He stands there nearly a full minute, scanning the place with a slow gaze, and then drags his heavy stare to me. I try to hold it, but I'm halfway through a drink order and have to focus on what I'm doing.

I finish my work as quickly as I can, trade the glasses for a credit card, and find the stranger standing alone at the far end of the counter when I've finished swiping the card at the register. The card's owner doesn't notice when I try to hand it back because he's too busy staring at my newest guest. I don't blame him, and I'm grateful for the excuse to follow his gaze.

I don't know what to look at first: his eyes, which are so red they look like they're glowing, or the white Celtic cross that is tattooed upside-down across half of his face. He looks young, maybe twenty at the oldest. Messy black hair hangs to his shoulders and he's dressed in an all-white ensemble that complements his olive skin. A half-dozen rosaries of different colors and sizes hang around his neck in an ill-advised fashion statement.

I jump when the credit card is plucked from my outstretched hand, but I can't scrounge up the decency to apologize or smile at my first customer. I can't look away from those strange eyes. I know they must be contacts, but the prickling at the back of my neck warns me they're not.

This man is from Society, and he is definitely not safe. But there is something familiar about him, something I can't quite put my finger on. It's like bumping into a customer in line at the grocery store, knowing I've

28

seen them somewhere but unable to pin it down for sure, or catching a whiff of a perfume I loved as a child but haven't ever found again.

I resist the urge to wipe my sweaty palms on my pants and move down the counter to meet him. "Evening," I say, and pride myself in how calm I sound. "What are you starting with?"

"You are Evelyn of Elysium," he says, "and you have something that belongs to me."

THREE

Jinx is never a quiet place, but the silence between the stranger and me feels a thousand miles deep. When it's obvious he's not going to explain himself without being prompted, I put up a hand for him to wait and go around the counter. I check once to make sure he's paying attention, then cross the room to open the main door. I give myself a solid ten seconds to study the lit sign boasting our name, nod an exaggerated confirmation, and return to my original spot across from my uninvited visitor.

"You say Elysium," I say, "but turns out you're standing in a bar called Jinx. That's a problem, because I thought I made it clear Society isn't welcome here."

He makes a grab at me, moving so fast I'm sure he must be part snake. I attempt to recoil out of reach but slam into someone who wasn't there a second ago. Luckily whoever is behind me is faster than I am, and a hand clamps down on the stranger's wrist. His hand is hauled up and away from me before he can catch hold of my throat. My heart pounds so hard at that near-miss that my temples ache, but then Betty's tight voice is at my ear.

"Please," she says. "We talked about this."

He wrenches out of her grip and levels a black look at her. "You said she would cooperate, Alexandra. Have you lied to me again?"

Betty presses a hand to my shoulder, neatly pushing me aside so she can step up alongside me. I glance between them, noting the hostility on his face and the wariness on hers. She is quick to drop her stare to the counter but she raises her hands palm-out in either an apology or a calming gesture. I've never seen her give ground to anyone before, and I'm positive that sick feeling in my chest is my heart skipping a half-dozen beats. I swallow hard against my own prickle of fear and look the man over once more.

"After all this time, you still doubt me?" Betty asks.

"You were wrong about him," he insists. "Are you wrong about her?"

"She is human," Betty says. "They are contrary by nature. She will come around."

Movement in the corner of my eye gives me an excuse to walk away. I

30

put space between us as fast as I can and fill a couple orders further down the bar. There's only so long I can avoid them, though, because Betty has answers I need and I want to know what that man is doing here.

I'm not going over there again without a pick-me-up, so I grab a bottle of whiskey from the closer well and carry it with me. Betty has three glasses ready by the time I make it back to her: rocks glasses for her and her guest, and a Collins glass for me. She's even considerate enough to wait until I've drained half of my glass before speaking again. She's had a couple minutes to calm down, so she almost sounds like herself again. I'm not fooled, because there's lingering tension evident in the line of her shoulders. Last I checked, vampires aren't afraid of anyone.

"We have a few questions for you," Betty says.

"There shouldn't be a 'we'," I tell her. "You know they're not allowed in here."

He shifts like he's considering coming at me again, but this time he stays put. He hasn't touched his drink but is slowly turning it between his hands on the counter. "You have exactly one more chance to cooperate, and then I will rip your head from your neck and check your skull for the answers I need."

"No, you won't," I say. "I'm Elysium's linchpin. You can't hurt me without bringing the gatekeepers down on you. You can't find what you're looking for if you're dead, right? So threaten me again and see what happens."

He pushes his glass aside like he's about to call my bluff, but Betty is faster. She hauls me around to face her. Her fingers dig into my shoulders so hard I'm sure she's going to break skin in a second, and my first attempt to shrug her off does nothing.

"Evelyn, this is important," she says, and gives me a small shake to emphasize that point. "I usually find your attitude entertaining, but tonight is not the night for it. Just tell us what we need to know, and we will be on our way."

"I have questions," I insist.

"Ours are more important," Betty says.

"Go to hell." I try shrugging out of her grip again, then settle for jabbing a finger at her chest when I fail. "When have you ever given me a straight answer in all the years I've known you? But now you show up here, you bring someone from Society here, where you promised they'd never come, and you expect me to help you out? I don't think so.

"No," I say, louder, when she looks about to argue with me. "Tell me the truth, first: was Thomas right about Chronos? Was he—" I can hear my voice start to crack, so I clear my throat before finishing. "Was he right about who was responsible?"

The look she gives me is calculating, like she's trying to determine why the answer matters so much. She knows as much as Casper now knows: that Notte destroying Elysium changed my life forever. But she was on the other end of the phone when I begged Thomas to retract his words. It's a toss-up if she stayed on the line long enough to listen to him die, or if she gave him up as a lost cause and used her mind tricks to empty out Jinx so she could come home.

I drive my finger harder into her chest. "Yes or no?"

She lets go of me. "Yes."

All the air goes out of the room, and without Betty to hold me up I crumple to my knees. I clench my hands into fists on my thighs and stare through Betty's legs at nothing. The heat in my face might be tears, might be that scream that's eating my chest from the inside-out. I choke on the first breath I finally manage and almost bite through my lip to keep from wailing. I don't know why I thought the answer would make me feel better. I'm so sorry I asked that I think I'm going to be sick.

Adam's alive. He survived what he did to me and Elysium, and he's been out there doing who-knows-what for sixteen years. Raising Ciara? I don't know—knowing Adam was spotted again doesn't confirm whether or not Ciara is alive. And even if she is, I realize with a horrible lurch that there's nothing I can do about it either way. Unless Adam comes within five miles of Elysium, I'll never see him or her again.

Betty digs her thumbnails into the corners of my mouth, forcing me out of my thoughts, and I find her crouched in front of me. She waits until I focus on her before asking, "Are you listening to me?"

I have to punch my thigh a couple times before I can keep my thoughts where they need to be right now. When I nod, she glances over her shoulder at her guest. He's edged around to the narrow entryway Betty and I use to get out to the main floor, since with me down here on my knees he couldn't see me properly from his stool. He gives a short jerk of his chin in an order to proceed, so Betty turns back to me.

"We are looking for someone," she says. "Brimstone has reason to believe he's at Elysium—"

"He is," the man cuts in, so harsh Betty's mouth thins to a hard line. "I can find him anywhere inside fifty kilometers. He's there when you said he wasn't."

"I said I've never seen a trace of him in the three years I've been a tenant," Betty says in as placating a tone as she can manage. "That's why we're here to talk to you, Evelyn. You've been here much longer than I have and your unique ties to the house means you have a better chance of finding him. You know everyone who's come and gone from Elysium, isn't that correct?"

I know where this conversation is going, but all I say is, "Yes."

"He went missing—"

"He was stolen," Brimstone interrupts.

His tone is savage, but this time that heat isn't directed at either of us. Betty's mouth twitches, not in fear but sympathy. She looks back at him and says quietly, "We will get him back. I promise."

"I shouldn't have to get him back," Brimstone snaps, but he gives a sharp jerk of his hand before he can continue that train of thought. He half-turns away from us and rakes his fingers through his hair with so much force he leaves scratches along his temples. He spits outs something I don't understand but which I think is Spanish, then brings himself back with a tight, "Ask her where he is."

Betty turns back to me. "He was stolen eighteen years ago, and it is imperative we retrieve him tonight. Society has no future without him. So please tell us: is there a guest at Elysium that you've never told me about, that no one else has ever seen on the premises?"

"You mean Rose," I say. She shakes her head, not following, so I explain: "Gray kid with red hair, right? Casper found him comatose in the cellar last night. I was going to ask you about him, but you disappeared to Utah to investigate Chronos as soon as you got home. What is he, Betty? Has he really been asleep down there all this time?"

Betty opens her mouth, but Brimstone speaks first with a low, "What the fuck did you just call him?"

I look up at his too-blank face. "Rose. Because of Sleeping—"

Brimstone lunges for us, and although Betty tries to push me to safety she's not fast enough. He picks her up by her shirt and arm and tosses her over the counter to get her out from between us. There's a crash of tables and chairs, either Betty's rough landing or my customers' terrified reactions or both, and the crackling pop of shattering glasses. I scramble to my feet, but Brimstone is too close for me to run from.

He gets a hand around my throat and throws me at the back wall. The counter only slows me down a little, and I slam my back and head into the shelving along the wall. Bottles hit my shoulders as they topple off their perches, and one glances my head. I claw at the hand around my throat, fighting to loosen his grip enough that I can breathe. Customers swarm him, hooking their arms around him in an attempt to pull him off of me, and I think I hear Dallas shouting in the background. Betty shoves through everyone else to grab at Brimstone's arm.

"We have to go," she says. "Right now."

It's too late. Falkor and Smerg appear above him with a crackle of power, and they dive for him with harsh shrieks. Bright blue fire rips along the counters, catching my customers who are standing too close to it. There's a jagged pulse in the air and the fire goes black.

The heat is like nothing I've felt after a lifetime of southern summers. Liquor bottles explode in the well racks, and the bottles along the wall aren't far behind them. I think I'm melting; I don't know if that's skin or sweat that's beading up on my hand and making my fingers slide against Brimstone's arm. Everyone is screaming as fire tears the bar apart.

Falkor goes for Brimstone's face with fangs and claws but is thrown aside like he's a gnat. Smerg has better luck by swooping in from behind, but the black fire on the counter isn't his. I watch it catch one of Smerg's wings, and he takes to the air with a ragged scream that's deafening.

My hand slips free of Brimstone's arm and I don't have the strength to lift it again. Everything's black at the edges as asphyxiation overrides my panic. We're all going to die in here, and I'm never going to know if Ciara survived.

I don't remember falling. I don't remember him letting go of me. But suddenly Falkor's legs are all I can see, and I realize I'm curled up on one of the sticky bar mats. I gasp for air so hard my lungs feel like they're tearing. I crane a look up, trying to see where Brimstone has gone, and it takes me a moment to realize the ceiling is gone. It's been completely torn from the building, and the sky is full of gatekeepers.

Smerg crash lands at my side, and I painstakingly push myself up on an elbow to look at him. He's no longer on fire, but half of his body is a charred mess. As I watch the shadows spread further across his body. He wails a ragged tune as he tries and fails to get to his feet. Falkor stretches his head to his brother, keening, but can't quite reach and won't leave me unprotected to close the gap between them. Smerg tosses his head, thrashing about like a wild thing, as the darkness reaches his throat. He can no longer speak, but gasps silently up at the open sky. Then the burn reaches his jaw, and he collapses limp against the floor.

Falkor is still making that awful sound. In my shock it takes me a minute longer than it should to understand why I can hear him. The roaring fire is gone, and my customers' screams are silenced. Either everyone has fled the scene, or everyone is dead. I have the horrifying feeling I know which answer it is.

Talons land a scant inch from my face, and I flinch closer to Falkor. Falkor lowers himself to his haunches so he's practically lying on top of me, and he brings his keening down to a grumbling roar that I feel more than hear. I expect the gatekeepers to demand explanations, but they stay silent. They've figured things out for themselves, perhaps, or they're arguing where I can't hear them. I chance another look up at the sky, and the sight of so many of them has my stomach turning inside out. The last time I saw so many of them was when Elysium fell.

I press unsteady fingers against Falkor's side, and he eases off of me. It takes me two tries to get to my feet, because the first time I catch at the counter my nearly scald my fingers. Finally I'm up, though, and I stare in numb horror at the wreckage that used to be Jinx. The walls and floor are soot-black, and glass has reshaped into spiked piles everywhere the bottles and cups were. The metal counter and well racks are warped from the heat.

There are no bodies, but the front door is still closed. No one made it out of here. That frightened wail has to be mine, but I don't recognize my own voice. I clamp my hands over my mouth like I can stifle the next horrible noise, but I'm choking on the memory of my customers' screams.

Sirens fill the air as the gatekeepers fade from sight one by one. The firefighters and police are on the way, too late to save anyone. The fire came and went too quickly to be stopped, too hot to not destroy everything under this roof. I am the only one left standing when the firefighters kick the door in.

The first man's just made it a few steps inside when the kitchen door slams open at my side and Betty stumbles in. She's too unsteady to catch herself but crashes into the bar counter. Her hair has been mostly burned away, leaving just a dangerously short mess around her skull, and she's soaking wet. Water streams over her torn clothes, and blood wells up in sluggish lines along her back and abdomen. I know in the first look that those injuries are from the gatekeepers' talons. I recognize those ugly swipes anywhere.

"Alex!" Jude pushes through the firefighters, ignoring the hands that try to pull him back to safety. "Evey!"

Betty draws a rattling breath and looks at me. "Evelyn, we have to go."

She doesn't give me time to argue, doesn't even look at Jude, but grabs my wrist and hauls me into the kitchen. The kitchen's mostly unharmed, as that black fire was centered in the main room, and I choke on a sob when I see Dallas crumpled against the stove. He's so still I'm sure he's dead, but the only hint of injury on him is a bloody hand print on his shirt. He was shoved back here when he tried to investigate up front, thrown to safety by someone with inhuman strength.

"Betty," I say, choking on her name. "You saved—"

Betty heaves the back door open and drags me to my bike. Shouts behind us say we're being pursued, but Betty's looking toward the Savannah River. The gatekeepers have moved from Jinx to the river and they're hovering over its surface in a long line. Looking for Brimstone, I realize, and I suddenly understand why Betty is wet. She dragged him out of Jinx before the gatekeepers could get hold of either of them. Betty's told me before that the gatekeepers hate water, though she only shrugged when I asked for a reason. But if Brimstone's really in there, he's going to have to come up for breath at some point, and I know that's what they're waiting for.

"We can't just leave," I say.

Betty grabs hold of my bike lock and breaks it with one fierce tug. "I will not let your mouth get us both killed. Get back to the house right now, and I will meet you there as soon as I can. Awlyn," she calls, and Falkor materializes beside me. He bares wicked fangs at her and leans heavily against my leg. For a moment he looks almost frightening, which is a mean feat for a translucent baby dragon. "Keep her safe. We've only a few minutes before the Lymanczyc realize Brimstone isn't in the river."

"Biters bites off more than they can chew, oh yes, they always does," Falkor says, angrier than I've ever heard him. "Biters think they cannot die. We thinks they forget how easily they burned last time."

"Now is not the time," Betty says in a tight voice, because the rest of the rescue brigade is coming up on us.

Leaving makes me feel like trash, in part because it makes me look guilty and mostly because I can't believe I'm walking away from the people Betty got killed, but I get on my bike and pedal for Main Street as fast as I can. I don't know if Betty can really control so many people long enough to cover my escape, but I trust her to know what she's doing and I refuse to look back. I don't want to see what Jinx looks like on the outside now. I don't want to see the firefighters starting after me before Betty reels them back in or see the gatekeepers floating in a silent, furious line over the murky river.

I don't want to kill myself slamming into a car, either, so I'm forced to obey most of the traffic signals between Jinx and Elysium. Relief is a stabbing ache in my gut as I turn down my street, at least until I see the gatekeepers waiting for me in my front lawn. I coast past the last few houses, fingers white-knuckled on my handlebars, and slow to a stop near

36

the mailbox. I'm slow to dismount and wonder if they're waiting for me or simply guarding their property. I take a cautious step forward and recoil when one throws its wings wide open.

Gatekeepers fall from the sky like stones, filling Elysium's front lawn. **YOU WILL RUN**.

It is the only warning I have before black fire explodes around me. I scream and duck. My bike falls over onto me, glancing off my arm and clattering off to one side, and I throw a look back. Brimstone stands right across the street from me, leaning against my neighbor's car for balance. An arm around his middle is the only thing keeping him together, if the amount of dark blood staining his white clothes is any indication. His fire lasts only a few seconds before sputtering out.

"I will not let you have him," he says, in a voice thick and wet with blood. "I don't care what Notte wants. I will kill you before I let you have him."

Adam's name freezes me where I am, and Brimstone seizes on his last chance. He shoves off the car and runs for me. Pain and injuries have slowed him down, but he's still faster than I am. He catches hold of my face, but his hands are so slick with his own blood he can't get a good grip. Falkor takes a chomp at his wrist to weaken his grip further, and I manage to wiggle free. I drive my shoe into the gaping wound in his middle, nearly knocking myself over with the force I put into it. It's enough to throw him back, and that's all the opening the gatekeepers need. They spring forward as one. Black fire snarls into life around him like a shield before he and his magic are buried beneath their writhing bodies.

I retreat up the sidewalk, unable to look away from the mountain of white monsters, and nearly trip over the porch. I catch at the doorway for balance, and Elysium comes to life at the first touch of my hand against the wood. The roar of magic through me is louder than the explosion of fire at the bar, almost strong enough to shake me to pieces, but it's not just the house that's responding. The ley line is a bolt of unforgiving heat through my veins, and it rockets from me to the front lawn. The force of it is enough that I have to sit down or fall over.

Power spikes up through the grass in bursts of white light, and the front wall of the house starts falling apart with thick rumbles and violent cracks. Chunks of plaster and brick rip free and fly at the mound of bodies on the lawn, and I realize too late that the house isn't defending me—it's protecting Brimstone. I watch in wide-eyed shock as the jumpgate turns on its own keepers and sends them scattering.

A crackle of ice along my fingertips is the only warning I get that a gate is opening. I've never seen Elysium open a gate of its own volition, but when I look back I'm almost blinded by the silver glow filling the doorway. That's an open-ended gate, an emergency exit with no predetermined destination. I haven't seen it in over a decade, not since the gatekeepers first descended on my tenants for speaking Notte's name, but the faerie who called it couldn't make it to the door fast enough to survive.

For a wild moment I think the gate is meant for me, but I know better. I look down the sidewalk at what's left of Brimstone. He's crumpled on his hands and knees, face almost pressed against the concrete. His fire shield has held so far, but it's starting to look as weak as a soap bubble. Too many assaults, perhaps, or too much blood loss. If not for Elysium's intervention, I have no doubt that shield would have lasted only a few more seconds. I blink and see Thomas Weather's remains scattered around my kitchen. That was done by only two gatekeepers. I'm betting there'll be nothing left of Brimstone but blood when this giant flock is done with him.

I have every intention of leaving him to die. After what he did to my customers at Jinx and after what he's tried to do to me, I have absolutely no reason to step in and help him now. But there's a desperate, almost fearful, cadence to Elysium's magic as it shudders through me and my ears still hear the echo of Notte's name on his lips. I struggle to my feet, try to ignore the babbling chorus of *Don't do it* that's ricocheting around my brain, and start down the sidewalk toward Brimstone.

This man knew the risks of following me back here, but like Thomas he came anyway. He wants the boy that's sleeping under Elysium's foundations, the creature Betty thinks is the key to Society's survival. I can't say I care much for Society after how my life has turned out, but I need to know where I fit into this. Adam warned Brimstone about me, which means Adam has always known I survived Elysium's fall and that I've been trapped here ever since. He brought me here and left me here for a reason.

Brimstone's fire sputters and goes out when I'm halfway to him. A gatekeeper dives for him but is thrown clear across the street by another piece of Elysium's wall. Two more try and are repelled with equal force. I make it to Brimstone unchallenged, and I grab his arm with both hands and pull.

YOU WILL STOP.

"Fuck you," I say, but I don't know if I'm talking to Brimstone, Elysium, or the gatekeepers. I tighten my grip and drag Brimstone forward a step. He wheezes something at me that somehow manages to sound unfriendly. I give his arm a violent shake. "Help me or die here!"

He can't get to his feet, but he can sort-of crawl, and he lets me yank him up the sidewalk. Talons snap a scant inch from my face before Elysium crushes that gatekeeper against the lawn.

Gatekeepers bleed blue, and that new knowledge gives me strength.

This time I look back to see where I'm going so I don't trip over the porch. Reaching it is only half the battle, though; Brimstone is at the end of his rope and I don't have the upper body strength to lift his dead weight up the last seven inches.

I look to Falkor, but he's hunched on his pedestal and watching the chaos in my front lawn with a slack-jawed stare. I barely get a "Please" out before he leaps to his haunches and shrieks. I look out at the yard again in time to see a gatekeeper narrowly miss taking Betty's head off. Elysium is out of front wall to throw and has moved on to flinging furniture. The couch spins as it flies past Betty, and she ducks her head and runs for us.

She makes a wild swipe of her arm in a silent order for me to move. As soon as I stumble out of the way, she grabs Brimstone under his arms and throws him. He disappears into the silver light in the doorway, and Elysium's magic snaps in my chest as the gate connects on the far side of the world. The gate vanishes a heartbeat later. Betty winds her arms around me so tight I can barely breathe and drags me into the house with her.

Elysium's magic rumbles as it dies down at last. It's done what it needed to do by getting Brimstone out of here, and now it sinks back into its usual state of rest. The gatekeepers aren't so willing to call things off, though, and I can hear them screaming as they continue their attack on the building. Betty and I make it as far as the living room before the gatekeepers try to follow. One dives through the open front wall, but since they can't enter any room Betty is in, it rebounds outside before it can reach us. Betty lingers a moment, as if making sure the protection is working, then drags me toward the stairs.

She says something, but I don't hear her, and later I won't even remember she spoke, because the gatekeepers don't need to reach me to hurt me. I'm connected to their gate, after all, and that's a link Betty can't save me from. They're still screaming, but now they're screaming in my head, a chorus of furious betrayal and murderous intent. Their magic feels nothing like Elysium's; it's a jagged and oily mess that fills my lungs and chokes me.

I clap my hands over my ears like that can keep them out, but the chorus swells until I'm screaming, too, and my world is nothing but blinding pain.

I wake up between a dead body and a ghost and immediately wish I was either one of them. Everything hurts, from the first breath I take when I open my eyes to my foolish attempt to sit up. It's like someone took a rolling pin to me in my sleep and worked me over top to bottom, pulverizing every inch of me. Hell, even my eyes ache and feel crusted over. Closing them again gives only the illusion of relief, because I'm too sore to fall asleep again.

"Evey?" Casper asks from somewhere right over me. "You awake?"

"Yes," I try to say, but my tongue is a piece of chalk and my throat is sandpaper. It stings for a split-second before my breath catches at the back of my mouth, and although I try to fight it I can't swallow a few wracking coughs. That hurts so much that I'm finally able to move, and I curl up on my side into the tightest fetal position I can manage. I hope it's my imagination that my ribs feel like they're crumpling in on each other.

Casper talks me through it, murmuring reassurances that are not at all helpful. I'd tell her to shut up, but I'm afraid of opening my mouth again. I lie there, miserable and silent, until I can finally breathe without my throat itching. I risk opening my eyes again only to find Casper has come off the bed and is kneeling beside it where she can peer at my face.

"You look like hell, Evey," she says.

I've got just enough strength in me to flip her off. She cracks a grin that doesn't reach her eyes and points over to the nightstand. I follow her finger to see a pitcher of water, a bottle of painkillers, and a letter written in elegant cursive. I bypass the note in favor of tossing four pills into my mouth. The first few gulps of water hurt so badly I want to cry, but eventually my throat loosens up enough that I can chug to my heart's content.

"Alexandra says you're not allowed to leave the room until she wakes up again," Casper says. "I'm supposed to keep an eye on you. She was really worried, you know? She couldn't see that I was right there next to her so she called for me over and over. Told me at least seven times to keep an eye on you. Good thing I like the sound of her voice or I would've gotten tired of the spiel.

"What I don't get is why she didn't bother to actually explain anything," Casper continues, disgruntled. "She didn't tell me why the gatekeepers lost it or why your tenants bailed or why—"

"Wait," I cut in, staring at her. "What?"

"What what?" Casper asks.

Now that she's said it, I recognize that raw feeling to Elysium's magic. The house reads only two residents: Betty and myself. Everyone else gave

40

up their asylum in favor of getting the hell out of dodge. I'd say the gatekeepers spooked them, first by dismembering a representative of the Atlanta Nest and then by attacking Elysium, but gatekeeper violence against Society is not a new thing.

"They're all gone," I say, needing to hear it aloud to believe it.

"You don't remember?" Casper asks, then waves that off and presses on before I can answer. "We were all waiting in the hallway for you two when Alexandra finally dragged you inside. The others wanted to know why Elysium was fighting with the gatekeepers, but then you freaked out. Couldn't get any answers until you finally passed out, and then all Alexandra had to say was the Brimstone Dream was in town.

"Poof." Casper claps her hands together, but they make no sound. "Your Wyrn didn't even stick around to argue. He was out of here like the house was on fire. It took the others a little longer to make up their minds, but the last one left just before you woke up. I wanted to listen in on them, see if they said anything interesting, but Alexandra had already asked me to watch you and I couldn't refuse a beautiful damsel in distress."

"Betty is no damsel."

"But she is in distress. She's asleep at full dark," Casper points out. "She was torn all to shreds when she got you in here, but it looks like she's finally healing."

"She's not sleeping," I remind Casper as I look over my shoulder at Betty. My vampire tenant didn't even bother to change before climbing into bed. Her sheets are stained almost black from her blood and her ravaged clothing is held together more by luck than thread. But Casper's right: the ugly gouges the gatekeepers ripped in her are shallow gashes now. I assume she's going to wake up ravenous after losing so much blood, and I rethink my desire to be in this room when her eyes open.

"So what's a Brimstone Dream?" Casper asks.

"An asshole."

"In more details, maybe," Casper suggests while I gulp down more water.

"I don't know," I admit, and scrub my mouth with the side of my arm. "Betty brought him by Jinx tonight and..."

Thoughts of Jinx are enough to make me lose my train of thought. I dig my phone out of my pocket and flip it open. My battery's nearly dead, but my notifications say I've missed twenty-one calls. There are also several text messages, and I scroll through my inbox without opening any of them. I see Dallas's name and that's enough to make me weak with relief. I can't believe Betty thought to save him. I don't know if it was intentional or if he was in her way when she tried to get Brimstone out of the bar, but honestly I don't really care about her reasons. It's enough to know he's still alive.

The last thing I note is the time: it's barely past midnight, so I've only been out maybe five hours. I set my phone aside without responding to anyone. I don't know what story Betty gave them, so I don't know what to say to corroborate her lies.

"And?" Casper asks, sounding a little annoyed that she has to keep prompting me.

"And he burned it down. He—" I swallow hard and try again. The words are knives burrowing in my chest. "He killed seven customers and one of my dragons to get to me." I can't leave it at that, because I don't want to think about it and can't stomach Casper's shocked demands for a more in-depth explanation. I swallow hard against the ache that feels a bit like betrayal and push Jinx solidly from mind. "He was looking for Rose."

She shakes her head at me and I remember I never shared my final decision on a nickname for our mystery tenant. I don't explain because I'm distracted thinking about Rose. Rather, I'm thinking about Brimstone's reaction. Betty had kept Brimstone in check throughout most of the conversation, carefully deflecting his anger and violence, but she'd failed the second I gave them what they wanted. Not because they no longer had any use to me, but because I'd given the supposed savior of Society a silly nickname.

"The savior of Society," I say quietly, because that presents a disturbing new question. "Hey, Casper. If Rose is really that important to Society, why would the gatekeepers bury him alive?"

"You lost me," Casper says.

I reach for Betty's letter, hoping there'll be some answers for me, but all the note says is: "Evelyn, attempt not to get anyone else killed while I am resting. When I rise, you and I will have a conversation about what you almost cost Society with your carelessness. Until then, stay close to me so the Lymanczyc cannot harm you. You chose sides tonight whether or not you intended to, and it is questionable if they will see fit to forgive you."

"Sometimes I really can't stand the people in my life," I tell Casper.

She leans forward to read the letter, and I turn it so she's not looking at it upside-down. She hums a bit when she's finished and finally says, "Guess that's that, then."

"No," I say, and crumple the letter into a ball. "I'm tired of having to wait on answers, especially when I don't think she's going to be straight with me. We're going to the source this time. Do me a favor and see if the gatekeepers are still here."

She hops to her feet and leaves. She's gone for a minute, then comes back with a grim look on her face. "Two in the kitchen, one in the living room. They've never waited around like this before, at least not since I came here. They're really mad at you, huh?"

"Glad you noticed," I mutter as I get to my feet. It hurts to be upright, but I slowly stretch the gnawing ache from my limbs. I talk as I work, partly to distract me from the pain and mostly because I need to hear this aloud to make heads and tails of it. The picture I'm painting doesn't make me feel any better about what I've gotten myself into tonight.

"I think this has to do with the war," I say. "I can't make this make sense any other way, not with the timing or the players involved. On one side you've got the gatekeepers, and on the other there're the vampires and Brimstone. And Rose," I add. At Casper's frown, I finally clarify, "The gray kid downstairs. There have to be more like him, if Falkor and Smerg wanted to blame Chronos on a sleeping *they*, but Rose is the key somehow. Betty said Society's future hinges on him. That's why he was stolen from them eighteen years ago. The gatekeepers buried him on the line under their watch."

"That's why Elysium was destroyed," Casper concludes. "The vampires were trying to get him back, but they failed. Why didn't they try again?"

I have no answers for that, just a sour burn in my throat that makes me queasy. I know Adam fought in the war. He came to us seeking solace from his nightmares, and Mom let him in without missing a beat. She gave him poultices and gems to keep the worst of it at bay and warned me not to ask him about it. It would be cruel to claw at healing wounds, she said. Being sixteen years old and in love for the first time, I was determined to obey. I never stopped to wonder which side he'd been on.

The childish knot in my chest says there's no hard evidence that Adam is allied with Brimstone and Betty against the gatekeepers. There are other reasons for what he's done, surely. Maybe Adam had been trying to kill Rose, but the gatekeepers couldn't forgive his methods or failure. Maybe he left me behind because I was safer here than on the run with him. Maybe his words to Brimstone were a warning that I would do the right thing and keep Rose out of reach. Maybe Betty recognized his handiwork in Salt Lake City only because she'd faced Adam on the battlefield.

But beneath that foolish attempt at self-delusion is at least one unavoidable truth: Adam destroyed Chronos, the same way he destroyed Elysium sixteen years ago. I don't know why or why he waited so long before making a second strike, but that's not the sort of thing an ally of the gatekeepers would do twice.

I want to shake the answers out of Betty, but the undead are unbelievably inconvenient. Nothing can stir Betty from this stasis but Betty herself. And like I told Casper, I'm not going to drive myself mad with half-answered questions and what-ifs in the meantime. I need the missing pieces of this story. I need the whole truth.

I catch Betty's arm to haul her closer to me. I'm too sore to be lugging her weight around, but I'm pretty much out of options at this point, so I grab her under her arms and drag her off her bed. She makes a sick thud on impact.

"Ouch," Casper says in sympathy. "Rude."

"She can't feel it," I remind Casper.

"It's the principle of the thing," Casper says, and repeats, "Rude."

"Shut up and go find the basement door," I tell her. When Casper hesitates, looking like she might argue, I cut her off with a firm, "We're going to wake up Rose."

FOUR

Getting Betty downstairs is harder work than I expected it to be, but I know I can't leave her behind if I want to survive the short trek to my living room. The upside is Casper has plenty of time to find the trapdoor, and she's waiting half-in and half-out of the floor when I make it to the doorway. The downside is that the gatekeeper who's repulsed from the living room the second I pull Betty into it only retreats as far as the kitchen.

What I didn't take into consideration when I angrily set this reckless plan into motion is that the gatekeepers can still reach me. Foolish, really, considering I've just survived an attack from them. It's a little late to turn back now, though, and all I can do is flinch as their voices dig into my brain.

YOU WILL RENOUNCE THE VAMPIRE AND SUBMIT YOURSELF TO US.

"That's what I'm doing," I lie, lifting my voice so they can hear me. "I'm putting her outside and seeing if Elysium will cut ties with her."

YOU HAVE CHOSEN UNWISELY TONIGHT.

"Maybe if someone had told me all the facts a couple years ago I could have made the right one. Something to think about."

The subsequent pain has me toppling over onto Betty's lifeless body. I gasp for breath against her throat and snap my fingernails against the wooden floorboards of the living room. I think I hear Casper's voice, but I feebly wave at her to stay put. I can't lose track of that door, not now, not with the gatekeepers so riled up. I close my eyes as tightly as I can and try to ride this out. I know they have to stop eventually, because they want me to be telling the truth about tossing Betty out.

The click of claws against wood makes me flinch, but the familiar smell that reaches my nose a second later startles me into opening my eyes again. Falkor has entered the house, reacting to my pain, and stands over me. He bares his fangs at nothing in particular, torn between his need to protect me and his keen understanding of the hierarchy between himself and the gatekeepers. I stroke a hand down his pebbled side and focus on the intricate details of his translucent wings until the gatekeepers' magic finally ebbs.

I can't get to my feet again, but I can crawl, so I do. I push Betty along

45

in front of me, grunting a little under the awkward weight of her, until we've reached Casper. Casper traces the line of the door for me, expression tight with worry, and I follow her path with an unsteady hand. I'm halfway around the border before I find the board I'm looking for. The trapdoor lifts a few inches, enough for me to get my fingers under it, but I'm too sore to lift it.

Falkor ducks his head to investigate, inadvertently nudging the door further open when he stuffs his snout under it. He gives a few noisy sniffs before saying, "We thinks she goes the wrong way."

"Quiet," I say, but of course it's too late.

The second slap of gatekeepers' magic is acid against my brain. I taste blood from screaming so hard. I think I'm screaming myself to pieces. Everything is just noise and jagged heat and shadows, and then there's the distant sensation of falling. The magic disappears a split-second before I crash against a cold stone floor. Betty is dead weight when she lands on top of me, knocking what little breath I had left out of my lungs..

Casper crouches beside me, hands a cold, faint weight against my face. Through her I can see Falkor. He's got Betty's arm in his mouth still, but he opens his jaws and lets it fall away when he feels my eyes on him.

"You saved me," I say, though my words are so slurred I don't know if he can understand.

"She is precious to us," Falkor says.

I laugh, but it sounds more like a sob. "I'm starting to like you."

Falkor catches the hem of Betty's pants leg with his teeth and starts dragging her down the stairs. Casper waits until I'm sitting up before moving out of my way, and she lets off a faint glow as she precedes me into the darkness. I start to stand up, decide I'm too numb to risk it, and settle for sliding down the stairs on my ass. After ten steps my back hurts and my butt is numb, but I keep it up until my feet finally hit the ground floor. Falkor leaves Betty at the base of the stairs and walks the perimeter of the room, snuffling at the red piles of glop. When he's satisfied there are no threats, he waddles to the table in the center of the room. He has to rear up onto his hind legs to get a good look at the sleeper, and he barks a little in either surprise or alarm.

"Oh, it begins again, begins again, or never ends."

I use the wall as support to get to my feet and limp toward him. "You know him?"

"We knows of him," Falkor says. "Everyone knows the gods' favorite child."

"He keeps saying 'we'," Casper says, "like he doesn't know he's

46

missing someone."

I wave at her to be quiet, never mind that Falkor can't hear her. Falkor didn't say those words with any sort of reverence, but it might not be reaching to call that edge fear. "Who is he?"

Falkor clacks his jaws together with a wet chomping sound, as if wondering how much he wants to answer me. For a second I think I'm going to have to drag an explanation out of him, but in the end he lolls his head back at an unnatural angle to face me. I guess he understands he's signed his death warrant by helping me tonight, so helping me helps us both in the end.

"He is Brimstone."

"No," I argue, and let the table take my weight. "Brimstone left. You were there when Betty threw him through a gate."

"Humans know nothing," Falkor says, and drops back to his haunches so he's not looking at Rose anymore. "The Dream comes for what he's lost, for what was taken so long ago. His other half, his responsibility, his precious irreplaceable thing. His Nightmare. But too late now, yes, too late. The Dream is gone, and the Nightmare sleeps still. She should not have come here. They will never forgive her for this one."

That's what Betty said, too. From Betty it could've been theatrics, a condescending reaction to a night that didn't go how she wanted it to, but from Falkor it sounds like truth.

"Society's Nightmare looks a little young for such a title," I say, buying myself time to calm that flutter in my stomach. I don't want to be intimidated by such a name, but it's a sharp reminder that I'm missing most of the story here. It's not like I have a lot of options anymore, but this is starting to feel a bit like frying pan and fire. "Do I want to know what he did to earn that?"

"Nightmares do as they are," Falkor says.

The plural has me looking at him. "I was right, then? There're more than one?"

"We does not know how many are left," Falkor says.

"Any more vague advice you want to not give me before I wake him up?" I ask.

He gnashes his teeth at me. "Stupid human, stupid, stupid. She cannot wake what isn't hers."

"I'm getting a little tired of people telling me what I can't do."

Despite that bold dismissal, it takes me a minute before I can reach for Rose. He is still a block of ice under my hands, an odd contrast to his Brimstone name. I brace myself and give him a short shake. There's no

47

reaction. I glance at Casper, who shrugs, and give him a harder shake. Falkor's tail winds around one of my ankles in either protest or support, and Casper puts a little more distance between herself and the table. I shake Rose until his head is rocking on the table, but his eyelids don't even flutter. I slap his cheek, light at first and harder each successive time, but there's no response.

"Hey!" I say, and louder, "Hey!"

I put a hand to his throat and wait, but his heartbeat is still ticking away at that eternally slow pace. I seize his shirt in both hands, lift him from the table, and let go. He falls like a dead thing and his head sounds too loud against the table's cold surface. I grab his shirt again and give him another violent shake.

"Hey! Damn you, Rose, *wake up!*"

Power sizzles up my arms like a violent static charge. A second later the floor gives out beneath my feet. I fall so fast the air is ripped from my lungs, strangling my scream before I can voice it. I expect to hit the ground at any moment, but I plummet through an inky darkness for what feels like an eternity. I've dreamed this every night since I was first trapped at Elysium but it is no less terrifying now than it was at the start. I claw desperately at the air, looking for something to catch myself on, and come up empty on all sides.

Wake up, I tell myself. *Wake up, wake up, wake up!*

There is another roil of power along my skin, and I am standing in a living room. I don't remember landing—I just go from that abyss to this tidy apartment with no transition. Shock tips the scales and kicks my balance out of sorts, and I fall heavily to my rear. I cast a wide-eyed look around, taking in the scenic paintings hanging equidistant on cream walls and the leather furniture set that screams expensive. The solitary lamp on the end table is too small to be lighting the room like this, but there are no overhead lights or windows to aid it. There's not even, I notice on a bewildered second check, a door leading in or out of here.

I scramble to my feet and feel the walls, but two laps around turn up no exits. I make a third lap anyway and take all of the paintings down. No secret tunnels are hidden behind them. This room is a box. I have no idea how I got in, and no clue how I'm supposed to get out. I hang onto the last painting like it'll somehow help me make sense of this. It feels real under my fingers, a cool wooden frame protecting coarse paper, but this can't be real.

"Casper?" I call.

The voice that answers isn't hers. "This is unexpected."

I whip around, brandishing the painting like a weapon, and find a young man standing in the same spot I'd landed. Eighteen at best guess, maybe a little younger, with bronze skin and dark hair cut jagged and short. His eyes are two spots of coal on his face. Equally unnerving is the black tattoo taking up half his face: an intricate and upside-down Celtic cross identical to Brimstone's save for the color color. This kid looks nothing like the creature sleeping in my cellar aside from his dark outfit, but somehow they are one and the same.

His stance is casual and he keeps his hands buried in his coat pockets as he surveys the room, but I keep my painting raised in case Society's so-called Nightmare turns violent. At last he turns his full attention on me, and his stare is a weight I feel on every inch of my skin. I don't know how much is from the creepy factor of his jet-black eyes and how much is from the raw power radiating from him. My throat clenches in instinctive fear and I have to swallow four times just to breathe without choking.

"I'm dreaming," he says.

"Common side effect of sleeping," I answer. "You couldn't have dreamed up a door?"

He doesn't move, I'm sure of it. I'm looking right at him. But suddenly I'm flat against the wall with the painting the only thing between his body and mine. Despite the age difference between us, he's got a couple inches on me. This close his eyes almost look like holes on his face, and I have the distinct feeling I'll fall into them if I stare too long. My stomach jumps at the thought and I wrench my attention to the bridge of his nose. It isn't much safer, but I refuse to drop my gaze.

"Personal space," I say.

"I'm dreaming," Rose says again, a little louder, "but where is Pharaoh?"

"Pretty sure the last pharaoh died out a couple thousand—"

Rose cuts me off. "Where is my Dream?"

"Brimstone?" I guess. "Mexican with a white tattoo and a shitty attitude?"

Rose wraps his fingers around my throat one at a time, just firm enough to be a warning. "Careful," he says, soft as a breath of air. "You should know better than to speak ill of him to me, especially when you've come here with his scent on you."

I've spent too many years at Elysium to let him threaten me, so I lift the painting until the frame is digging into his Adam's apple. Meeting his eyes puts that sickening drop in my stomach again, but I stare him down like I've stared down every other upstart beast that's come under my

49

jurisdiction. The trick is to not think about what the hell a Nightmare might be or why Falkor called him the gods' favored child.

"Let go," I say.

"I will ask you one last time."

"I'm not asking," I say in as hard a voice I can manage. "You let go of me right now, and then I'll tell you who killed your dirtbag boyfriend."

The lamp snap-crackle-pops behind Rose, casting us into a heartbeat of darkness. I ignore it, more interested in the half-second of shock that has his fingers going slack against my throat. I press the advantage as soon as I have it, shoving myself off the wall and using my weight and the painting to throw Rose away from me. He's too rattled to resist but catches himself on the chair to stare at me.

"You're lying," he whispers.

"Maybe," I admit. "We got him through an open-ended gate—India or Russia, I think, judging by how far away the connection felt—but I doubt he survived long on the other side. The gatekeepers were trying to turn him inside out on my lawn."

"No," Rose insists. "No! I would know."

"Sure about that?" I ask.

"You're lying. This is just another dream."

"Then wake up and ask me again."

He takes a step toward me but goes still as stone as soon as his shoe touches the ground. For a moment I think the world has stopped, but then Rose slowly turns his attention downward. I follow his stare, half-sure this is a trick, and stare in consternation as the carpet darkens under his foot. It takes another second before I can understand. Water is seeping into the room from who-knows-where, soaking through the beige fibers and lapping at our shoes.

"No," Rose says again, and takes a faltering step back. "Not this. I'm not—"

"Guess you should've dreamed up that door." I toss the painting aside as useless and make a fourth lap of the room, this time hunched over with my fingers jammed into the edge of the carpet. There's no hole that I can feel, nothing we can plug to stop this place from filling up. I'm so intent on my task I don't realize how quickly it's coming in until I reach my starting point again and straighten. My knees barely have time to adjust to the cold before the water's halfway up my thighs.

Rose is perched on the back of the couch like an oversized cat. I follow his lead and clamber onto the nearest chair. "Now what?"

"Pharaoh," Rose says, and on his lips it sounds like a prayer. "Pharaoh,

50

wake me up!"

"He's dead," I remind him, maybe a little too sharply. The water's at my knees again, and I don't think the arm of the chair will support my weight for long. I attempt it anyway and reach toward the ceiling for a bit of extra balance. I kick water at the unresponsive Nightmare standing across from me and snap, "Wake up and get us out of here. Hey! *Rose!*"

His gaze snaps to mine immediately. I know it's my imagination, but for a moment I'm sure the plaster I'm touching is his comatose body. He's too far away for me to hear his breath hitch, but I feel it catch in my own throat as if we're sharing the same skin. The abyss in his eyes suddenly doesn't seem so far down. If I let go now, I think I can fall through to the basement where I'm standing over his pedestal.

"How dare you," Rose says with a terrible anger.

His power is a crackling heat on every inch of my skin, a static charge waiting for permission to break free. It isn't mine, but I know with inexplicable certainty that I can redirect it. I lower a hand from the ceiling and press my palm flat against the water now lapping at my ribcage.

"Pharaoh's not here, but I am, and I am not dying down here," I tell him.

"No," he says. "Don't you dare—"

He lunges toward me, but the water slows him down, and I only need two words: "Wake up."

The air fills with white noise. I barely hear two ticks before a concussive wave kicks me from my perch. I slam into the wall so hard I'm sure I've broken every bone in my body. The water that eats its way up my throat is now scalding hot. I open my mouth to scream and the fire swallows me whole.

I come awake in the basement, still standing over Rose's dark form, and only Falkor's presence behind my legs keeps me retreating from the stone bed. My throat aches like I've been screaming again, but Casper is watching me with interest, not alarm. I press careful fingers to my neck, wincing at the lingering soreness, but forget my pain when Rose shifts.

Falkor spits and books it to the far side of the room. I'm tempted to join him but settle for taking two careful steps back. Rose takes his time getting up, starting with a twitch of each gray finger and then a painstakingly slow twist onto his side. He needs two tries to boost himself up on an elbow, and when he coughs, black fire curls along his lips.

Around the room the jelly piles pop and deflate, leaking a dark red blood across the stone floor. Rose waits until the room has gone quiet again before finally pushing himself into a sitting position. His power is almost suffocating, somehow heavier out here than it was down there, and I almost can't stop myself from rubbing at my arms.

"Pharaoh," he says, so sleep-slurred I barely understand him.

"Is not here," I remind him.

Rose goes perfectly still. It is an eternity before he tilts his head to look at me. Meeting that creepy stare of his makes my spine itch. I wait to see if he picks up where we left off, but instead of making another grab at me he takes a long look around the room.

"This must be another dream, but even my mind has never been so cruel," he says. He turns his hand and considers his palm as if it holds all the answers he's seeking. One by one he curls his fingers into a fist so tight his knuckles go silver. "This is impossible. I reject this. I reject you."

"Ingrate," I say. "Did I or did I not just save our lives?"

"I am not yours to use," Rose says, with a heat I swear I can feel. "How dare you try to claim what isn't yours."

"All I want from you are answers. Tell me about—"

Adam's name catches in my throat. It's instinctive by now to swallow his name, even though I know we're safe down here. I'm inside the range of Betty's unusual protection, and Falkor's intervention earlier proved the gatekeepers' power can't reach past the living room trap door. I work my jaw, clawing for the last scrap of courage I need, but then Rose is sliding toward the edge of his bed like he's going to get up and come at me. I change what I wanted to say.

"How you can move?" I demand. "Shouldn't your body have rotted to pudding after all this time down here? Why are you down here in the first place? What is a Nightmare?"

Rose goes still and echoes, "All this time. How long have I been sleeping?"

"Eighteen years, last I heard."

That drives him to his feet, but I barely have time to tense before his legs give out on him. I guess he's not in such tiptop shape after all. I keep my distance and watch as he steadies himself with his hands. Casper climbs onto his newly-abandoned pedestal and sits cross-legged in the center to consider him. Falkor hunches low to the ground, and it takes me a minute to realize he's retreating. He's moving slower than molasses, as if he fears drawing Rose's attention by going any faster.

"No. I was only supposed to—he said he would wake me up when we—" Rose shakes his head and digs the palm of a hand into one eye. "He never would have let me sleep this long. What went wrong?"

"You were stolen," I say, but it's as unhelpful an answer to him as it is a proper explanation to me. "I'm hazy on the rest of the details, but you can ask Betty when she revives."

Rose slants a sharp look up at me, then follows my gesture to Betty's limp form. It takes him two tries to push himself up onto his knees and he sinks back onto his heels when he starts to tilt to the side. He points at Betty, and my first thought is he expects me to drag her dead weight over to him. Instead his power sends a searing heat ricocheting through my gut. Betty comes back to life with a strangled yell and immediately rolls into the fetal position.

"That's," I start, and since I can't say "terrifying" I settle for, "pretty handy."

Betty is too fresh from death to have her full voice back, but she somehow still manages to pack venom into her raspy, "Evelyn."

Rose interrupts what is sure to be an unjustified lecture. "Vicereine Alexandra."

Betty's head jerks up at the sound of his voice. She stares at him for a moment in unabashed shock before a wicked grin cuts her face in two. I find it pretty interesting that her smile doesn't reach her eyes, especially considering how determined she was to find this kid. I'm not sure if it's tension that brings her onto her knees so slowly or if she's still aching from whatever magic trick Rose used to call her back from the dead.

"Brimstone," she says. "At last."

"I will give you one chance to explain this to me."

Betty spreads her hands in a calming gesture. "Ask anything."

I expect him to ask about Pharaoh, but he swivels his finger toward me. "Start with her."

Betty barely glances at me. Whatever this Nightmare is to Society, he is worth her full attention. "Evelyn Downey. Mediocre psychic, surly bartender, and sour landlord, but she is worth tolerating most of the time. She is the one who found you down here."

"I found him," Casper protests, but I'm the only one who can hear her.

"Thanks for the glowing review," I mutter.

Rose ignores me. "She is alone?"

It is an odd question to ask when they're both right here with me, and the frown that tugs at Betty's lips says she understands it as well as I do. It takes her a moment to come up with a response, and then all she has to offer is, "She keeps a pet ghost on hand and usually has four to eight tenants here any given day."

"I'm not a pet!" Casper argues. I wave at her to shush and she subsides grumpily.

Rose continues to stare at Betty, as if expecting more than that. Betty risks another glance my way like I know what she's missing. I shrug.

At last Rose says, "Then she is now under Brimstone protection, and we will retaliate with extreme prejudice."

I take a page from Casper's book. "You keep saying 'we' like you haven't—"

"He lives," Rose interrupts me savagely. "I would know if I'd lost him."

Betty gives him a second to see if there's more, then says, "You will need to contest the Lymanczyc for custody. They have bound her to the Elysium gate."

"This is not Elysium."

"This is what is left of it after your master attempted to destroy it sixteen years ago. Evelyn was sacrificed to stabilize the line."

For a moment I can't feel my body. "What do you mean, his master?"

Rose's response is much quieter. "The Lymancyzc did what?"

I put myself between them and snap my fingers until Rose drags his stare up to my face. "They tore me inside out on the floorboards until Elysium rebuilt itself around my blood," I say in a voice too cold and terrible to be mine, "because *my husband* left me here to die. What do you mean, he was your master?"

Rose matches me fire for ice. "Notte isn't yours, you ignorant child."

Fingers clamp down around my wrist. Adrenaline makes my head spin. I didn't realize I'd drawn my hand back to strike him; I didn't hear Betty bolt across the room to stop me before I could make that fatal mistake. I suck in a breath that shakes me open all the way down, make one half-assed attempt to calm down, and settle for kicking Rose in the shoulder. He's too weak from sleep to brace against the blow and goes crashing into his pedestal. I try to wrench out of Betty's grip and nearly break my wrist in the process.

"Fuck you," I snap. "Fuck you! What do you know?"

Rose takes his time getting to his feet. There is death in his bottomless stare when he turns on me again, but I lean toward him instead of away when he reaches for me. He makes a fist in my hair that has half of my scalp screaming in protest. If he yanks hard enough right now, I will lose more than just my hair.

"I know that if you weren't what you are, you would be dead now," Rose says. "There are allowances for unforgivable transgressions, but we can only stay our hands for so long. It is not in our nature to be understanding. You will learn restraint before you meet Meridian or she

54

will kill you, and we cannot afford to lose you."

"Meridian is dead," Betty says. "We lost her seventeen years ago."

Rose's fingers go slack and slip from my hair. "No. Notte still lives."

"According to several witnesses outside Chronos, yes, but this is the first sign anyone's seen of him since Elysium fell. We're not sure where he is now," Betty admits. "He appeared only long enough to wake your Dream, then—"

"Wake," Rose repeats, so softly I probably imagined it.

Maybe not, because Betty falters too and stares at him a moment. When nothing else is forthcoming, she presses on. "He vanished shortly afterward. We've got the witches looking for him now, and the old channels are being reestablished in case he's spotted again. We've asked the sirens to collect your brethren, but your name has always been the better bargaining chip in getting their cooperation."

"I am nothing to them without Pharaoh," Rose says, and Betty tips her head in either agreement or acknowledgment. "Now: an explanation. You said he woke Pharaoh."

Betty clues in too late that she's made a mistake. "I am only repeating what was said to me," she says, slow and careful. "The Salt Lake Nest retrieved him from the wreckage of the Chronos gate and brought him to safety. When they expressed appropriate relief for his return, he asked how long he had been missing. Eighteen years, same as you. We had always assumed you two went underground together."

Rose might look mostly human, but he is definitely not, and the savage power he packs into his fierce "*I will kill him!*" is a frightening reminder. The room contracts under the weight of his unholy magic until the air is a vise around my body and a scorching heat in my throat. My eyeballs scream under the pressure and even my toenails are trying to bend deeper into soft flesh to escape. I taste blood where my jaws are driving my teeth back into my gums.

I try to speak, to yell at him to stop this, but the best I can manage is a slight crack of my lips. A second later my nerve endings go numb, short-circuiting under too much pressure and input. In the absence of my body, I can feel a second power that will forever run deeper than Rose's: Elysium's. Why it hasn't struck out against him for hurting me, I don't know, but I claw desperately at the line that's twisted through my soul. I think of how it felt when it lashed out against the gatekeepers and pull that thought to the forefront of everything else.

The room snaps open; the pressure vanishes with a fierce crackle. I gasp desperately for air and curl my fingers into my mouth to check on my teeth. They feel fine, and my fingertips come back without any blood on them. I look to Betty to see how she's holding up, but she looks unfazed and untouched. I turn my glare on Rose, who's now looking at me like he's seen a ghost.

"If this is your idea of protection, I'm safer off with Elysium. But!" I jab a finger at him for emphasis, and he's still off-guard enough that I land it in the hollow of his throat. Betty hisses a warning at me that I ignore. "I'm assuming when you say 'I will kill him' that you are not talking about your bratty little Pharaoh, which means you're going after Adam. And since I'm under your protection you are obligated to take me along, and I am therefore obligated to tell you that he is mine to kill."

"My quarrel is with Notte."

"Adam Notte," I say, and it's as exhilarating as it is terrifying to say his full name aloud.

"Do not call him that," Rose says. "He is not yours to name."

"Oh," Betty says, sharp with surprise. She's finally put the pieces together, but the look on her face says she and I are drawing very different conclusions. I'm not sure I want to know what track her mind has taken, because there is more than a little hunger in her intense stare. It's made even creepier by the new urgency in her voice: "Brimstone, I did not know. I never would have brought him to her if I'd known."

"You could not have known," Rose says, "but the Lymancyzc will understand the truth when they realize I am awake again. We are leaving."

"Can you get me out of here?" I ask. "I have a five-mile leash attached to Elysium's front door."

"You are tied to the line," Rose says.

It takes me a moment to realize that's all the explanation he thinks I need. "Yeah, I was there when it happened. The gatekeepers don't want me going anywhere. Are you strong enough to break what they did or not?"

Betty puts her hand out in a calming gesture. It's a move I've seen a lot from her in the last twenty-four hours, as defensive as it is supportive, but she has never turned it on me. She's always treated me with an irreverent tolerance. I don't know if it's the news of my relationship with Adam that's changed things or if she's toeing the line because of Rose's promise to protect me, but it's a little eerie to see this change in her.

"The Nightmares have more rights to the lines than the Lymancyzc ever will, Evelyn. They cannot stop him if he chooses to take you along. There is still the matter of the draconian faerie," she adds, with a glance toward Rose. "She was gold to a pair; Brimstone killed one but the other remains."

56

"Falkor saved our lives tonight," I point out when Rose's heavy stare finally swivels to the last living occupant of the room. Falkor has made it to the far wall and is lying so flat against the ground he looks like a shiny puddle. "He's not going to be a problem."

Betty waits a beat to see if Rose argues, then says, "I will get you a gate to Madtown, but I cannot follow you yet. Give me a day, maybe two, to lose the Lymancyzc and pull the right strings in Atlanta, and I will join you there. We will rally the Nest and the Guard. A moment."

She is across the room faster than my eyes can track her and flies up the stairs.

Casper puts her hand up as soon as Betty is gone. "I have no idea what just happened."

"You and me both," I say.

"Was all that true?" Casper demands. She slides off the pedestal and comes through Rose to stand in front me. "The guy that broke the gate, that the gatekeepers just killed a dude over, he's your husband? He just.. left you here to die? Did this to you?" She waggles her hand near my abdomen. "Jesus, Evey. Were you ever going to tell me?"

"Probably not."

Rose slides a hooded look my way. "Pet ghost," he guesses.

"Still not a pet," Casper says. "Correct him, Evey."

"I named her Casper," I say instead.

"Your ignorance is dangerous," Rose tells me. "You name what isn't yours and create binds that cannot, should not exist. Did Notte teach you nothing?"

"I guess he was too busy stabbing me in the back."

"He will answer for it," Rose says, and it sounds so much like a promise my heart aches.

Elysium's magic stirs under my skin and I glance instinctively to the stairs. I haven't felt Madtown's gate in ages; Elysium is a refuge, after all, and most of its tenants only came because no place else would take them.

It strikes me then that this might actually be happening, that Rose really might be able to break the gatekeepers' chains and get me out of here. Sixteen years trapped in Augusta, serving drinks and avoiding my tenants, and it's all about to end. I'm lightheaded at the prospect, and on the heels of excitement is a gnawing guilt. Jinx is a burned husk; Dallas barely avoided getting killed tonight. Now I'm just going to vanish on all of them without a word?

Betty darts back downstairs, and I blurt out, "What about Jude?"

She draws up short with her hand halfway to Rose. I half-expect her to brush it aside and confirm that Jude has just been an entertaining pastime these last couple years, but instead she says, "Right now you have to go, Evelyn. There is too much at stake. Trust me to cover our tracks."

She presses a black coin into Rose's waiting palm. "This should get you into Pariah. I will contact you as soon as I make it to the city."

"Find Pharaoh," Rose says.

"Whatever the cost," Betty promises. "The Nests will call him home."

Rose catches hold of my wrist with his free hand. "Stay close."

He hauls me after him toward the stairs. I risk a look over my shoulder and manage to stub my toe on the first step. "Ouch! Falkor, Casper, we're leaving!"

I say it, but I can't believe it, and as I follow Rose up through the pitch black stairwell all I feel is fear. My heart hammers bruises into my ribcage and lungs and I know beyond a doubt that Rose is wrong, that we'll reach the gate and he'll go through and I'll be left here staring after him. I think about Adam and Ciara and Madtown, and I need him to be right so badly I could cry. Desperation is a knot eating me alive from the inside out, and then Rose is letting go of me.

"Wait," I cry, but he's just boosting himself out of the trap door in our living room. He hauls me out after him like I'm a sack of potatoes and I stare at the wreckage around us. Without Betty or me around to protect Elysium, it has been reduced to rubble. The sky is hidden behind a flock of furious gatekeepers. Somehow the gate still holds, though the frame around it has been ripped away by angry talons. Up here away from Rose's tomb it's easier to feel Elysium's pain; the line and house twist around each other like mangled caterpillars.

It takes the gatekeepers only a moment to realize I've returned—and less than that to see who is with me. They scream a chorus of outrage as they launch for us, but Betty is just fast enough. She appears at my side and brings Elysium's protection with her. The first gatekeeper to dive is repelled off an invisible barrier. Elysium starts pulling itself together around us, brick by brick, taking advantage of our presence and the gatekeepers' distraction. Betty shifts aside as Falkor leaps out of the hole and plants himself against my leg.

"Oh, God," Casper says when she sees our welcome committee. "Evey?"

DREAM, the gatekeepers say, a sibilant and hate-filled accusation. **KILL THE DREAM**. Above it all one trumpets **BRIMSTONE, BRIMSTONE** like a call to arms. This has to be all the gatekeepers Society has to offer, but as I watch more of them appear to fill in the scant gaps.

Rose pulls up a hood that wasn't there before and tugs it low over his face. "You must not stop."

"Promise me," I say, because there are so many of them and so few of us.

"You belong to Brimstone," Rose says. "I will not leave you."

His hand around my wrist is the only warning I get before he runs for the gate. It's run or be dragged, so I nearly kick his heels in my attempt to keep up. I don't look back; I don't look up. I look only at the shimmering gate that feels a world away from us.

Let me go, I think at the gate. *Let me go, let me go.*

I close my eyes at the last second, bracing myself for heat and the agony of a forced rebound. Rose's magic surges through me, smothering Elysium's familiar crackle, and I hit something so cold it knocks the wind from me. There is a split second of resistance, but then we are through.

I am free.

FIVE

We hit the streets of Madtown at a run. I try looking back to see if Casper and Falkor have made it through the gate behind us, but we're going so fast I just trip over my own feet. Rose hauls me up right before I crack both kneecaps against the sidewalk. I swear up a storm over my stubbed toes, then swear at Rose when he digs his fingers harder into my wrist. He doesn't waste his breath responding but drags me after him past the line waiting for Madtown's gate to reset. I see the crowd as a mostly indistinct blur, horns here and scales there, and hope we're just as hard to make out at this speed.

We're almost to the corner when the gatekeepers arrive en masse above us, still roaring hate and outrage. Their anger actually works in our favor, as Madtown's denizens panic and scatter at the sight of so many. Rose and I are just a couple more bodies diving for cover. We make it six streets up and two over before Rose finds us a narrow alley to hide in. He lets go of me at last and goes to check at the mouth for any sign we've been followed.

I press my hands against my abdomen and inspect them for blood. I expected pain. I thought I'd feel different, lighter maybe, with Elysium's chains cut. Instead I feel the same as I did yesterday and last week and six years ago.

"Is this a dream?" I ask. "Am I really free?"

"None of us are truly free," Rose says. "We're going."

I glance at what sliver of the sky I can actually see from here. "Maybe we should wait."

"It is safer there than here."

I look over my shoulder at the innocuous alley but don't argue. Rose catches my wrist again when I scoot close enough to him and leads me out into the street.

Madtown is as much a part of San Francisco as Chinatown or Little Italy, but it's not going to show up in travel brochures anytime soon. The stronger gates warp reality around them, same as Elysium can contract and expand on the inside to accommodate a fluctuating number of guests. Madtown is strong enough that it has pulled three square miles of Earth a half-step out of sync. If you don't know exactly where the entrances are and don't have enough magic in you to survive that jump, you'll never set foot in Madtown proper.

Some five thousand beasties call Madtown home, making it the largest community in all of Society and a crowded hellhole I never wanted to visit. The streets and doorways are wide to accommodate bigger monsters, and the buildings are a mismatched mess dependent on occupant needs. The vampires' tower is an eyesore in the near distance, a black skyscraper building with no windows and only a solitary door.

"We lost the others," I tell Rose.

"They are of no concern to me," Rose says.

I won't risk calling out to them, not with the gatekeepers just a street or two over. I have to trust the invisible leash that binds me to Falkor—and hope that Casper is smart enough to stick close to him.

We don't get far before Rose stops us again. PARIAH is etched into a stone front door, and I belatedly remember Betty name-dropping it. Rose turns my hand over, presses the black coin Betty gave him into my palm, and lets me go. I turn the coin over in my hands, studying the unfamiliar markings.

"Money?" I guess.

"A favor," he answers. "We need two nights. Do not give him our names."

"Two nights," I echo. I give the door a skeptical look. "Preternatural bed and breakfast?"

"Close enough."

Rose keeps his hood down and head low when I push open the door for us. There is some pretty sharp magic built into the doorway. It crackles over my skin and snarls over his when he follows me inside. The foyer is expansive, but its furniture is limited to the front desk and a small corner fountain. Instead there are a good two-dozen pillows piled haphazardly on the wooden floor. Five teenage humans are sprawled there, gossiping about recent tests, while a lion dozes in the back corner. The only one who acknowledges our arrival is the man at the front desk.

I go to him. "We need to stay two nights. How many people to a room?"

He quirks a too-fuzzy brow. "How many are staying?"

"Three and a draconian faerie," I say. "The others will join us later. Is this enough?"

I show him the coin. He moves faster than a blink to snatch it from me. It turns green when he presses it to his forehead. I assume that's his way of judging its authenticity, because he pockets it and grabs an oversized key ring from his top drawer. He hoists himself out of his chair and turns toward a stairwell I swear wasn't there a few seconds ago. I look to Rose to see if he notices anything strange, but his hood hides his face completely.

Our room is on the fourth floor. Our guide unlocks the door by pressing the keys to the wood, and he plucks the appropriate key from the ring like he's pulling a petal off a flower. I turn it over in my hand, but the metal feels solid, and the ring he's holding looks unbroken. I decide not to ask and let him leave us uncontested.

When he's disappeared into the stairwell again, I push the door open and let us inside. Two steps in I realize we're standing in an empty room. Before I can cry foul, the floor rumbles and sprouts beds. A tinted window spreads into existence on the wall. Clanging and groaning in what must be the bathroom is the appropriate plumbing falling into place. It's the same magic Elysium uses, though I rarely got to watch it in action.

Rose spits something that isn't English and swats at his shoulder. I dodge a couple steps to the left and check the floor, but there's nothing there. When I check Rose next, he's picking at his coat like he's peeling something off of himself. Spiderweb from the alley, I assume, but the threads are too small for me to see them between his fingers.

I leave him to his work and claim the closer bed for my own. It isn't until I'm sitting cross-legged on the mattress that I realize I didn't pack anything before abandoning Elysium. I've no toiletries or spare clothes. I rock side to side and pat at my ass, checking my pockets for my wallet, and am satisfied by the weight of it.

I glance up when Rose crosses the room. There's a panel on the far wall that flips up to reveal a set of dials. A couple quick clicks and the vents start blasting hot air into a room that's already almost uncomfortably warm.

"Is that really necessary?" I ask.

"It's cold."

"No, you're cold because you were passed out in a meat locker. Did the gatekeepers do that?"

"Only a Dream can put a Nightmare to sleep."

"Pharaoh did that to you? That's a little messed up, don't you think?"

"We had no choice." Rose moves to the bed beside mine and sits in the center. He hugs his coat tighter around himself and stares into the distance. "And that is not where he put me to rest. I do not know how I ended up in Elysium."

I give him a couple minutes to his thoughts, then say, "Promise me

62

we're going to find Adam."

"Stop calling him that," Rose warns me. "You cannot name him."

"Technically I didn't," I point out. "He went by Notte until he asked me to run away with him. I told him I couldn't marry him until he told me his first name. He said if I was Evelyn, he'd be Adam to my Eve. I knew it was a lie, but I loved it. I was sixteen," I add, a little defensively. "I thought it was romantic."

"No. Nightmares are not allowed to name themselves," Rose insists. "That right belongs to their Dreams."

I put a hand up. "What?"

"He could not have named himself," Rose says. "You are mistaken."

"*You're* mistaken," I say. "He wasn't a Nightmare."

"Says the Dream who stakes a hundred claims where there should be none," Rose says with an edge in his voice. "You will learn restraint before we find your Nightmare or you will leave him with no choice but to kill everyone you've linked yourself to. Nightmares cannot share. Our existence depends on us being the one and only person of import."

My laugh is short and startled, sharp enough to hurt my throat. "You've mixed me up with someone else. I'm just a two-bit psychic from the south."

"You cannot be both," Rose says, "and yet you are what you are." He tips his head to one side and stares so intensely I have to clench my hands in my lap to keep from fidgeting. "You waste your breath on ignorant protests. Nightmares can always find what's theirs; we see you when no one else can. It is a necessary fail-safe to keep you alive until you are paired."

"No," I insist. "I don't even know what a Dream *is*."

"How can you not know?" Rose demands. Before I can snap something rude back, I realize it's not me he's angry at. His words get sharper as he bulls on: "He put you at risk. He put us all at risk. How is he still so—" He makes a cutting gesture and shuts up, but I can see the rest of his angry rant in the hard line of mouth and the tension in his shoulders.

Betty called Notte his master, but Rose's angry *I will kill him* was not a heat of the moment outburst. There is a deep and toxic hatred in him toward my not-so-late husband. It takes him four deep breaths before he can forcibly calm down, and then Rose says, "Tell me what you do know, and we will go from there."

"Nothing," I say. "I didn't know your kind existed until we found you in the basement. Falkor called you a Nightmare, but he didn't explain. Betty seems to think you're some sort of savior, but last I checked the vampires were fighting the gatekeepers for control of the lines. It looks like you're allies, but I don't know what you want with the gates. To destroy them, if Adam's anyone to judge by."

"Do not," Rose says, cold and low, "judge us by him."

"Should I judge them by Pharaoh?" I shoot back. "He murdered my customers and Falkor's other half for no reason."

"Not for no reason," Rose says as if he was there. "He has no quarrel with humans."

I'm raring up for a good argument when I remember what set Pharaoh off. He'd been on the edge of an outburst our entire conversation, but it wasn't until I mentioned Rose that he completely lost his chill and tried to kill me. "Just out of curiosity, when you say Nightmares can't handle nicknames from other people is that because it's offensive or because there really is more to it? You keep implying that it's a little more complicated somehow."

"No," Rose protests, but there's more horror than anger in his denial. "You did not call me this in front of him."

"There's more to it," I conclude.

Rose crushes the heels of his hands against his eyes and moans something in that other language again. I can't even begin to hazard a guess as to what it is. Not the Spanish Pharaoh was using, or the Chinese I've heard around Augusta once in a rare while. I consider asking, but I bite my tongue and wait for a proper explanation.

Rose digs his fingernails into his forehead so hard his knuckles go white, takes a steadying breath, and drops his hands to his lap. "We will start at the beginning. You are too dangerous when you know nothing."

"Not my fault," I point out.

Rose ignores me. I let it slide because of where he starts his story: "These creatures you erroneously call gatekeepers are not the originally guardians of the ley lines. The Lymanczyc are sole survivors from another of Earth's nine realms, vultures who must be exterminated. They feed off the living essence of a realm, eating it down to the bare bones, and then move on to the next Earth to repeat the process. We are not yet sure how many worlds they have destroyed, but we know what will happen if we cannot wrest them free of this one."

"Okay," I say when Rose pauses, though none of that sounds okay whatsoever. "That's a, uh, that's a hell of a place to begin."

"The realms are connected in five places we call the Fingers," Rose continues. "This is how the Lymanczyc came to us. This is also how Gaia felt the death of Her brethren realms. Her veins were already poisoned by

64

the deeds of humans; coupled with this new sickness She had no choice but to purge Herself to survive.

"She birthed the Nightmares: living incarnations of Her corruption, physical manifestations of Her wounds, charged with the single task of clearing the Lymanczyc from this realm. But Gaia exists on a system of balances, and where we are poison we must have a cure. Dreams are the answer to this: a people born to save us from ourselves, to act as anchors for our sanity when our power would otherwise tear us apart. They are what takes our magic from here," he gestures to his temple, then moves his hand out between us with his next words, "to here."

"You told Betty you were nothing without Pharaoh," I say. "Truth?"

"The longer I am without him, the greater my chances of getting devoured by my own power," Rose says. "My grasp on reality will weaken, my defenses will crumble, and my mind will be eaten by those who once called me master. I know Pharaoh survived the Lymanczyc because I remain in control, but his absence will not go unnoticed for long."

"And you think I'm one of these—these cures."

"I do not think," Rose says. "I know."

"I'm human."

"You have never been human."

"My mother was a psychic," I insist. "My father was a witch."

"Irrelevant. Why else would Notte have come to you?"

"Because he—" My strident *loved me* dies in my throat. It is a lie I stopped believing the first morning I woke up alone in Elysium, glued to the floor by my own blood and shredded organs. The wounds the gatekeepers carved in me had already been healed to hideous scars by Elysium's magic, but the ache remained—the lingering agony of a rough childbirth barely smothered by the stabbing pains of a recent evisceration. If Adam had ever loved me, he certainly hadn't loved me at the end.

Which leaves only Rose's "why", and there are so many whys behind it. Why did he come to my house in Orlando? Why did my mother not question a grown man's intense interest in her sixteen year-old child? Why did Adam sweet-talk me into running away with him, only to lead us on a winding path to Elysium? Why did he steal Ciara from me and leave me behind to die?

That's the question that sticks the hardest in my throat, because now I know Adam always knew I'd survived. Pharaoh knew of me from Notte. He thought I was going to take Rose from him—and apparently I confirmed that fear by calling him "Rose".

"If I really am a cure, why did he leave me?" I ask in a low voice.

65

Rose actually considers that, but the best he has is, "I do not know. It is a crime we cannot forgive. Dreams are too important, too precious. Even if he fulfilled his obligation by saving me, he should have known better than to abandon you."

I stare at him for a hard minute, then give a sharp jerk of my hand. "We'll come back to this, because I don't even know where to start right now."

Rose doesn't argue but picks up where he left off. "Those in Society whose lives are longest tend to stand with us, as they better understand the consequences of a drained world, but most either will not believe the truth due to the make-up of our alliance or are too short-lived to honestly grasp what will happen to Gaia should this continue. We refer to ourselves as the Guard. GLOBE refers to us as a menace to be monitored. If the vampires were not the financial backbone of Society as well as our allies, there is little doubt they would be actively hunted down by those who oppose us."

"Betty said she would rally the Guard," I recall. "Do you think anyone is left? The war's been over a long time. You lost."

"Pharaoh and I disappeared for too long, and Notte lost Meridian," Rose says. "It is unsurprising that the Lymanczyc were victorious. But there is too much at stake for the Guard to ignore a call to arms. We will get a status report tonight if the old rooms are still open, and then we will at least know what we are starting from."

"You mean to go to war again." It shouldn't be so surprising, not after Adam destroyed Chronos, not after everything I've patched together over the last couple days, but fear is cold fingers on my spine. I was too young to understand the last war, but there is no way to avoid it if Rose is playing bodyguard. "Betty called you the savior of Society. Truth?"

"I am the strongest of the Nightmares," Rose says without an ounce of pride. "I am as valuable to them as I am dangerous. My strength is why Pharaoh put me to sleep."

"That seems counterproductive."

"We are Gaia's children, and Gaia is dying," Rose says. "As she could feel the realms die around her, they can feel her growing weakness. Gods have little reason to linger over ruined worlds and no way to sidestep to more prosperous lands—or they had no way until the Nightmares were born. We are walking pieces of Gaia, and so we are also connected to the Fingers. The stronger we are, the harder our power pulls at her, and the greater the chances of us sidestepping the wrong way. The gods wait for us to cross realms in hopes of following us home."

"Falkor called you the gods' favorite child," I tell him.

"I know the gods by name," Rose says. "I know their faces and their lands. I know the feel of their fingers on my throat when I cannot outrun their reaching hands. The only way to reset my connection is for Pharaoh to put me to sleep. When I am sleeping, I cannot dream, and so they cannot find me."

It's my turn to rub at my eyes, because this is all almost too much to take in at once. Gaia's children and nine realms and the attempted invasion of foreign gods? I'd kill for a drink to wash this news down with, but I'm an entire country away from Jinx and what booze we had on those shelves exploded in Pharaoh's black fire. My thoughts threaten to derail to seven cremated customers. My throat burns with bile and I forcibly pull myself away from that memory.

"So what, Pharaoh put you to sleep because these gods were trying to take over Gaia via you, and then he just forgot to wake you up? And just like that the war was over."

"No," Rose says, very quietly. "Pharaoh never puts me under for longer than a day, which means Notte did not wait long before interfering. He touched what is mine and mine alone, and he will answer for it. I will tear him to pieces and you will have to be satisfied with the scraps I leave behind."

"So much for that whole 'master' bit."

"Every Nightmare has a master," Rose says. "The rules of the Nightmares are few but they are ironclad for our survival and sanity. The second rule is the rule of one: each Nightmare is required to find and save at least one other. Notte fulfilled his duty by protecting me until we could find Pharaoh. This gives him a unique power over us and influence against our bond, but he will lose that power when I find your Nightmare. You are the key to my freedom from him—and perhaps the reason he is even still an issue. He should have died when Meridian did."

I'm not jealous. I'm not. "Meridian?"

"Meridian was Notte's Dream," Rose says, "which brings us back to your transgressions. The first rule of the Nightmares is simple: for each Nightmare, a Dream, and each Dream, a Nightmare. Even if our powers overlap, there is only one in the entire world who is a perfect cure for our particular poison. Whatever you are, you have enough connecting pieces with both of us that you were able to wake me and keep Notte alive in Meridian's absence. But you cannot, must not, stake a claim on either of us."

"That's not going to be a problem."

"It's already a problem," Rose insists. "The bond between us is sealed by our names. By naming me you tried to put a collar around my throat where Pharaoh's already rests. He is my survival. He is my sanity. My world stops and starts with every breath he takes and you have dared put your claim atop his. He should have killed you to protect me."

The thought that a dumpy little bartender could be a legitimate threat to one of Society's Nightmares, an actual child of Gaia, is as ridiculous as it is thrilling. "He tried," I remind him. "Betty stopped him, and then the gatekeepers showed up to chew on him."

The reminder that they hurt Pharaoh puts a vicious look on Rose's face. He works his jaw for a moment, visibly warring with his temper. "I would not hesitate to do the same and worse should something threaten my ties to Pharaoh. You will understand one day, but for now you must stop overstepping your boundaries. It is in your nature as a Dream to name that which you keep close to you, but I am not yours to control and call to action."

"You'd rather I call you Brimstone?" I ask. "Because that's a terrible name, by the way."

"Pharaoh and I together are Brimstone," Rose says. "Our names are not common knowledge to those outside our circles, and those within rarely risk speaking them aloud for fear of implying intimacy. This is how it goes with most Nightmares. Notte and Meridian were the exceptions, as Meridian thought having names would somehow help soften humans to our cause. They wanted to be the face of the Nightmares in the war. 'Fathom' was unknowable, but 'Notte' was perhaps someone to rally behind."

"You guys really should not be in charge of your own call signs," I say. "Those both suck."

"We are called by the nature of our powers," Rose says.

"Brimstone," I say, a little skeptically, and then think about the black fire Pharaoh used against us in Jinx. I take a steadying breath and hold the rest of that memory at bay by sheer willpower alone. "Wait. That means you named him Pharaoh, doesn't it? What did he name you?"

Rose is quiet so long I think he's not going to answer me. Then: "Soul."

"Do you even have one?" I ask.

"Sol," Rose corrects me, "as in sun."

"Oh. Spanish," I say. "Pharaoh spoke Spanish at the bar, but that's not what you keep using."

"I was born in Egypt."

I guess I should have figured that one out, considering Pharaoh's name.

68

Instead of copping to my own ignorance, I stray toward too-personal territory and ask, "I imagine the long-distance fees are astronomical, but are you going to call your parents and tell them you're awake again?"

The way he looks at me is all the answer I need, but after a beat he says, "Our people do not have families. Whatever Pharaoh's parents were to him once, they are not even a footnote in his life now because of me. It creates a conflict of interest," he says when I start to argue. "I must always be the most important person in his world, and he in mine. Once the bond between us is sealed, everything in the world outside of us is background noise."

"Because that sounds healthy." It sounds like a lot of rubbish to me, but I'm emboldened by what he didn't say: "I asked about your parents, not Pharaoh's. You're not at all concerned with them?"

"I do not remember them," Rose says. "They had me committed when my power manifested."

It takes a beat for the words to make sense, they're so unexpected. "Like actually committed?"

"It is a common fate for our kind. Our power manifests between our seventh and eighth birthdays, and our parents do not know what to do with our sudden change. We see horrors they cannot see, things they'll never know, and they cannot protect us from ourselves. They try, though: hospitals and asylums, electroshock and exorcisms, anything to make us human again when we were never human to begin with. Most Nightmares never realize the madness they see and feel is not madness but the strident cries of a bleeding god; the weakest ones die when their minds give out on them. It is why we instated the rule of one, but it is so very hard to stay alive and sane until we are saved."

"How old were you?"

"I was nine when Notte and Meridian found me, and twelve when we found Pharaoh," Rose says. "That I survived so long is in large part due to Fathom's hold over me."

"Adam saved your life," I say. "But you hate him. Right?"

"With every breath I take."

I put a hand to my stomach and dig my fingers in, trying to feel my scars through my shirt. "Me too. Do you think—"

Rapid scratching at the door has me casting it a hunted look, question forgotten. Rose shifts in my peripheral vision but doesn't get up. A moment later the door unlocks itself and swings open, and Falkor comes loping in with his funky ferret gallop. Casper is on his heels, looking more than a little bewildered.

"I've never met a door I couldn't walk through," she says. "The hell is this place, Evey?"

It's jarring how relieved I am to see them. I reach for Falkor when he bounds onto my bed. He neatly avoids an actual pet but noses at my hand and cranes his head every which way as he checks me for injuries. His huffing breath comes fast and short, with a wheezy undertone I chalk up to anxiety. I don't know how much of it is from him misplacing his prized possession and how much is due to our recent rebellion against the gatekeepers' control. I choose to be comforted regardless.

"Your guess is as good as mine," I tell Casper, and grunt when Falkor curls his bony body around me. "Right now I'm leaning toward Society's version of a Days Inn."

"The ghost," Rose guesses.

"I have a name," Casper insists. "Evey, tell him."

I roll my eyes at her but obediently turn on Rose. "Casper says to use her name."

"An accusation she should level first at you," Rose points out.

"Casper's more appropriate and it's clever. Are you even old enough to get the reference?"

"It is not her name," Rose says. "You must learn to let go of this habit of yours."

"I asked you how old you are," I say, because now I'm thinking of how young he looked in that first dreamscape. Rose only stares back at me, so I huff a sigh and say, "I'll tell you what her real name is if you answer the question."

"Seventeen," he says. "Maybe eighteen. I cannot remember."

"Seventeen," I echo. "What the hell?"

His eighteen years in Elysium didn't leave a single mark on him; whether it was Gaia's interference or some strange twist of his power, he spent that entire time in stasis, his existence paused until Pharaoh could call on him again. And on the tail-end of that is an unwelcome thought so painful it squeezes the breath from my lungs: he is barely older than Ciara would be.

And suddenly it doesn't matter that he's a Nightmare or a legal adult by American standards. He is almost young enough to be my son, and Notte put him at the frontline of a war where all of Earth's gods could find him. My need to get my hands around Adam's neck is almost blinding.

Rose flinches and rubs his hands together. "Stop it."

My mouth feels as numb as my chest, but I ask, "Stop what?"

"Whatever you are doing. I can feel it tugging at me."

I'm not doing anything, but he looks too unsettled to actually believe that, so I distract him with my half of the bargain. "Her name was Emily White. She was a high school English teacher until she got hit by a drunk driver. Didn't even survive to see the ambulance, she says. She likes teaching her children creepy stories."

"Edgar Allan Poe is a literary genius," Casper points out. A second later she hums and says, "Emily. You're right. I'd almost forgotten. Weird, isn't it, that I could forget my own name?"

"Emily," Rose says, and beckons to thin air. He doesn't waste his time trying to look in her general direction, knowing he's more likely to just stare past her, but watches me for any indication that she's obeying. I don't have to encourage her. Being acknowledged by someone other than me has her traipsing across the room in a heartbeat. I nod an okay to Rose, and he uses his fingertip to trace a symbol on the mattress at his side. He waits a beat, then does it again. "We need you to find this mark. Look for it in doorways and on streetlamps. Can you do it?"

"One more time," Casper says, and I relay the message. Rose complies, and Casper offers a thumbs-up. "Got it. Am I just supposed to tell you where it is, or?"

"Remember where you found it," Rose confirms when I pass that question on. "We will need to get there after full dark. This marks the safe houses of the Guard," he says, more for my benefit than for Casper's. "We will show our faces and see what we have to work with, and hopefully have news from the Nests regarding Pharaoh's whereabouts."

"Roger that, over and out," Casper says with mock gravity. The farce doesn't last long before she giggles like a daft child, and she winks at me on her way out of the room. It takes a minute, but finally the bedroom door swings closed of its own accord, and the lock snaps into place. I look at Rose to see what he thinks of this, but his hooded gaze is on the draconian faerie curled around my hips.

"Your Nightmare is going to kill it," he says. "It cannot keep its claim to you."

"I don't want a Nightmare," I point out. "Life is enough of a nightmare already."

"Don't be selfish," Rose warns me in a low voice. "Your Nightmare's sanity and survival depend on your acceptance."

"If I meant anything to my so-called Nightmare, my happiness and safety would not be afterthoughts," I retort.

"You will be happy," Rose promises. "You will love him or her because you will not know how to do anything else."

71

"A, that sounds like brainwashing," I say, "and B, are there female Nightmares?"

"It is brainwashing, in a sense," Rose confirms, and the fact he can say it without an ounce of shame makes my skin crawl. "That code is hardwired into us from birth. And yes, there were several female Nightmares the last time I was awake. If you are unlucky enough you will meet Wrath before this is all over. They are the second strongest pair after Pharaoh and me, but they lost faith in us when Notte crossed too many lines. They would have us fall for the cause just as he would."

"Charming."

"Stop it," Rose says.

"Still not doing anything," I tell him.

Rose only stares balefully at me. I roll my eyes at his suspicion and turn my attention to Falkor, whose breathing is only now starting to even out. In the new stillness I'm keenly aware of how exhausted I am. I don't think I can handle further conversation with Rose, and we're obviously not going anywhere until Casper gets back, so I shift until I can use Falkor as a pillow. I expect an annoyed protest from him at being appropriated, but he keeps a wary eye on Rose and says nothing to me. I have only a moment to wonder if these unhappy truths will keep me up, and then the world slips away into a sleep that is—for once—dreamless and deep.

SIX

Nightfall brings out a side of Madtown I do not like at all. There are very few streetlamps so as to respect the nocturnal beasts who call Madtown home, and the sparkling pixies that bounce this way and that do nothing to illuminate the darkness properly. The creatures we pass are ink black shapes barely discernible from the rest of the shadows around them, and more than once I brush against a body I didn't know was there. I smell animals and dead flesh and blood, and I tighten my grip on Rose's coat until I'm sure I'm leaving permanent wrinkles. I wish Rose had let us bring Falkor or Casper, but Falkor is tasked with guarding our room and Casper is meant to be eavesdropping on local gossip.

The further we go, the quieter it gets, and the silence is worse than the constant press of unseen bodies. That prickle at the back of my neck is the weight of curious stares, and even as I tell myself it's my imagination I hear what sounds like rustling laughter on the wind. I'm about to do something ill-advised and call out a challenge to our unseen watchers when Rose makes an abrupt turn. A dim porch light flicks on as soon as we are close enough to it, and the sudden light has me squinting in displeasure. It keeps me from tripping over the stone steps leading up to the front door, though, and I finally let go of Rose.

Rose presses his thumb to the doorbell and holds it. I look to the door and its intricate engraving of flowers and thorns. Buried in the middle, almost lost to the rest of the design, is the symbol Rose sent Casper to find earlier. No wonder it took her so long to finally find this place.

It's nearly three in the morning, but someone answers immediately. I hear no less than four locks snap undone before the door opens outward. A pink-skinned woman stands in the doorway, cradling what looks like a mix between a rocket launcher and a shotgun. Judging by the size of the barrel she doesn't even have to have good aim to liquefy us both on the spot.

Rose pulls his hood down. "You will let me in."

She props her gun against her shoulder and disables the ward in her doorway with a few quick words. Red light crackles through the air like spiderweb before falling to the ground between us and fading. Rose precedes me inside and we wait to one side so she can reestablish her ward and secure the door again.

I miss most of the spell, because she didn't come to the door alone. A halfling is standing just out of eyesight of the door with a crossbow in his hands. I wonder for a moment why they risk living in Madtown if they've got to come to the door armed to the teeth and in pairs, then attribute tonight's paranoia to the gatekeepers' earlier invasion.

"Come," the woman says, and leads us down the hall to the kitchen. She has an actual pantry that is impressively stocked. She pushes aside a few bags of sugar, revealing the same mark as what was on the doorway, and presses a button built in right beside it. The back wall of the pantry swings open on silent hinges to reveal a well-lit stairwell leading down. Rose goes to it without so much as a thank-you, and I spare the woman one last look before following after him.

We're only two steps into the stairwell before the door disappears behind us, replaced by an unbroken wooden wall, and the walls of the stairwell are replaced by open air. We're on a flight of stairs down into what is very obviously a bar. Tables are set comfortable distances apart, but the bar counter itself is a circular thing in the center of the room. Tonight most of the tables are crowded, and people huddle close together. Their gestures are sharp, agitated, as they react to the trouble we've brought to their city.

The jukebox sputters to a stop, and one by one all heads turn our way. Conversations falter and die, and in the new silence a single voice says: "Nightmare."

It's echoed in quiet murmurs around in the room. I hear surprise mostly, but there's an *a-ha* satisfaction to more than a few faces as they finally understand what set the gatekeepers off. Rose walks past all of them, aiming for the bar counter. The bartender watches our approach with obvious relief, and he materializes two glasses and a bottle from thin air as we take the stools right in front of him. Conversation starts up again once we're seated, but now there's an actual energy to it, and scattered laughter carries through now and then.

I scoop up the glass and down it in one desperate go. It goes down smoother than water, with the faint aftertaste of smoke and molasses. As soon as I set it down it refills itself. I cradle the cup closer with a bit of hungry greed.

"Is it the cup or a spell?" I ask, because if he says cup I'm walking out of here with my glass.

Rose makes a dismissive gesture and asks, "Where is Barley?"

The bartender looks surprised. "He's been gone six years now."

Rose breaks his glass with one fierce clench of his fingers. Liquid spills across the counter, but it stops after a time. I guess it isn't a magical cup after all, and while that's a little disappointing it doesn't stop me from emptying mine a second time. The bartender places both hands flat on the counter and keeps his stance as nonthreatening as possible. Rose uncurls his fingers slowly. Glass sparkles like glitter on his skin, but his hand remains unbroken somehow.

Despite that flash of temper, Rose's voice is calm when he says, "Gone."

The bartender uses his middle and ring fingers to draw a spell on the counter. Liquid evaporates, and the glass pulls itself from Rose's skin and the counter to tumble end over end toward a trashcan. Once it's clean, he risks putting another cup down in front of Rose. This time Rose picks it up without breaking it, but he holds it to his lips and doesn't drink.

"He disappeared into the lines," the bartender says. "Went too quick, is what they were saying, because the Lymanczyc were closing in on him. Stepped sideways instead of forward. They sent ten in after him when he didn't come back, but no one's heard from him since."

"Someone important?" I ask.

"Barley was one of the elementals," Rose says.

I shrug ignorance, and the bartender takes pity on me. "Elementals can tap into Gaia's magic in a way few others can. They do not need gates to traverse the lines. Their primary task is to clean the lines as best they can, to support the flow of magic and try to heal all weakening spots. The strongest ones are trying to remap the lines and find their guardians."

I assume by guardians he means the original gatekeepers. I look to Rose. "So the elementals are your cousins."

"In a sense," Rose says. "They are what She was capable of making before She started dying."

"Cinder is who you'll want to speak to now," the bartender says. "She's of the fire strain, so she's convinced she can succeed where Barley failed. Something about being one with the earth's core, I think? I didn't catch all of it. She was here a couple weeks ago but didn't stay long. Never does. Kid's not all here," he says, tapping his temple, "but she's on to something. The faeries say they can already feel a difference along the coast. She might be the answer we're all looking for. We just have to keep her alive."

Rose considers that, then sets his glass aside. "We are leaving the city as soon as we have the West Council's backing, but if you find her keep her close. We will come back for her. In the meantime, I expect you to cooperate and coordinate with the Nests. I require the Nightmares' return to North America. Put out the call on every channel you have left."

"If I may ask which name I can sign?"

"I am Brimstone," Rose says.

Betty called him savior; Rose declared himself strongest. The reaction in the bartender is immediate and confirms both stories. He looked at ease for most of our conversation, but Rose's name takes so much tension out of him he looks fit to crumple. It's the bone-deep weariness of the losing side of a war, of a rebellion forced underground by powers outside of their control. He looks at Rose now like Rose is the moon and stars in his sky, a constellation upon which he will hang every fierce wish and whispered prayer.

I look from him to the scattered bodies at our back and understand. This is the Guard Betty mentioned; this is the resistance that wants to wrest the gates from the gatekeepers before it's too late. They are worn and tired and spread thinner than paste, but they are here and ready to go.

"You live," the bartender says, so quiet it might be my imagination.

"For now," Rose says. "Tell me who is left."

Most of the following conversation goes over my head, a list of names and places I do not recognize and don't care to demand a hundred explanations for. I attempt to keep up with it at first, then settle for sipping my drink and studying the rest of these underground rebels. Even that is starting to get boring when the bartender says something that makes me spit out my drink:

"—Shannons are currently being supported by the Downeys along the Canadian border."

My coughing fit derails their conversation. The bartender lifts a hand like he's considering thumping me on the back while Rose just watches me suffer. I finally manage a breath that doesn't taste like liquor and pound my own chest.

"The Downeys," I gasp out, "are where?"

"Near the Great Lakes, last I heard, but I don't have an exact location."

Rose gestures at me, but I don't need encouragement to explain my interest: "My maiden name is Downey. My mother disappeared from Orlando after I eloped with—" I think better of saying his name, even though this bartender is obviously on our side. I don't want this conversation to turn into another argument about Notte. "Is there any way to get in touch with them? I want to know if that's where she went."

I don't add the *and why*, because I have a sinking feeling I finally know what that reason is. She told me leaving with Notte meant goodbye, but I know it wasn't disapproval of our relationship. After all, she never

76

lifted a finger to stop Notte from courting me, no matter the grievous difference in our ages or the fact that he was supposedly suffering PTSD from the war.

She cut ties with me because she knew then what Rose told me tonight: that Dreams have no room for family once they've bonded. She expected me to leave with Notte and forget all about her. Mom has always known I'm not fully human. Betrayal is a sick and oily heat low in my gut, and I empty my glass twice more in quick succession.

"I can call around," the bartender promises. "Who am I looking for?"

"Keandra Downey."

"I will see what I can find."

I nod a silent thanks to that, and once they're sure I'm done interrupting they pick up where they left off. This time I pay a little more attention, because I had no idea the psychics were involved in the war. Mom never implied that she had friends and family facing off against the gatekeepers; she mentioned the war in passing only and raised me on her own in Florida. It's a little eerie finding out there's more to her that I ever thought possible, that she went straight from being my mother to being a frontline rebel in the fight for Gaia's survival.

They've nearly gotten through all seven of the psychics' tiers when Rose stops mid-sentence. His gaze goes vacant for a heartbeat and his hand stills mid-gesture. I've almost had enough to drink that shaking him seems like a good idea, but he moves before I can reach out. He turns his hand over and curls his fingers, in one at a time and then out again until his hand is splayed open as far as he can make it. He raises it to his shoulder and picks at the cloth. Another invisible thread stuck to him like he had at Pariah, I'm guessing, but I don't understand how he even noticed its sticky weight. He picks them off one at a time, but stare as I might at the counter I can't see what he's putting down. Maybe the bartender can, because he takes two very careful steps back away from the counter.

"You're a Downey," the bartender says, catching on far too late. He looks from me to Rose and back again. "You're a psychic. You're not the Brimstone Dream."

"It is time to go," Rose says, very quietly.

I sneak one last sip from my glass before getting to my feet. The world is a fuzzy heat against my skin, and the bar is tilted a little bit sideways, but I have enough coordination to reach for Rose. Rose follows my tug to his feet and says nothing when I lean against him for balance. He glances up, looking past the bartender to the far corner of the room. I follow his stare, and for a half-second I think I see something hanging from the ceiling. It's a blur of shadows and sharp angles, there and gone again in the time it takes me to blink.

"The door disappeared," I say.

Rose tips his head without taking his eyes off the corner. I follow the gesture to see a new door in the far wall. Somehow I get us there, and Rose eases me out into the night ahead of him. I have to straighten away from him so he can turn and get the door, and when I do I'm hit with an icy breeze. I blink up at the half-full moon, then turn a concerned look on the ocean washing ashore not even ten feet from my shoes.

"We're at the beach," I say, like saying it aloud will make it make sense. "Why are we at the beach? I'm pretty sure Madtown is on the other side of the peninsula."

"The Lymanczyc hate water. This is a safe exit."

I would point out that that doesn't explain how we teleported so far, but the sight of someone walking across the water toward us kills that concern really quick. Rose goes out to meet her and speaks quietly with her for several minutes. I hug myself, trying to stay warm, and wait until she finally turns away. She heads back out to sea and sinks beneath the waves as soon as the water is deep enough to swallow her. Rose returns to my side and I plant myself against him once more. It is a mistake; he is colder than the breeze.

"You know a lot of strange people."

"The sirens have always been on our side. Those of the sea have no reason to fear or respect the Lymancyzc."

"What happened back there?" I ask. "In the bar, I mean."

"I have to find Pharaoh," Rose says in a low voice. I feel his words more than hear them despite how close I am to him. "My power is starting to notice his absence."

"How much longer until that's a real problem?"

"Unknown," Rose admits.

"Lovely." I turn him away from the ocean, and we trudge across the sand to the highway. The streets are empty thanks to the ungodly hour, but eventually I see headlights. I fumble Rose's hood into his face before waving desperately for the driver to pull over. I half-expect to be ignored, but the car slows and crawls into the shoulder. The man inside is dressed for a long day at the office, and he does not look at all impressed by our shenanigans. I rethink my options of asking for a ride.

"My phone died," I say. "Can you call a taxi for us?"

He makes a show of checking his watch before collecting his phone from the cup holder between the front seats. It takes a minute before a dispatcher picks up, but the driver gets through and gives his best guess at our current whereabouts. As soon as he hangs up I take an exaggerated step back from his car.

"Much appreciated."

He heads off, leaving us to the night's mercies, but ten minutes later a cab finds us. I have no idea where Madtown's physical entrance is, so Rose has to give directions. It's a longer drive than I expect, and since I'm apparently the only one carrying a wallet I'm the one who has to fork over cash when we finally reach the piers. We take the last two blocks on foot and disappear into the narrow space between two buildings. I have a half-second to wonder if my hips will even fit, and then reality spins away from us and we're through to Madtown's wider streets.

Rose takes the lead again since his night vision is better. I'm relieved to see Pariah, and Falkor and Casper are equally pleased to see us. Casper tries to relay all the things she overheard in our absence, but I can't pay attention to her once I see my pillow. I mumble a half-hearted "Uh-huh" as I kick my shoes off and crawl into bed, and Casper's indignant voice fades to a meaningless blur as I fall asleep.

I wake up because it's hotter than a Georgia summer in our room. My throat is too dry for me to even groan in protest, and I feel glued to my sheets with sweat. I fumble my way out of bed and stumble across the room to the controls Rose was messing with earlier. I crank the central air on as high as it can go and shoot Rose a mean look. He misses it, as he's buried unmoving beneath three quilts in the center of his bed. There's not a kitchenette in here, so I settle for gulping water from the bathroom sink. Falkor is in the tub, the only cool thing left in this room.

"He's trying to kill us," I say.

Falkor pants open-mouthed at me, tongue lolled out between long teeth. "She is our precious thing. Ours, ours. We will not lets him hurt her."

It's bold talk from a dragon who is scared to death of Rose, but I'm in no mood to correct him. Instead I motion for him to look away so I can handle my business. Falkor gnashes his teeth and ignores that silent command. Casper has about the same respect for privacy when she barges through the door a few seconds later. She's walked in on me so many times that she doesn't even try to gloat about catching me with my pants around my ankles.

"When is Alexandra going to get here?" she asks.

"Hopefully tonight," I say.

Casper sighs dramatically and leans over the sink. She has no reflection but she tilts her head this way and that like she's checking for flaws on the mirror. It buys me time to finish up, and I reach through her to wash my hands.

"Rude," Casper says.

"You're one to talk."

"We do have to talk," Casper insists. "You fell asleep on me last night before you could tell me how your super secret meeting went. I want all the details."

"And I want breakfast," I say. "We can't talk about this outside the room, so you'll have to get your answers when we get back. Come on."

I can't talk to her, but she has little fear of being overheard and so talks my ear off as we leave the room and head downstairs. We've just reached the last flight when a cool energy crackles over my skin. At my back Casper falters and goes quiet. Most kinds of magic go right through her, as few people and creatures have a power that can effect the dead. I send a sharp look over my shoulder at her and see her rubbing at her heart with a troubled look on her face.

"What is that?" she asks.

"One way to find out," I say, and lead her down to the lobby.

It is a decision I regret immediately, because there are seven robed figures standing at the front desk. Their hoods are up, but their hoods aren't the reason I can't make out their faces. There's an infinite darkness where their heads should be, and I recognize that yawning abyss as easily as I recognize the symbols sewn into their sleeves. It's been over twenty years since I last saw a hoxie, but my mother made sure I could recognize them on sight.

The dead are no safer than the living are. Those who can't or won't pass over quickly are prey to any of a dozen races who know how to harness soul energy. If they're not picked up by harmless psychics or reckless kids with ouija boards, they risk being forcibly sorted by the Justices or getting eaten by one of four races that consume souls to stay alive. Hoxies are the most persistent race of the latter bunch and learned long ago that psychics can act as a fishing line for them. Mom squared off against them more times than I can count until she finally hired someone stronger to build barricades around Orlando.

I look to the woman who's now guarding the front desk. "They aren't staying."

"They've paid their passage," she says. "I have no grounds on which to decline."

"I was here first," I snap back, "and I included a ghost in my party.

That's grounds enough."

"Pariah cannot and will not guarantee the safety of any of its guests."

"Evey?" Casper asks, quiet and nervous. "Evey, what are those things?"

The hooded figures confer with one another in sibilant hisses. It takes them only seconds to reach a decision, and the closest one to me lifts a skeletal hand. Hoxies have skin, but little beneath it, so their bodies look like plastic wrap pulled too tight over bones. The three fingers extended my way have hollow tips meant for pulling a soul in one scrap at a time.

"Draw your lines, psychic," it says in a voice like leaves on asphalt. "Drive your stakes deep and well. What strays outside your borders is ours to take."

The words are familiar the way a nursery rhyme is, but so far buried I barely remember how this is supposed to go. It's a ritual greeting, the closest thing to a warning and respect the hoxies can manage, but this fight was always my mother's problem. Since I wasn't supposed to inherit her power, she never wasted her time teaching me her side of things. The best I've got to go on are fractured memories, and I don't know how important it is that I get the response exactly right. Something about anchors and crossing lines? I shake my head as if that'll force the pieces into place.

"Evey, please," Casper says. "They don't feel right."

"The psychic claims none," the hoxie says when I'm quiet for too long.

"Don't rush me," I insist. "I'm working on it."

They start toward us with slow steps. Their magic curls along the ground at their feet, a hazy green cloud that turns darker the closer it gets to us. By the time it reaches the bottom step it's liquid, and it snakes up the wood toward us. I put an arm out, warning Casper back, but can't take my eyes off the hoxies to see if she's obeying. The pained noise she makes means she isn't moving fast enough. I put my hand out next, like I can somehow ward them off, but my hand keeps moving of its own accord. Fear flips the switch I need most, and I trace desperate symbols into the air between us.

"I am Evelyn Notte of the fourth-tier Downey clan. Where my feet stand my territory begins. I anchor my corners on the people I've brought with me: the draconian faerie, the ghost, and the Brimstone Nightmare."

As I say it, I feel a wiry web spiraling out from me. It streaks through Casper's familiar energy before vanishing upstairs to Falkor's inescapable leash and Rose's black magic. I clench my hand, yanking the threads tight, and pull the knot to my chest. Proof that this is working puts an edge in my final warning:

81

"You stand inside lines you were never meant to cross. If I am to take this as a declaration of war against me and mine, make it known right now."

It is not the response they wanted from me, especially with a meal so close, and the front hoxie dives like it'll plow straight through me to Casper.

I panic and yell, "This is mine!"

It's as effective as a punch—the hoxie goes flying back and crashes into its brethren. They retreat past the front desk to argue amongst themselves in angry, spitting voices. I can barely see them through the energy that's humming through me. Light stabs out between my clenched fingers and when I turn my hand over to look there's a swirling orb no larger than a quarter spinning in my hand. I close my fingers over it again, partly because it's too blinding to look at for long and partly because I'm afraid I might drop it.

One by one the hoxies fade, conceding Pariah to me. The light goes out in their absence, and the lobby feels strangely bare without it. I put my hand to my chest as if I can hold my pounding heart still.

"Evelyn Notte," the woman at the desk says, sounding like she's choking on it.

I shouldn't have used Adam's name in public, but sincerity and will are the keystones of magic and no matter what Adam did to me I can't think of myself as Evelyn Downey. For better or worse everything I am is grounded in his love and betrayal.

"Evey," Casper starts. "That was—"

A hard hand on my shoulder scares ten years out of me, and I look back to see Rose standing half-inside of Casper. He looks positively murderous. "What did you just do?"

"I don't know," I admit, though that's only half the truth. I look down at my now-empty palm and feel sick to my stomach. "My mother said I didn't have magic. She said the best I'd ever do was speak to ghosts. I shouldn't have been able to do that."

"I told you to never lay claim to me!"

"They were going to eat Casper," I protest. "What else was I supposed to do?"

"Get it off of me."

"I don't know how." When he draws his hand back like he intends to knock my head off my neck, I insist again, "Mom said I didn't have magic. She didn't teach me how to do that, so I don't know how to break it. I just knew I had to keep Casper safe. If you want me to remove it you'll have to find someone who actually understands what the hell just happened."

He snaps his hand back and rakes it through his hair in violent and helpless frustration. "We're leaving. We cannot stay here anymore."

"Casper, get Falkor," I say, but Falkor comes bounding into sight a moment later, drawn by my web just like Rose was. He slows to a creeping crawl to sneak past Rose but headbutts my thigh as soon as he is close enough.

"Oh, perhaps she is not human after all," Falkor says.

"Perhaps not," I agree quietly.

"What has we done, taking such a piece into our hoard," Falkor muses, with a sidelong look up at me. "Too precious to let go, too dangerous to keep. She will be the death of us after all."

"No," I say. "I'm not going to—"

Rose doesn't give me time to finish but catches my shoulder and shoves me around toward the front door. I lead us out of Pariah and into a too-bright midday in Madtown. Rose is not angry enough to be careless, and he pulls his hood up before following me out into public. I step off to one side to let him take the lead and he sets off through the crowd without hesitation.

I keep a careful eye on the people and creatures we pass, unsure how much they've learned since our rowdy arrival yesterday. I didn't think Society was keen on Wanted posters but if the gatekeepers stopped to give anyone a description of our faces we could have some serious issues. Every time a stare lingers for a half-second too long I inch closer to Rose, but we press on uncontested.

We end up at the same house we visited last night, and the pink woman lets us into the bar downstairs without a word. The bartender is missing, so I let myself behind the bar counter. The setup is nothing like Jinx, down to the complete lack of a proper well, but I find glasses in the third cabinet I open. Rose stares hard at me the entire time I peruse the collection of bottles on the back wall and it's all I can do to feign ignorance to his smothering disapproval.

Rose doesn't speak until I'm pouring my first drink, and even his question sounds like a hateful accusation: "What level psychic do you need?"

"Mom is a fourth-tier and can do what I just did," I say into my drink, "so that or higher."

He pushes away from the bar and goes to sit alone in the back corner. He doesn't take his drink with him, so Casper dips her fingers in it and leans across the counter toward me.

"You saved me," she says. "I don't know how, but I'm not going to

83

question it. Thank you."

"I dragged you into this," I say. "That kind of makes you my responsibility."

"He doesn't approve."

"That has nothing to do with you," I say. When she waits for a better explanation, I sigh and say, "It's a long story."

"English teacher," Casper reminds me. "I like stories."

I look from her to Rose's now-distant figure and empty my drink. "It starts with a war."

SEVEN

When I wake up the bar is packed. I only dimly remember putting my head down sometime after my tenth or twelfth drink, but I know we were the only ones here when I needed to crash. I rub clothing crinkles out of my forehead as I survey the crowd. Some faces I think I recognize from yesterday, but the majority are new. Rose is easy to pick out where he stands in the center of the room. His hands move in agitated gestures as he speaks to an attentive group. I turn my back on him and note that my glass has obediently filled itself.

I expect to feel a quiver of nausea at the sight of more liquor, especially considering I've already had enough today to pass out once, but my head is clear and stomach steady. There's not even a twinge at my temples to mark a lingering hangover. I'm doubly determined now to learn the magic the bartenders cast in this place, even if I'll never be witch enough to pull off this kind of spell.

The first thought of magic gives me a headache of a different kind, and I knock my glass back.

"Really, Evey?" Casper asks as she slides onto the stool beside me. "Starting up again?"

"After everything I told you, you wouldn't be drinking if you could?"

"I don't drink," Casper says. She corrects herself before I have to point it out: "I mean while I was alive, so don't look at me like that."

"How long was I out?" I ask, then remember who I'm talking to. "Never mind."

The weight of someone's stare has me looking down the length of the bar. Yesterday's bartender is at the far end of the counter. He has a coworker with him tonight who's human one second and a tree nymph the next. Why she's bothering with a glamour down here of all places is beyond me, but it's a little disorienting watching her skin shift to tree bark and back again every time she breathes.

They're too far away and the bar is too loud for me to hear what they're saying, but they're both watching me. The man holds my gaze for a few more moments, unworried at being spotted, and then turns his attention toward Rose. The nymph gestures toward me, but he answers with a firm shake of his head. She tolerates his hesitation for only a few more moments before slipping around him and coming toward me.

"Evelyn Downey-Notte," she says in greeting.

I go perfectly still. "I didn't give you that name."

"You gave it away at Pariah," she says. "Where it goes now is outside of your control."

"Is it going to be a problem?"

My tone says it better not be, and the thin smile on her face says she hears that warning loud and clear. It doesn't reach her eyes, but it tugs just enough at her cheeks that her facade slips once more. Soft moss trails through the cracks in dark bark, and ivy twines together in a farce of an intricate braid. She's back in the space between two heartbeats. It's more dizzying up close than it was with her at the end of the bar, and I'm too tired to tolerate this nonsense.

"You're going to give me a headache flicking in and out like that," I say. "Why even bother with a glamour if you can't keep it together for more than a second at a time?"

It's her turn to go still, and her eyes go dark as onyx. "Excuse me?"

"What glamour?" Casper asks. "She's just a human, isn't she?"

I give a slight shake of my head in answer but don't look at Casper. I can't, not when the faerie is staring me down like I'll be the first to blink. I didn't spend all that time lording over Elysium to lose to an unstable nymph here in San Francisco. Indeed, it takes less than a minute before her gaze flicks away. She's quick to look back at me, but she and I both know who won that challenge. She finally addresses my warning with a calm:

"We have no quarrel with Notte. We are only concerned with the company you keep."

"The ghost, the dragon, or—" I almost say Rose; how I catch myself is a miracle I know better than to question, "—Brimstone?"

"We have by now heard of what transpired in Georgia," she says. "We know the Brimstone Dream left empty-handed, and we know now via the Nest that no one knows where he is. Not even his own Nightmare," she says, with an edge in her voice.

She glances past me and I don't have to follow her stare to know she's watching Rose. I look at her colleague instead and find him equally distracted. I think of how he reacted when he realized I wasn't Rose's Dream, and how Rose admitted that his power is going to be a problem if we can't catch up to Pharaoh. I say nothing, though, and wait for her to make her point.

"We only ask for your guarantee," she says, bringing her attention back to me with obvious effort. "I will not condone the Guard's revival if we cannot rely on him to see this through with us until the very end. His abrupt disappearance last time was catastrophic. I will not ask my people to commit to a lost cause a second time."

I could tell her the truth: that I have no say in what Rose can and cannot do, that the war is such a secondary concern for me that it barely registers on my radar, that the only thing I care about is getting my hands around Notte's throat and finding out what truly became of our daughter. I get the feeling honesty would be a horrible idea right now, but I'm not about to lie just to make her feel better. I'm weighing just how vague of a response I can get away with when Casper perks up at my side.

"Alexandra!"

I twist on the stool and follow her pointing finger. I don't need the help to spot Betty, even in this crowd. She turned heads and killed conversations in Augusta, and she does the same here. It's an interesting reaction considering these people live in the shadow of the West Council's high tower. It isn't her species that puts that shock and reverence on their faces this time, though: it is because of who she is.

Betty left Madtown twenty years ago but the Guard recognize her on sight. I understand when she and Rose lock eyes across the room. She maintains a fearful respect for Rose and Pharaoh, but I remember her words to Pharaoh at Jinx: "*After all this time?*" She's been in this war for decades.

For a dizzying moment I wonder how well she knows Notte.

Rose extricates himself from the crowd and starts my way, and Betty takes the hint to meet us at the bar. Casper has to abandon her stool before Betty can sit inside her, but she doesn't go far. She rests her hands on Betty's shoulders and half-buries her face in Betty's thick hair.

Betty dismisses the forest nymph with a cool look and flick of her fingers before turning to me. "Did you get us our rooms?"

"I got us kicked out," I say. "Did you bite Jude?"

"Kicked out?" Betty frowns at me. "Are you incapable of behaving for one day?"

"Pariah and I had different opinions on Casper's rights as a guest. She says hello, by the way."

"Get your pet away from me."

Rose doesn't have the patience for this kind of back-and-forth. "Do you have news?"

Betty knows what he's asking, judging by how carefully she considers him. "Not yet, but I've asked the Nests to forward all information and rumors to the West Council." She glances at her watch and says, "The tower doors will be open for visitors soon. I have secured us an audience with Councilor Freeman."

Rose frowns. "Not Matthias?"

Betty's expression goes so removed and distant she finally looks like the undead thing she actually is. It takes her a minute to answer, and then her voice is so quiet it's a wonder I can hear her over the music.

"Matthias burned when the Lymancyzc subdued Madtown."

Rose pinches the bridge of his nose and snarls something I can't understand. I tune him out, more interested in translating Betty's reaction. That's a loss too personal to simply be a colleague, but in the years I've known Betty I've never heard her mention anyone from her time in Society.

"Friend of yours?" I ask.

Betty cuts me a look so full of loathing I almost expect her to attack me, but she is quick to school her expression. "Matthias was my maker and a Grand Duke of the Madtown Nest. He held a seat on the West Council for two hundred years. His was one of the oldest names in North America; we came to this country together."

It clicks. "That's why you didn't return to the Madtown Nest after the war. You didn't want to be here without him."

"Uselessly stating the obvious has always been one of your character flaws."

I don't roll my eyes, but it's a close call. "A 'yes' would have sufficed." I should probably leave it at that, but I jerk a thumb in Rose's direction and ask, "You lost Matthias because the Guard lost the war, and the Guard lost the war because he disappeared on you. You trust him to make it through the entire thing this time around? Because they don't," I press on when Betty opens her mouth. She hesitates for just a moment, and I switch my attention to Rose. "They know I'm not your Dream. Some of them understand what that means and don't want to throw their weight behind you yet."

"What they believe in and fight for is for the vampires to manage," Rose says. "My concerns extend only to Pharaoh, Gaia, and my Nightmare brethren. Society's support is useful but it is inconsequential in the end. As someone with equally narrow vision you should not waste your time stirring up additional trouble."

"Just want to make sure we're all on the same page."

"We are not even in the same book yet. Pharaoh is our first priority, and then we must deal with Notte. Only then can we turn our full attention to the war."

This is probably not the best time to tell him I have no plans on getting involved in the war. Rose will probably launch into some lecture about selfishness and my role as one of Gaia's children, but I know the truth: I'm just a homeless bartender who can talk to ghosts and win a staring contest with Society's beasts. I have no place in this conflict and nothing real to contribute. Once I have the answers and revenge I need, I'm finding a quiet place as far from Society as I can go. It's the least I deserve after what I've been through.

Rose mistakenly takes my silence for agreement and looks to Betty. "Get us into the tower."

Betty slides off her stool and motions to the bartender. The man comes without hesitation. Rose and I follow them to the nearest wall, and Betty presses her hand flat against the wood. The bartender uses three fingers to draw an invisible spell around her and connects the end points to her wrist. A door groans into existence to our right and Betty keeps her hand where it is until Rose has gotten it open.

This time the bar lets us out into Madtown instead of dumping us on the beach. I knew Betty being up meant it was nightfall, but it's still disorienting to step out into Madtown's poorly-lit streets. I must have slept longer than I thought.

Betty's assistance in the spell made our exit the most convenient thing in the world, it seems, because when she leads us around the corner I realize we've come out right alongside the West Council's tower. The front doors have no handles, but Betty makes eye contact with a security camera overhead and the doors swing open on silent hinges. We're let into a small room with another set of doors that remain closed.

"Ouch!" Casper says behind me. I look back and see her with her hands flat against open air. "Evey, I can't come through. What's with the doors in this city? They suck!"

"You have a Ghosts-be-gone up?" I ask Betty.

"Spirits are not welcome here," Betty says. "We do not trust them to not spy for our competitors and enemies. Most of the buildings in Madtown use the same protections."

I look to Casper. "Looks like you're sitting this one out."

"That's not fair!" Casper complains. "I don't want to wait outside."

I motion to Falkor. "Keep an eye on her, would you?"

"He can't even see me," Casper says.

"We cannot leave our shiny alone with the biters," Falkor says. "We only trusts them so much."

Betty doesn't have time for this. "Councilor Freeman thinks faeries are a delicacy."

Falkor gnashes his teeth for a few moments, then declares, "We will protects the ghost."

He waddles back out onto the sidewalk and settles down to wait. Betty motions to the camera pointed inside the entrance and the front doors swing closed. Once the locks have slid into place, the second doors open. Considering how flammable the tower's inhabitants are, I'm not surprised by these safety measures, though this setup borders on paranoia when it turns out there's a third door to get through.

Finally we are in a lobby that looks more like a museum exhibit than a business foyer. Marble statues line the path to the front desk, encased in glass boxes, and there are framed paintings hanging on the wall that look positively ancient. A silk black banner hangs halfway between us and the receptionist and lists a series of tour dates. Seems the Nests rotate their treasures from one hub to the next. I'm undecided if it's a show of wealth or if they're genuinely interested in sharing the world history they've protected for hundreds and thousands of years.

Betty checks in with the well-dressed receptionist, who summons the elevator for us with the press of a button. The presence of mirrors on the inside of the lift are unexpected, and I stare at the gap between Rose and me where Betty's body should be. There's no elevator music, and no lights to tell us what floor we're passing. We just go up and up like we're heading for the clouds, and even though I have no problem with tight spaces I start to feel a little claustrophobic.

"A little disappointed there's no spooky mansion," I say.

"Do you know how much property costs in San Francisco?" Betty asks.

I let that slide and look to Rose. "You never told me why we're here."

"It is rude to start a fight within the Nest's territory without proper warning. Seeing how I am relying on them to bring Pharaoh home to me, I would prefer not to step on more toes than is strictly necessary. Yet," Rose says, with a sideways glance at Betty. She only lifts her shoulders in a faint shrug, accepting and dismissing the implied warning that he will not take the Nest into consideration for long. If she's not going to properly react, then I have to.

"Start a fight," I echo. "You told the bartender we were leaving as soon as we checked in. Which one is it?"

"Yes," Rose says. I consider smacking a proper answer out of him, but he elaborates before I've worked up the courage: "We are going to start it, but we cannot finish it. I cannot finish it," he corrects himself, "without

Pharaoh here to ground my power. It will fall to the Nest and the Guard."

The elevator finally slows to a stop. Betty precedes us off and barely slows to check in with Freeman's secretary. The man only needs a second to realize who's arrived and he immediately buzzes us through to his boss's office. I'm the last one in and I take a moment just inside the door to inspect my surroundings.

Aside from the lack of windows, it looks like any businessman's corner office. Certificates hang in neat rows on the nearest wall, degrees from a couple dozen universities, and a painting of a woman sits on his desk in lieu of a photograph. The other two walls are lined with bookshelves full to bursting. There's even a little mini bar to one side, though I sincerely doubt that's grenadine in the largest stoppered bottle.

Freeman doesn't stand up at our entrance like I half-expect him to but greets us with a smooth, "Vicereine Alexandra. Brimstone. And... guest," he adds, with a glance at me. "Please, make yourselves comfortable."

There are only two chairs, but Betty presses her hand to the small of my back and concedes the second chair to me. It's an unexpected deference, and Freeman gives me a long look as he reconsiders my importance. I stare back and am not at all surprised to feel the cold prickle of vampire magic down my spine. I have a half-second to worry that it'll work on me now that I'm so far from Elysium, but it dissipates before I can get good and concerned. Freeman's eyes narrow a bit as his power passes straight through me and I don't bother to stifle my smug smile.

"You have traded familiar company for strange things," Freeman says.

"She is strange," Rose agrees, but leaves it at that.

Betty is more accommodating when Freeman looks expectantly to her. "She is Elysium's linchpin and an unmatched Dream. She exists under Brimstone's protection."

Freeman accepts this without argument and turns on Rose. "Society presumed you dead, Brimstone. I speak for the entirety of the West Council when I say your survival is welcome news. You are always so very entertaining." His smile is slow and close-lipped. I'm startled by that self-censure, as it means he keeps a life outside Madtown's small borders. "So: entertain us. You would not be on our doorstep so quickly if you did not want something from us."

"I am going to take Madtown's gate apart," Rose says.

I stare at him. "You're what?"

Freeman's eyebrows creep up his forehead. Rose ignores me in favor of waiting out the Councilor, but the silence stretches so long it goes from awkward to uncomfortable. Finally Freeman blinks, and his expression relaxes.

"Interesting," he says. "Do you honestly believe you can?"

"I am the only one strong enough to," Rose says.

"It appears death is as temporary a setback to Nightmares as it is to vampires," Freeman muses. "Yet you must admit your disadvantage. Alexandra has already filed reports for a rescue and retrieval of your missing half. Without him at your side, you cannot expect this campaign to be successful."

"I am giving the city back to the West Council," Rose tells him. "It is not my campaign; it is yours. Tell me you can take it if I leave it to you. Breaking the gate will take almost everything I have and I cannot stay here once it's fallen."

Freeman turns his gaze on the ceiling as he mentally ticks through the Council's resources. At length he says, "I will put it before the board and see how they rule. Do you require anything else?"

"Support," Rose says. "Most immediately, transportation."

Freeman inclines his head and rests his hand on his desk phone. "I will not be long."

It's a dismissal, so we follow Betty back out to the waiting area. There are enough chairs here for all of us, but I wait until Rose is sitting and then loom over him.

"What do you mean, you're going to break the gate?" I demand. "Did Elysium teach you nothing? Madtown's the largest gate on the west coast—what makes you think San Francisco will survive a blast like that?"

"It will hold," Rose says. "The Lymancyzc will come in droves to protect it."

"Last I heard, protecting Gaia was *your* job."

"The Lymancyzc are at their weakest when their food source is threatened," Betty says. "It's estimated a fifth of their entire flock are hooked into Madtown's power. If the gate comes down, so will they. We can't afford for them to keep Madtown," she says, speaking over my next indignant protest. "The war must start here. It must always start here."

"It will hurt Gaia," Rose admits, "but it is no more harmful than applying leeches to a wound. We must bleed her now so she can heal later."

"A, gross, and B, no."

"It serves the secondary purpose of finding Notte and Pharaoh," Rose says. "Such news is undiscriminating; it does not have to be coded or passed along from safe house to safe house. If they are anywhere within earshot of Society, they will hear what has happened within a matter of hours and know who is responsible."

"And with no gate, they can't come through," I say.

"We are not staying here," Rose reminds me. "The majority of the American resistance lives along the northern border. When Pharaoh and Notte hear we are on the west coast, they will know to look for us in the pacific northwest."

"I have trouble finding both my socks in one room, and you're talking about finding one man on the entire west coast. Didn't think you were an optimist."

"I can sense Pharaoh inside three hundred kilometers," Rose says. "I'll know exactly where he is at fifty."

"Creepy," I say, but I remember Pharaoh saying something similar to Betty when they showed up at Jinx. I suppose it's necessary, considering their survival depends on one another, but it's still weird. Not that I have any room to argue the point, considering what I did to Rose back at Pariah. I can still feel my magic stretching between us like a taut thread. "Also, we use miles in the US. Just saying."

"Your ignorance has been noted."

"One-eighty," Betty says. I frown at her, not following, and she shrugs. "Give or take a few miles."

I tuck that tidbit aside for later and consider Rose again. It's continue the argument and risk hitting him in front of his vampire minions or bite my tongue for now. I choose the safer route of silence and pick the chair furthest from him. Betty stays with Rose, and despite how obviously uncomfortable he makes her she doesn't hesitate to take the chair right beside his. We ignore each other until Rose is summoned back to Freeman's office. Betty watches the door close behind him, then immediately comes to sit beside me.

"Evelyn Notte," Betty says, enunciating each syllable.

She studies me with an intensity that makes the hairs on the back of my neck stand on end, but I stare back and wait her out. The look on her face says she's not sure she wants to press this conversation, but at last she glances at the receptionist and lowers her voice.

"It seems it wasn't a car accident that took them from you after all, hm? But you have always said you lost your husband and daughter on the same day. A daughter," she says again, barely audible. "Was it his?"

I swallow hard against the gnawing heat in my throat. "Yes."

"I have been around for a very long time, Evelyn," Betty tells me. "I remember when the Nightmares were born. I have watched generations of them rise and die. I have never heard of one having a child." She motions me to lean closer but doesn't wait for me to obey before asking, "What happened to the child, really?"

"I don't know." The truth is almost more painful aloud than it is ricocheting around my brain. "Adam and Ciara were caught in the backlash when Elysium blew. I assumed they burned away in the blast, but now everyone's saying Adam survived. I don't think he would have stolen her from me just to leave her behind, which means there's a chance he took her with him. I have to find him, Betty. I have to know what really happened to her."

"What an interesting conflict of interest," Betty says. At my frown, she elaborates: "A Dream with a child. I imagine it will put a strain on your pairing."

"There is no conflict of interest, because I'm not going to have a Nightmare," I say. That's not a conversation I'm getting into here, though, so I attempt to distract her. "I didn't tell you I was a Dream, but you knew anyway. It's how you introduced me. When did you figure it out, and when were you going to tell me? You let me find out from him of all people."

Betty gives me a pitying look. "You woke Brimstone."

I did what Falkor said a human couldn't. Looking back I can pinpoint the exact moment Betty clued in: the moment I called Notte Adam and tried to hit Rose for denying my relationship with him. She'd apologized to Rose for bringing Pharaoh to me and treated me with the same cautious deference she afforded the Brimstone pair. Rose said the gatekeepers would understand as soon as they saw him up and about, and indeed they'd called out *Kill the Dream* as soon as we climbed out of the basement. They'd been talking about me.

"At least we finally know why Elysium saved you," Betty muses.

"Why what?" I ask, thrown, but then it clicks.

Sixteen years ago the gatekeepers turned me inside-out atop a broken gate. I'd never understood why the line repaired itself by making me its anchor, but maybe Betty's right. Maybe Gaia latched onto me because of what I am. Betty said the Nightmares have more rights to the lines than most; Rose said we are Gaia's children. The gate saved me because I am a Dream, and I saved it because I am as much a part of Gaia as the line is.

"I'll be damned," I say quietly, but it takes an extra minute for that to really sink in. When it does, the rest of it finally makes sense: "It'd also explain why Elysium tolerated you when no other gate will suffer a vampire. It recognized you as an ally because I was linked into the line and he was sleeping at its base. You've known him a long time, haven't you?"

"I remember when Notte found him," Betty says, and tips her head back to consider the ceiling. "The Nests are a solid network the Nightmares can lean against, as we cover significantly more ground. We put out the call when a Nightmare or Dream is found so that the other pairs know to look for the missing half. I was the one who told Notte about the Brimstone Dream."

"You knew him," I say. "How well?"

"I fought at his side for years in the war," Betty says. I swallow hard and resist the urge to ask what he was like. It turns out I don't have to, because Betty says, "You have terrible taste in men, Evelyn."

"I noticed," I mutter.

Freeman's door opens, and Rose steps out. Betty gets up, hesitates for just a moment, and sends me an inscrutable look. For a moment I think she might mention Ciara to Rose. Instead she goes silently into Freeman's office and closes the door behind her. I wait for Rose to take his seat again, but he goes to the elevator and presses a button to call it back to our floor.

"We're leaving," he says.

"Back to the bar?" I ask.

"Leaving," Rose says again and holds out his hand.

I take a wallet and key ring from his palm. "What about Betty?"

"Vicereine Alexandra's place is here," Rose says, and steps into the elevator as soon as the doors open. I balk, and he is forced to hold the doors open for me. "She cannot go north with us. We cannot take her condition into account."

"She's staying here?" I ask. "But—"

I don't know how to finish that. I've seen a lot of tenants come and go, but Betty was one of my longest-lasting. Not a friend, not necessarily an ally, but still a constant. Now she is gone without so much as a goodbye.

"Our path is not hers, though they will intersect eventually." Rose says. "It is inevitable that she will return to us. Now: we're going."

I send a last look at Freeman's door and then step into the elevator. The ride down feels no shorter than the ride up was, and I soundlessly follow Rose across the lobby and out into the night. Falkor and Casper fall in alongside us immediately and I can feel Falkor leaving a snuffling trail along my thigh as he checks me for new injuries.

The tower is close to Madtown's entrance, which I guess makes sense considering San Francisco's residents are the Nest's main food source. Rose leads me to a garage two blocks down. Because of the hour it's locked up for the night, but the fob doubles as a key card that lets us in. Rose waits until I have the door open before speaking.

"Find the car and start the engine," he says. "The Lymancyzc will swarm when the gate comes down. We must be ready to leave as soon as I return."

He turns back toward Madtown, so I take Casper and Falkor into the garage. I aim the fob every which way as I smash the unlock button, and finally headlights flash in response. I open the back door first to let Falkor in, and he turns in circles on the cushion. Casper makes no move to join him but gives the car a leery look.

"The last time I was this close to a car it was literally sitting on top of me."

"Falkor will protect you. Get in."

Casper heaves a put-upon sigh and eases into the backseat. "Speaking of Falkor, you have no right to critique my reading choices when you named him—"

I close the door on the rest of her accusation. She sticks her tongue out at me, and I roll my eyes in response. I'm immediately distracted when the thread between Rose and me snaps tight. I send a sharp look over my shoulder as if somehow I can see through Madtown's barriers to where Rose is heading for the gate. Fear and anticipation are a ball of ice lodged in my stomach. I remember what it felt like when Elysium broke. More than that, I remember the backlash from Chronos. Madtown is bigger by several magnitudes.

"This is going to suck," I whisper. I set my back to the car and slide down it until I'm crouched. I fold my arms tight across my chest and squeeze, bracing for the inevitable blow.

When it comes, it is actually easier than Chronos was to ride out, if only because that first ferocious crunch fries every nerve ending in my body. I stop breathing, stop existing, stop being anything but a numb husk with too much power rebounding through me. The only thing that keeps me alive is that web between Rose and myself. He is an unyielding pressure burning hotter than even Madtown's destroyed magic does, and bit by bit that fiery thread pulls me back to my quivering body.

Pharaoh.

It is a desperate whisper at my ear, clear as day despite the distance between Rose and myself, and I remember how to breathe again. I suck a ragged gasp into aching lungs and swear I feel my chest rip open beneath it. I squeeze my arms tighter and gasp again, more carefully this time. The spots in my vision have nothing to do with the night and everything to do with my slow asphyxiation. I blink rapidly, feeling big and clumsy in a body I'd already forgotten I owned, and then Rose's voice comes again:

Help me.

I don't remember deciding to move. I don't remember getting up. I just feel the slap of metal against my palms as I throw the garage door open and know I'm moving. Rose's fear is a jagged weight on the line between us, kicking my heart into a panicked overdrive, and I race up the sidewalk as fast as my legs can take me. The half-step up into Madtown is sudden and disorienting enough that I trip over my own feet. I catch myself with my hands and feel the telltale sting of torn skin along my fingers. It's going to hurt like hell later, but right now Rose's call is more important.

Madtown's streets were half-abandoned when we left, but the gate's explosion has brought a shoulder-to-shoulder crowd to the streets. I shove my way through them and am knocked around in turn by bigger, heavier bodies. I wrench my ankle a bit when someone steps on my foot but finally manage to stumble to the front edge of the crowd.

I take the last corner to Madtown's gate and am almost immediately blinded by the light pulsing out of it. Rose stands alone at the gate with his hands buried inside the nebula. The sky is full of screaming gatekeepers. Why they haven't swooped for him yet, I don't know, but I don't trust them to keep their distance for long.

"Run," I whisper, but then Rose flickers. He's here and gone and here again. I take a half-step forward, sure I'm seeing things, and he does it again. "Rose, run."

There's no way he can hear me over all this chaos, but Rose looks over his shoulder and catches my eye. He flickers in and out a third time, and this time he's gone for longer than a blink. I pound on the wall closest to me, warring with my fear, and then launch myself at him. I don't know if the gate is trying to pull him in or if there's something worse at play, but I've only got a couple seconds until the gatekeepers notice his distraction and realize I'm here too. Whatever Rose is doing, I'm safest with him, so I run for him and refuse to look up at the murderous flock overhead.

Rose flickers twice in quick succession, and then I'm close enough to catch hold of his elbow. I yank at his arm, meaning to haul him away from the gate. Instead the street gives out beneath us, and we fall into oblivion together.

EIGHT

We land in a tangled heap, me on top of him. My first confused thought is that we survived such a long fall and didn't liquefy immediately upon the landing. The second is that the world is far too quiet to be Madtown, and that I can't feel the shattered gate anymore. I use Rose's shoulders as a brace to push myself up and look around.

The building we're in might have been a church at one point, but it's more ruins than anything else now. A handful of pews survived the test of time, but none of them are complete anymore. Support beams are scattered haphazardly, barely held up by piles of rubble, and all but one window has been reduced to empty frames. If there was ever a door, it is hidden now by the half-collapsed walls.

I look down at Rose, a little surprised he hasn't tossed me off him yet. His eyes are closed and he lies so still I'm half-sure he's dead. Only the heartbeat jack-hammering against the magical leash between us tells me otherwise. That pulse kills any vague interest I might have had in our new predicament, because anything that can scare a Nightmare is not something I want anything to do with.

"Hey," I say.

"Quiet," he says, barely louder than a breath of air.

He reaches up without looking and finds my arms on the second try. Carefully, oh so carefully, he guides me off of him. His caution is contagious, and I check where my feet are before standing. Rose stays on his back for another minute, then opens his eyes. The look that twists across his face when he notes our surroundings is equal parts agony and defeat, and he digs the heels of his hands into his eyes. I can still see his mouth, though, and the silent snarl his lips curl into sends a chill down my spine. I rub at my arms and wait for him to get up.

Finally Rose drops his hands and sits up. He's got his expression under control, but I'm not fooled.

"This isn't—" I start, but swallow Madtown's name when Rose sends me a hot look.

He gets to his feet and creeps to the window on cat's feet. I follow close enough that I almost step on his heels twice. He leans against the wall by the window for an endless minute, then works up the nerve to ghost his fingers along the window frame. When nothing happens, he does it again and again, sliding more of his fingers outside on each pass. He gets his entire hand outside with no response, so finally risks a look out. I wait a beat to see if he recoils, then lean forward to see where we are.

The town we're in is unfamiliar and in as bad of shape as this church. The neighboring buildings are skeletal remains, and shadows cling to the rubble surrounding them. The place looks abandoned, but that does nothing for Rose's composure. He taps my shoulder and hoists himself out the window. I follow, albeit much less gracefully. Rose steadies me on the landing, fingers digging in tight as he tries to keep me as quiet as possible.

I assume we're going to stick to the walls and hide in the shadows, but Rose catches hold of my wrist and pulls me out into the middle of the street. I keep a discreet eye on the buildings as we set off. I have the unsettling feeling we're being watched, and I don't know if it's my imagination fueled by Rose's fear or if there really is something else here with us. I check every dark window and alleyway we pass and see no one else.

It's because I'm looking that I realize we're walking in a loop. We've gone about five minutes down the road when we pass the church again, and the next buildings we pass are familiar. I look from Rose to the road we're on, but there's no curve I can see and no forking path to explain how we're getting turned around. Five minutes later the church is back, though, and this time there is a new shadow on the ground outside the window.

I can't risk tugging my hand out of Rose's, so I grab at him with my free hand and give his arm a quick prod. He keeps his eyes forward, but the tight look on his face says he knows what I've spotted. I send a wild look over my shoulder at the shadowy mass getting further behind us. Each time we pass the church, the shadow has shifted closer to the road, and there are more and more gathering on the dead lawn behind it. I lean against Rose, trying to shift him further across the road. Instead he pulls me around him until he's between me and the curb.

The next time we come up on the church, the shadow is waiting for us in the middle of the road. It's a lumpy undefinable shape, as if someone's thrown a black cloth over a pile of rubble and given it permission to move, but it's half-again as tall as I am and has five bright white eyes. I twist my hand in Rose's grip and slip my fingers through his, squeezing a silent plea into the backs of his hands with my blunt fingernails. He nearly crushes my hand in response but keeps us on collision course. At the last possible second he pushes us off to one side.

99

The shadow lunges and glances Rose hard enough to nearly take us both down. I brace as hard as I can to keep us from falling and haul Rose closer to me. For a moment I smell blood, and then we are finally running. This time we make it to the edge of town, and we bolt into an open, dusty desert. We run until I can't breathe, then run until the stitch in my side feels like it's tearing a line all the way up to the corner of my mouth, and at last Rose slows down. I barely have time to catch my breath before he stumbles and falls.

The blood wasn't my imagination. His coat is torn from shoulder to hip, and blood splatters to the sand at his knees when he hits the ground. I grab at his coat and peel it down his shoulder to his elbow. It's a move I regret immediately, because Rose looks like he was nearly sliced in half. Skin curls up and away from the gouge in him, and I swear I see the flutter of a lung through the bloody wreckage of a shattered ribcage.

"You need a doctor," I say without thinking.

Rose smacks his good hand over my mouth, but it's too late. A breeze picks up and carries whispers to us, a chorus of voices and tones I feel more than hear. Rose lets go of me immediately and scrabbles for handfuls of sand. He packs it into his wound like somehow it can keep him alive and motions for me to get him to his feet.

He's almost dead weight now, and I have to loop his arm around my neck to get him up. He stumbles into me and hisses in pain. We set off once more, but the wind picks up until it threatens to knock us over. I want to duck and cover until it passes, but I can feel Rose's blood soaking into my hip.

Abruptly two things happen: the wind dies, and the ground gives out only inches from our feet. I've been going so hard into the gale that I almost send us headfirst into the new chasm. As it is I have to practically throw us backward to change our course, and I drop Rose in the process. He hits the ground with a sick thud and doesn't even try to get up. I drop to my knees and give his shoulder a frantic shake.

"Up," I say, as quietly as I can. "Wake up! I need you to stay with me, okay?"

Rose's mouth moves, but I can't hear him. I have to lean over him and practically crush my ear to his mouth, and even then it takes a moment to understand: "He is coming."

"Pharaoh?" I guess.

"Nevere."

The sound of rocks crumbling has me looking to the chasm, and I watch as it stretches into the distance. It takes a moment to realize that noise is coming from behind us as well. I twist and watch as the chasm comes racing at us from the horizon. I make a solid attempt at hauling Rose up, as if I'm at all strong enough to carry him out of here, but then the ground goes still and calm. We exist on a sliver of land maybe fifteen feet wide, with who knows how long a drop bracketing us on either side.

"Escape plan," I say as the whispering wind starts up again. "Right now."

"I can't," Rose says. There's a gurgle in his voice, and I look to his ruined chest. Most of the dirt has fallen out, pushed free by blood. I don't know what else to do but grab more sand and try again. I shove it into the gouge in his chest and try not to retch at the feel of his lungs quivering against my palm. Rose tries to speak again, but he manages words only in bursts: "I can't—sidestep—without Pharaoh."

Sidestep, he says, and I suddenly understand where we are. We've crossed realms.

"Pharaoh isn't here," I say.

I almost forget what I'm saying when large white stones creep over the edge of the canyon. They're followed by white sticks as long and thick as trees. It takes a heartbeat to realize I'm looking at a massive skeletal hand, and then it's impossible to look away again. In a desperate bid, I dig my fingers too hard into Rose's injury. The pained noise he makes is harsh enough that I can finally rip my stare away from what's coming and look down at Rose again.

"I'm here, and I'm a Dream too. Use me."

"No," Rose says, with all the anger he can still muster. "No. He'll know."

"Don't keep me, just use me to get us out of here. You can, can't you?" Rose doesn't answer, but he doesn't have to. The look on his face reminds me of a cornered beast. "Rose, for fuck's sake—"

"Don't," Rose says. "Don't call me that. Not here."

A second hand makes it over the ridge. Bony fingers dig into the ground around us for purchase, and then a pair of spiral horns appear from the depths. They go on and on, each almost as tall as the West Council's tower, and finally an equine skull appears. Its eye sockets glow the sickly green-black of an infected wound. I can only face the god for a few seconds before panic threatens to send me running off the edge of the cliff. I forcibly turn my attention on Rose and hunch forward until he is the only thing I can see.

"Rose, please," I whisper. "Please, please, please."

Nevere's voice is thunder rolling atop that unintelligible chorus of whispers. "I see you," He says, and drums His fingers hard enough to shake the ground beneath us. "So very far from home. So very alone."

His hands snap up in my peripheral vision. I flinch, expecting to get crushed, but He only interlocks His fingers to make a bone cage around us. As I watch, the bones start to split and flake until they are covered in ragged scales. Nevere exhales a fierce breath at us, and the scales snap free. It's raining knives, and there's nowhere I can go. I scream as they sink into my shoulders and back. One goes clear through my hand and sinks into Rose's ribcage; another nearly slices my ear clean off. I scrabble at the scale buried in my hand and succeed only in slicing my fingertips off.

"Where is your Dream now?" Nevere asks. "Did you finally destroy him? I am jealous. I would have liked to play with him once more."

Rose doesn't answer. He can't answer, not with a scale buried in his throat. Blood wells up around it, dark and thick, and streams down either side of his throat. He lifts an unsteady hand to it, mouth moving on silent breaths he can no longer manage.

A heartbeat later the scales are gone, leaving only the wreckage behind, and a smaller version of Nevere stands inside the cage with us. The grotesque god crouches on Roses' other side and dips His bone fingers into the gaping wound in Rose's throat. I want to scream for Him to stop. I want to shove Him away and put myself between them. I want to, I have to, but I—who sassed gatekeepers and kicked Rose and kept my tenants in line for sixteen years by sheer attitude alone—can only watch in numb terror. He is a god, and I am nothing, and I can feel my own insignificance all the way down to my wrecked soul.

"No matter, I suppose," Nevere says, and pulls. Gray skin comes away with His fingers, stretching out away from Rose like elastic, and winds over Nevere's hand. Before my eyes Nevere starts stealing Rose's body for Himself. "I will find him."

"No," Rose says. It is more air than words, but I can feel his agony singing on the bond between us. "*No*."

"I will eat him," Nevere promises. "Bit by bit, I will eat him for everything he's done to thwart me, and he will allow it while I wear your face."

Rose screams in animalistic rage and lashes out—not at Nevere but at me. Bloody, broken fingers catch hold of my elbow and Rose's power comes awake with the roar of black fire. Nevere howls outrage, but we are already gone.

I thought the breaking gates hurt. I thought Nevere's cruelty hurt. But Rose's power is something else, something ugly and fierce and far too strong for my fragile body. My skin ruptures to vent it, and I fall to pieces when that is not enough. Color comes in jagged bursts, so bright and strong it sears my eyes, and the metallic taste of blood is sharp enough to break my teeth on.

As quickly as he takes me apart, he puts me back together again, and I come alive in a burning cornfield. I swat frantically at the flames that are licking their way over us until I realize it doesn't hurt. Quite the opposite, actually—the fire is burning our injuries away and leaving unmarred skin behind.

Rose puts cold lips to my ear. "Wake up."

We are back in Madtown in the midst of an all-out war. It's too many jumps in too short of time, too much pain and trauma. I can only stand there and stare at Rose in numb silence. I want to run from Rose and that horrifying magic of his, but I can't even breathe.

I can feel in him the same agony that's eating me alive from the inside out, and somehow that scares me more than anything. Maybe it's the Dream in me reacting to a Nightmare's unfettered power; maybe it's the ghost of a mother I never was responding to a child's unbridled fear. I don't know. All I can do is gasp out shaky reassurances neither of us believe: "We're okay, we're okay, we're okay."

"For now," Rose says, bone-tired and soft. "We have to go."

The fight raging around us works both for and against us, as most of Society is too deep in the fight to notice two more bodies trying to flee the scene. We have one near-miss with a werewolf, but the pink woman from the bar unloads a shotgun in its face. Falkor appears out of nowhere a heartbeat later, drawn as always to my pain, and clears us a path with claws and teeth. He leaves more than one person screaming in our wake, but I don't look back to see if he can differentiate friend from foe.

Rose and I leave Madtown at a run. The garage door is missing, blown off its hinges by Falkor's forced exit, and the car door isn't much better off. Casper is pacing tight circles by the trunk, but she goes still to gape at us as we rush toward her.

"Evey?" she asks, voice sharp with alarm. "What—"

"In, in, in," I say, and Falkor bounds through Casper to get in the backseat. Casper scrambles in after him, and Rose slams the mangled door closed with an inhuman strength. I spot the keys on the concrete near the front tire where I dropped them at Rose's call and snatch them up. Before I can get in the car three gatekeepers materialize around us.

I reach out without thinking and grab hold of Rose again. "*Kill them.*"

He bound himself to me to get us away from Nevere, so there is no way he can ignore my command. Black fire unfurls around us in a shockwave that melts the gatekeepers to nothing. I stare at the ashen shadows they leave behind, slack-jawed in surprise. Rose makes an awful noise and yanks free of me. I don't try to call him back but sink sideways into the driver's seat. Rose rubs desperately at his face, then puts a hand to his now-healed throat. He shudders so hard I expect him to fall over. I can't understand what he says, but I understand that agonized tone well enough.

"Hey," I say, knowing I don't have the right words for this.

Rose digs his fingers into his neck before dropping his hand to his side. When he starts around the hood of the car I turn in the seat and jam the keys into the ignition. Small mercies that the car is an automatic, seeing how I haven't driven a car since I first got my license. I take in the dashboard and pedals with a nervous glance, hope to god I'm remembering which control does which, and then almost forget to put the car in reverse. At least I was right about which pedal was the brake, but I scrabble for my seatbelt anyway.

"I didn't think you could drive," Casper says.

"I can. Kind of," I answer in a tight voice, but I get us out of the garage without crashing into anyone else's car.

"We're all going to die."

"You're already dead," I remind her.

Rose digs a handful of maps out from under his seat while I idle at the road. I stare up the street toward Madtown, silently willing him to be faster in his search. He finds the one for California halfway down and turns it this way and that until he can find San Francisco. A gray finger traces the route we need to get out of here, and Rose points. I trust Casper and Falkor to warn me if anyone comes for us and turn my entire attention on remembering how to drive.

It's almost four in the morning, so I expect the roads to be empty, but we pass a good two dozen cars at least before we make it to the Golden Gate Bridge turnoff. We're barely over the bridge before Rose has us turning off the interstate and onto a smaller highway. The lack of traffic makes me nervous, but Rose shakes his head when I mention it.

"Stay to the coastline as much as possible. The sirens will find us a place in Coos Bay to rest."

I have no idea where that is, but I guess it doesn't matter. At least driving down this smaller road means I have fewer people to run over and more time to figure out what the hell I'm doing. It takes a couple miles before even a straight line feels less nervewracking, and then I relax just enough to look over at Rose.

He hasn't put the map away yet, but the shuttered look on his face says he's staring right through it. I drop my gaze to his throat and feel my gorge rise as I remember Nevere's fingers digging into him. I reach across the space between us to touch the unbroken skin of his neck, and Rose flinches so hard I recoil back to my side of the car.

I jerk my gaze away and remember to pay attention to the road for a few more miles, but my thoughts continue their dark spiral down until I have to say, "Hey. That was—that was one of the gods, wasn't it? You took us into a different realm."

"It was not my intention to take you."

"I'm not asking for an apology," I snap back, because every time I blink I see Nevere crouched over Rose's broken form.

"It is not an apology," Rose says in a low voice. "You should not have been able to go with me. That I could pull you means this bond you've created between us is tighter than I feared. That I was foolish enough to respond when you called me in da-Vìncŭn is..." He trails off and gives a fierce shake of his head. "If the third rule did not make allowances for facing the gods, I would put us both to death for such a crime. A Nightmare cannot answer to two Dreams."

"You were going to let him have you," I accuse him. "You would have rather died than use me, except he threatened Pharaoh's life."

Rose doesn't answer, but his silence says enough.

"He slept eighteen years for you," I say, getting louder with each word. "He faced the gatekeepers and was eviscerated on my front lawn. You've sent all of the Guard and Nests to find him and bring him home to you. And you would have just died down there without a fight? You would have let us both die rather than use me. You can't be serious."

"He is my survival," Rose says, voice tight. "He is my sanity. He is the anchor of my world and existence. This is made possible by the sanctity of our bond. By answering to you and letting you into my world, I poison what I have with him, and that will kill us just as surely in the end. I cannot, will not risk him. You must stop calling me by this name. You can't deny it," he insists when I start to argue. "You can feel what you've done to us."

I clamp my mouth shut and turn a sullen look out the windshield.

Rose gives me a minute, then continues. "You are a Dream with too many near-misses. Your soul knows what it was born to do and it reaches for the piece to make it whole. But I am not that piece. You must learn restraint until I have found your Nightmare."

"I don't want one," I say. "I didn't want one before and I definitely

105

don't want one after what I just saw. I want to find Adam and then get away from all of this."

"You can't," Rose warns me. "Somewhere your Nightmare clings to life by his fingertips, trying to survive until you step into his life. You damn him to madness and a slow death with your refusal to accept the truth."

He gives me a beat to respond, then gets angry all over again when I don't immediately change my stance. "If we found your Nightmare tomorrow, what would you do? Would you truly let him die? Would you leave him chained up in the ward you found him in, screaming and crying in his restraints as his gift tore him apart again and again and again?"

The savage edge in his voice is too personal to be hypothetical. It takes me two tries to find my voice, and then the best I manage is a hesitant, "Like Adam found you."

"Finding a Dream is never so difficult as making one say yes," Rose says, sounding a bit like he hates himself for having to tell me the truth. "A Nightmare initiates the bond, but a Dream must accept of his own volition. It is very painful being this close to salvation," he reaches out and stops his hand just a breath from where my fingers are clenched on the steering wheel, "and knowing there is nothing you can do to close the gap. Nothing our power does to us hurts us nearly so much as waiting at that precipice."

"Pharaoh told you no," I guess.

"Of course he did," Rose says. "No Dream wants this power. Dreams are born ignorant to the truth of their existence and so create lives outside of us. They know what they are giving up by agreeing to us. It took Pharaoh almost a year to accept me, and I nearly destroyed us both in my desperation to convince him to give in. Do not do to your Nightmare what he did to me. Take this time to come to terms with your purpose in life."

I bite my tongue on everything I want to say to that and say again, "Like Adam found you."

Rose opens his mouth, closes it, and turns his gaze out the window. "Yes."

It's a horrible place to leave the conversation, but neither of us has anything else to say. I leave him to his thoughts and focus instead on following Highway 1 up the coast. Every time the road winds away from the Pacific Ocean I feel my heart kick up a few notches, but inevitably we return to the waves. We pass stoplight town after stoplight town, and as the sun comes up we start to see more traffic. Only the view and the promised safety of this route ease my anxiety over how slow we're going.

Eventually we have to stop for gas and food. Rose stays in the car but sends me into the convenience store to find breakfast. The clerk at the counter is buried in a book and mumbles a distracted greeting as I peruse the aisles. It doesn't take him long to decide I'm the more interesting thing in here, because I am picking up enough junk food that I have to make trips back and forth to the front counter.

"Thirty on pump three, too," I say as I make a beeline for the coffee. I fill the biggest cup I can find, then bleach it with enough cream and sugar to rot my teeth.

"Road trip?" the clerk asks when I return to him.

"Highway to hell," I say. "On a schedule."

He takes the hint and rings my stuff up in silence. The total comes to a ridiculous amount considering eighty percent of what I'm buying is sugar and fat, so I'm glad the vampires are footing the bill. I fork over cash, stuff the change into my own pockets instead of the wallet, and lug the bags out to the car.

The door Falkor broke and Rose slammed shut in San Francisco is still half-crumpled and very obviously not opening again any time soon, so I kick at Rose's door until he opens it. I dump the bags unceremoniously in his lap and go to fill the tank. When I'm done and back in the driver's seat, Rose is holding a jerky stick by the tips of his fingers.

"This is not food."

I snatch it from him and eat it in two bites. "I thought kids liked junk food."

"They do," Casper chimes in solemnly from the back seat.

Rose cranks the heater on as soon as I get the engine going. I poke his cheek and am unsurprised to find out he is as chilly as ever. I make a face at him when he turns a baleful look on me and ask, "How can Pharaoh stand to touch you? You're a block of ice."

"Pharaoh is my body heat."

"Seriously, though. What's the point of wearing a coat if it doesn't keep you warm?"

"This is a shield," Rose corrects me. "Protective spells are woven into the fabric. Pharaoh and I traded favors with the Arctic coven to get the set."

I think of the black coin we used at Pariah. "Favors being...?"

"It is what it says: it is a promise of future aid and the greatest bargaining tool in Society."

"An IOU."

"More dangerous, as it can be passed on without the original owner's consent or knowledge. There's no telling what the coven has done with ours, if they still have it or if they traded it for their own gain. Whomever ends up with the coin has the right to call on Pharaoh and myself for aid. We are allowed loopholes in answering the request, but we must honor our arrangement one way or the other."

He lifts one shoulder in a shrug and pokes his fingers into the vent. "The Nightmares were furious to hear what we'd done. Creatures as powerful as we are should never put our magic in others' hands. We hedged our bets on them being too afraid to summon us, but we will answer if they call."

"Why did you do it?"

"In all the world there is only one Pharaoh," Rose says. "I will not risk him."

"Pharaoh has one?" I ask. "He wasn't wearing it when he showed up in Augusta."

Rose looks at me. "You lie."

"Ask Falkor if you don't believe me. It could have come in handy, too, considering what the gatekeepers did to him."

Rose slams the side of his fist against his door. "*Damn him.*"

He's definitely not talking about Pharaoh. I give him a moment to collect himself, then say, "I know why I hate him. Why do you?"

"It doesn't matter."

"It does to me."

"It doesn't matter," Rose says again.

His tone warns me not to push it. I'm tempted to do so anyway, because backing down from arguments isn't one of my strong suits, but after a nagging internal debate I decide to let it slide. We've had a horrible enough day as it is and we're nowhere near the Oregon border. I'll ask again later, when we're not carrying the ghosts of Nevere's cruelty with us.

If I can't have answers, I can at least have the last word: "For now."

Rose ignores me, so I return the favor, and I focus instead on the unending drive.

NINE

We stop at a hotel that's thirty feet from the ocean. Considering we've just crawled into February, I'm not surprised the parking lot is mostly abandoned. The wind coming up off the ocean is cold as all get-out and I regret opening my car door immediately. I grit my teeth against the instant shakes and instead go around to Casper's door. Neither she nor Falkor seems to care they're stepping out into an ice box, so I grumble discontentedly and dig our snack bags out of the backseat. At least Rose is suffering, judging from how scrunched up and tense he is.

"Ask for Dean," Rose says. "He will have a room ready for us."

The lobby is small and abandoned, save for the woman sitting at the desk in the middle of the room. She's on the phone with a prospective customer, chatting about wake-up times and the hotel's complimentary breakfast. I eavesdrop unashamedly as I try to work warmth back into my hands. She's friendly but efficient and off the phone only a minute after I reach her.

"Welcome to Coos Bay," she says brightly. "Are you checking in?"

"I'm looking for Dean."

"Sure, hon. Let me call him out here for you."

She picks up the receiver, and I hear another phone ringing nearby. I look past her to the short hallway at her back, which presumably leads to the kitchens and management office. Wherever Dean's office is, it's far enough away that I hear the ringing stop but can't hear his voice when he answers. He's out here so quick on the tail-end of the call that I'm certain he dropped everything he was working on. I don't recognize him, but he smiles at me like we're old friends.

"Evelyn!" He tugs me into a quick, fierce hug under the clerk's curious stare. "You made it! Lily's going to be so excited; we weren't really sure you'd make it all the way out here. We know what a workaholic your husband is."

"Yeah," I answer lamely. "Here we are."

Dean looks to his employee. "Kristin, this is Evelyn, one of Lily's friends from back home. I believe Lily turned in her suite keys for them, if you can get them checked in? I'm sure they're exhausted after such a long drive." Kristin nods and starts pecking away at her keyboard. Dean turns back to me, still smiling. "Lily's got a huge deadline coming up, so she's going to be holed up at home until sometime tonight. I'll be out of here at six.

"Here," he adds, and fishes a business card out of his pocket. There's an extra number penned in along the bottom edge that's marked "CELL". "My office number, in case you need anything. Take some time to relax, and we'll get together tonight for sure. Drinks on us!"

"Yeah," I say again, much more enthusiastically. "Drinks sound great."

"Here we go." Kristin opens a drawer and pulls out a key card. She pauses on her way out of her seat to tap in a few last commands, then presents me the card with a smile. "You're in 512, one of the master suites. Ocean view, nonsmoking, top floor. We've got stairs to my left, or you passed the elevators near the door. Dial 0 on your room phone to reach me if you need anything."

"Thanks," I say, pocketing the card, and send a longer look at Dean. "And thank you."

"Anytime," Dean says.

He goes back to his office to work, so I go to the front door to let the others in. Rose steps through immediately, but Falkor hangs back until he's sure he can get in without getting within ten feet of Rose. Casper's the odd one out, standing near the trunk and staring off toward the Pacific.

"Casper," I call. "It's freezing out here."

"I've never seen the ocean," Casper says. "I'll come in after."

I don't expect the hotel to have the same spirit safeguards some of Madtown's buildings employed, so I just say, "Room 512, okay?" and then head back in to meet the others at the elevator.

Rose leaves his hood pulled into his face for the ride up but pushes it out of his way as soon as we're safe in the room. It doesn't surprise me he goes straight to the heater and cranks it up. I entertain myself exploring the hotel room. For a master suite, it's not much nicer than hotel rooms I've stayed in previously, but this place isn't exactly a glitzy kind of hotel. It's just a local chain trying to hold its own and clinging to premium beach property as its saving grace.

"Who are Dean and Lily?" I ask.

"Lily is the siren of Coos Bay. Dean is her human husband."

"He invited us out tonight."

"We will go," Rose says. "I need to know what they've heard since Madtown fell. They are our eyes and ears for the next two nights."

"I thought we were in a hurry."

"Being in a hurry does not require we rush," Rose points out. "There is only so much we can do when so many pieces have been scattered to the winds. We must buy time for Pharaoh to make it back to me and for the Nightmares to return to the fight. Moving too quickly without these safety measures in place just ensures our death."

I stretch out the kinks of a painfully long drive, then motion Falkor aside so I can sprawl in the dead center of the second bed. It feels achingly good to be flat. I rub my eyes and look for a clock. It's nearly half past five, so at least we don't have to wait long before we meet up with our newest contacts. I poke at Falkor, mumble at him to wake me up when it's time to go, and attempt to doze off for a precious hour or two.

I've barely gone under before I'm woken by the shrill ringing of the telephone. I resist its piercing call for a few moments, hoping Rose will reach it first, but it continues droning on and on. Finally I groan and roll over. I slap blindly at the nightstand until my hand hits cool plastic and drag the receiver to my ear.

"Hello?" I manage.

I'm greeted by a dial tone. I squint my eyes open to consider the phone, then set it back in its cradle and look at the clock. It flashes red zeroes at me. I scrub sleep from my eyes and finally push myself up enough to hang my legs off the edge of the bed. It takes more strength than I think I have to actually get up, and I head for the restroom. A couple splashes of cold water to my face only manage to take the very edge off my exhaustion, but a glance at the mirror has me coming wide awake.

The whites of my eyes are a very distinct and disconcerting shade of pink. I gingerly touch the skin around my eyes, looking for lingering soreness. The last time I cried was at four o'clock this morning when we came back to Earth from Nevere's realm. I shouldn't look like this still. I dry unsteady hands off on the nearest hand towel and go out to demand answers from Rose.

I forget everything I was going to say as soon as I see him, and I don't know how the hell I walked past him just a few moments ago without realizing something was very wrong. The Rose sitting cross-legged on the far bed has lost his gray skin and red hair in lieu of the natural look I saw in his first dream. He sits perfectly still in the center of his bed, eyes closed and fingers laced together in his lap. He's humming—except he's not. It takes a couple bars for me to realize that voice is female. I check my own throat for reverberations in case this is just a nervous response to a strange situation.

"Hey," I say.

He opens his eyes, and in the space of a blink I realize he's not alone. There are four women sitting around him on the bed. I get a brief glimpse of long, tangled hair and bare legs, and then they are gone. I shake my head to clear it, but that only brings them back. They flash in and out like a strobe light, and as they start to move they look more like a stop-motion animation reel than anything else.

One by one they turn their full attention to me. I take in too-wide mouths and sharp fingertips and too much skin, and I've almost decided they aren't quite human when they pull apart long enough for me to see their gaping abdomens. It's like they swallowed small bombs; their chests and stomachs are blown out, edges black and curling out away from the slush-red holes.

"What the fuck?" I demand sharply. Rose cuts a hard look at me. "What are those?"

"Oh," one girl whispers, and her sisters echo it until it almost sounds like laughter. "She can see us. What has our brother done now? Does Pharaoh know the deals you cut behind his back?"

"Get out," Rose warns me. "Right now."

"No, no, no." The girls curl toward him, taking hold with overly long fingers, and press ghastly smiles against his coat and hair. Long locks of hair spill over his shoulders and writhe against his coat like snakes. Rose carefully picks them free one lock at a time. It's a gesture I've seen from him several times since we hit the road a couple days ago. I always assumed he was picking at spiderwebs, but the truth is a hundred times creepier. "No, no. Let her stay a while."

I draw a steadying breath. "You're dreaming, aren't you?"

"You should not be here," Rose says.

The girl closest to me slides off the bed. "Let us say hello properly, won't you? We have been so very lonely without you. We appreciate that you have brought us a new friend."

"Yasmin," Rose says. "Do not."

"Come now, brother. We are doing you a favor."

"You're dreaming," I say again, because even if I'm sure I need him to confirm it. That hope is all that lets me hold my ground as Yasmin shuffles toward me. The damage she took to her spine in the explosion cocks her hips and shoulders at odd, contrasting angles. It gives her a shambling gait too much akin to zombies in horror flicks. I breathe slowly through my mouth, afraid I'll smell her insides otherwise, and keep my eyes on her face. "Yes or no?"

"Yes," Rose says.

"Then wake up and get these ugly things out of my face."

Cool fingers dance over my lip and test the line of my jaw. "Nearly as unkind as he is. Let us take her home with us, brother. She smells like I do."

"Yasmin," Rose says, in a tone that promises violence. "I will not say it again."

She lingers for a few moments longer, then finally withdraws. "You never let us have any fun."

Rose doesn't respond, but his silence hardly matters. One by one the girls fade, and as they go Rose's skin darkens to that familiar charcoal gray. I'm newly aware of Falkor asleep on the bed and Casper slouched in the chair by the window. They were here all along; I just couldn't see them through Rose's dream. Judging by the unsettled look Casper is giving me, she at least caught the real-world side of that freak show.

"Evey?" Casper says, slow and careful. "You all right there?"

Not in sixteen years, but I settle for a tart, "Peachy."

"Damn you," Rose says, with feeling. "Stop going where you don't belong."

I wave that aside as a worn-out argument I no longer have the patience for. "Why does your skin change when you're dreaming? I'm going to assume you're not born looking like this or your parents wouldn't have had to wait until your powers manifested to know something was wrong. That's what you really look like, right?"

"This is what I'm supposed to look like," Rose says. "Nightmares come in shades of gray. We change when our bond finalizes."

I bite my tongue on the obvious question and start instead with: "But Dreams don't change? Pharaoh looked relatively human except for..." My heart catches on before the rest of me does and thumps in fear. I reach for my face and dig my fingernails into my cheek. "His eyes turned red."

"Like yours are changing now," Rose says before I can work up the courage to ask. He says it like an accusation, like any of this is my fault, but I'm too startled to defend myself from his snapping anger. "You are not supposed to change until you find your Nightmare, but the bond you set up between us still stands. Incomplete or not, you have access to my powers, and mine is awakening yours in you."

"I have power?" I ask.

"You don't remember that cool thing you did at Pariah?" Casper asks.

"That's a psychic thing," I say. "Not the same."

"Discover your power with your own Nightmare," Rose says. "Stop pulling at me."

I could tell him I'm not doing it on purpose, but it's easier to go back to my paused question: "If Nightmares are supposed to be 'shades of gray', why did Adam look human? Is it because Meridian is dead?"

"Possible."

"You don't know?"

"Dreams and Nightmares are not meant to live without each other," Rose says. "Nightmares who lose their Dreams are consumed by their powers. Even if you worked as a stopgap for him, that you never saw him change means you were not strong enough to keep him sane. He should not be alive today. That he's survived this long means he's committed one of two unthinkable crimes."

"Besides trying to kill me?" I ask.

"The most likely solution is he disappeared into the wastes," Rose says. At the look I give him, he says, "It is easiest to think of it as Gaia's scar tissue, a vacuum where Her power no longer exists."

"Sure," I say. "That really clears things up."

He glances to his right and the way his gaze lingers makes me wonder if he can still see the girls. I resist the urge to swat the air in front of me. "But the wastes have too many rules and too many shifting landscapes. To survive sixteen years there is impossible, which means he would have retreated to the catacombs at their center. He must be half-mad or more by now."

"Just out of curiosity, do you ever go to nice places?" I ask.

"Nightmare," Rose says, with all the intonation of a *Duh*.

The phone rings. Rose makes no move to pick it up, so I cross the room and put it to my ear. I half-expect a dial tone to greet me, but when there's only silence I say, "Evelyn."

"Evelyn, hello," Dean says. "Just got word that Lily is almost home from work. Are you free to meet me downstairs in say, fifteen minutes?"

"We'll be there," I say. After I hang up I look at Rose. "At some point we really ought to get some new clothes, don't you think? I'll settle for a clean pair of underwear if nothing else, but I'm getting kind of rank and you haven't changed in two decades or so. Foul."

"It is a secondary concern."

"Oh, right, sure. I bet Pharaoh won't mind that you stink like a crypt. Seriously," I press when he hesitates. "Tell your contacts here to find us something clean to wear, or we're going to have to make a stop at the nearest store. We can't go another day like this."

He doesn't respond, but I opt to take his silence as agreement. Fifteen minutes is enough to shower, though it's depressing putting on the same

114

dirty clothes afterward. Rose leads the way out, with Casper and Falkor not far behind him, so I lock and check the door before following them to the elevator.

Dean is waiting for us at the front desk, and he leads us out to where his sedan is parked. Rose shakes his head at the silent invitation and redirects us to our loaner car. Rose takes the passenger seat, so I stuff the others in the back, and I follow Dean's car out of the lot.

We travel south a couple miles along the highway, out of Coos Bay proper and past the straggling houses on its outskirts. He pulls into the drive at a house with no lights on and collects two bags from the trunk. Instead of going inside, we head out back, where the yard goes all the way to the water's edge.

Sirens are nocturnal creatures who are unable to step on shore during the day. Despite the sun's absence, Lily seems in no rush to leave her natural habitat. She is waiting for us where the waves reach the shore, and the tide washes over her hips and thighs where she sits cross-legged on the ground. She doesn't stand at our approach but smiles and accepts the greeting kiss Dean dips down to offer her. He gets comfortable alongside her, never mind that he's still dressed in his work clothes. He motions to a cooler sitting further up on dryer land, and I unzip it to find it packed with ice and beer.

Lily gets right to the point. "Madtown burns, Nightmare. Are you pleased?"

"That depends on which side is winning," Sol says.

Lily lifts her shoulders in a dainty shrug. "It is too early to tell. Fortunately for us, the Lymancyzc are wasting most of their time trying to seal the gate. Society has turned on itself without their intervention. The vampires led the charge as you wished, but sunrise forced them from the frontlines and left the Guard unattended. My sisters will tally the dead as best they can and pass it on. We should hear within a couple hours how the day progressed." She looks south at that as if she can somehow see San Francisco from here.

"The sea sings of the Nightmares and your return," she says, returning her full attention to Rose. "Every gate felt Madtown fall, and it did not take your brethren long to answer. Tempest and Wrath have made contact. We have not gotten confirmation that they have arrived safely in North America, but we cautiously assume they will touch base with us soon."

"And my Dream?" Rose asks.

"We have heard nothing yet, and for that we are grateful. It is best that he fly under the radar with Society going up in flames." She hesitates,

115

answers Dean's subtle head shake with a firmer shake of her own, and says, "They know you are alone, Brimstone. Not all you passed in Madtown were your allies. There is a bounty on his head—who posted it and for how much, I have not yet heard, but enough sources have mentioned it for me to believe it. If the Lymanczyc's allies are afraid to face you directly, they will turn their full efforts to his whereabouts."

The look on Rose's face chills my blood in my veins. Survival instincts warn me to put space between us; ingrained habits from Elysium have me holding my breath until I know I can hold my ground. Dean leans forward to put at least part of himself between Rose and his wife, and Lily shifts just enough that I know she's prepping to bolt to the ocean.

"They will die for considering it," Rose says. "I need names."

"I do not have names yet," Lily says again, with a calm but quiet firmness that sounds like truth. "Treachery is a hard thing to sort out, Brimstone. You of all people—"

"Do not."

She shuts up immediately. Rose stares her down for another tense moment, then swivels his dark stare to me.

"Where is your ghost?"

It takes only a second to place her. Casper has made herself comfortable on the cooler and is watching the proceedings with blatant interest. I jerk a thumb in her direction and she leans forward, pleased to be remembered and included by someone who isn't me.

"Emily," Rose says, and I'm sure that earns him a dozen more brownie points. "You need to return to San Francisco."

Her jaw drops. "What? Is he serious?"

"He sounds serious," I say.

My response tells Rose she's not pleased, so he turns his head her direction. "There is rot in the Guard, and you are the only one who can safely act as eyes and ears for us. It is more than just Pharaoh and me at stake," Rose insists when he sees my expression. "Someone who is willing to betray us to the Lymanczyc could do irreparable damage to the entire Guard. We are too bruised and broken to suffer betrayal now, and the world will not survive a second loss in this war."

"So he wants me to go back to that bar and spy on everyone who's there?" Casper asks.

"Last I checked that's one of your hobbies," I say dryly. "Probably best to start with that bartender we saw the first night, if you remember what he looks like. He was the first one to realize that I wasn't—Brimstone's Dream," I say, biting off 'Rose' in the nick of time. I think I'm safe, but the foul look Rose gives me says he knows what that catch in my sentence means. I choose not to acknowledge it but ask instead, "Say she can actually figure out who's on the wrong side. How are you supposed to get that information from her?"

"Last I checked, you bound her to you," Rose says with cool disapproval.

"Do you know when's the last time I tried a séance?" I ask.

"The how of it is your problem to sort out," Rose says. "Is she willing or not?"

I look at Casper. "Well?"

She taps her fingers against her lower lip as she thinks about it, then says, "Supernatural super spy. It has a nice ring to it." She brightens and flashes me a toothy smile. "And Alexandra stayed behind in San Francisco, so there's that!"

"You can't even get into the West Tower," I remind her. That takes a little wind out of her sails, but I don't give her time to change her mind before looking back to Rose. "She'll do it. We heading back tomorrow?"

"We do not have time to double back," Rose says. "I leave it to Dean and Lily."

"Southwest Regional connects to San Francisco," Dean says. "I can drive her to the airport if she can find her way from there?" He tries looking at Casper but misses her by a few feet. I resist the urge to correct him and let him finish. "If I find a flight number, the screens should get her to the right gate for boarding, and BART will get her within a mile of Madtown on the other side."

"I've never haunted a plane before," Casper says.

"Sure you won't fall through it?" I ask.

She scowls at me, then gives a determined nod and sits up straight. "I can do it. If I could get across Georgia to find you at Elysium, getting to Madtown is no problem. By the time you remember to call me I'll have all sorts of news for you."

At my nod, Dean digs his phone out of his pocket and starts tapping away in search of the next flight south. Lily watches him work for a moment, then looks to me.

"We do have a message for Brimstone's companion," she says. "You sent a query for the whereabouts of one Keandra Downey. The Downeys were summoned to the Great Lakes four weeks ago to provide support to the Shannons. We have not heard and were not told what has drawn such a fierce concentration of psychics, but the official response is that the Shannons cannot afford to release anyone at this time. Three days," she lifts the appropriate number of fingers, "and Keandra will find you in Seattle."

I round on Rose. "Will we be in Seattle?"

"Unknown," Rose says. "We are passing through it, but we are unlikely to stay."

"It sounded like a question, but it wasn't really one," I say. "We have to go to Seattle. She can help me fix what happened at Pariah and give me a refresher on how to get in contact with Casper once we're separated."

"You are unsubtle in hiding your own needs and wants behind very real problems."

"It's a win-win situation."

Rose studies me for a few moments, maybe looking for a better argument to use against me, then settles for a simple, "Our search takes priority. If it requires we leave Seattle before she arrives, then there is nothing I can or will do to extend our stay. Do you understand?"

"Agreed," I say.

He hesitates just a moment, as if he expected greater resistance, but eventually nods and turns back to our hosts. I'm grateful, because I don't feel like explaining myself to him. As much as I desperately want to see my mother again, I honestly don't know what I'm supposed to say to her. I needed her when I lost Ciara. I needed her when the gatekeepers gutted me and when Elysium stole me for its own. I've needed her so many times these awful, many years, and she's been off fighting a war she never once explained to me. I'm as likely to hit her as hug her.

"There's an early flight tomorrow morning," Dean says. "I suppose it would be easiest if she spends the night, then."

"Stay out of their bedroom," I tell Casper.

"Hell no," Casper says. "I want to know if sirens snore."

Dean looks distinctly uncomfortable, even without hearing Casper's response, but I don't have the energy to tell him I'm mostly joking. Instead I chug the rest of my beer and clamber to my feet. "Restroom?"

"The back door's unlocked," Dean says. "It's the second door on the left in the hall."

I motion to Casper as I pass but don't look back to see if she's following until I've made it to the back porch. We take a silent tour of the first floor, inspecting cabinets and closets to kill a couple minutes, and then I finally turn on Casper.

"Be careful," I say. "I don't know how common hoxies are in Madtown but I won't be there to protect you next time they come looking for a meal. I don't know if the territorial bond I strung up between us will

118

stretch that far, and I'd rather not find out the hard way that it's a line-of-sight type of thing. If you can find a psychic of any sort, latch onto them as quickly as you can. Just, you know, don't tell them what you're doing in Madtown."

"I'm dead, not dumb," Casper says. She sounds annoyed at being told what to do, but the imaginary chill she rubs out of her arms means she's rightfully nervous. "What if I see a hoxie before I see a psychic? What do I do?"

"You run," I say. "Once they've taken a bite of you, you'll leave a trail wherever you go."

"That's... encouraging."

"I can come back for you after I've found Adam," I tell her. "Make sure you're settled in or take you with me, whatever sounds better at the time."

"You really planning on running away from all this?" Casper asks. "After everything you've told me about the war and everything at risk if the Guard loses, you'd just duck your head and run?"

"I lost everything that ever mattered to me and have only just gotten back my life," I say quietly. "Going with Rose means letting him pair me up with a Nightmare, and that's an arrangement I'll never be free of. I don't have it in me to be chained to anyone or anything else ever again."

"Even you've got to admit that you're being selfish."

"He's the gods' favorite, not me. The war doesn't hinge on me being the self-sacrificing one. Now come on," I say before Casper can press the argument. "Let's get out back out there before Dean decides I'm clogging up his pipes in here."

The look on her face is blatant disapproval, but she follows me without further argument. Rose is probing Dean and Lily for everything they know about Cinder when I settle in with another beer, and I am content to tune everything out. I stare out at the ocean and drink and try as hard as I can not to think about the truth of Casper's argument. I count waves, then stars, then any shadow that might be a seashell but is probably a rock, anything to keep my mind clear of my wretched situation.

It works long enough to keep me sane until we can finally leave. It's weirder than I want it to be for me to leave Casper behind, and I can't stop glancing at the rearview mirror. The ride back to the hotel is silent, and I'm loathe to follow Rose upstairs to our room immediately. It takes him only a moment to notice my absence, and I shake my head at him when he looks over his shoulder at me.

"Gonna hang out here for a bit," I say. The lobby is empty save for us

119

and the overnight desk attendant, so I help myself to one of the comfy chairs near the TV. "I want to try and sort out our options."

It's a lame excuse considering we both know what our limited options are, but Rose doesn't even question it. He simply continues to the elevator, and I wave at Falkor to follow him. I wait until the doors shut behind them before closing my eyes and letting my thoughts drift. I wish I'd taken more of Dean's beer. More than that I wish he'd had something harder to offer us, something that would make it easier to disconnect from everything that's happened these last three days.

In the end, the only thought that keeps me from losing my mind is that Notte and Ciara have to come first. I'll follow Rose north, help him find Pharaoh, and then discover the truth of my daughter's fate. Only then can I even pretend to seriously think about what Rose is demanding of me.

"Evelyn?"

I look up to find a security guard standing by my knee. "Yes?"

"There's a call for you in the office."

I assume it's Dean and Lily, still nervous over their invisible house guest and redirected to the lobby after an unsuccessful call to our room. Either way it's a welcome distraction from my shaky mental compromise, so I get up and follow him past the front desk. The desk attendant looks up as we pass, then glances a second time at the security guard and returns to his paperwork. We continue down the hall unchallenged, and I precede the guard into an office at the end. There is someone waiting for us in one of the closer corners, and I've just laid eyes on her when the guard closes the door behind us.

After having Marilyn and Hogan as my tenants, I'm too familiar with the process a werecreature suffers through to change. It's an ugly, awful thing that has an even worse ending. If they could shift into the animals they share distant DNA with, it'd be one thing, but human bodies can't transition enough mass to achieve a perfect form. Instead they look like the hulking beasts from older horror films. This woman is halfway through her change already, and the lean angles on her face are too sharp to be a dog's.

I turn on the guard, fist drawn back to fight my way out if need be, and am rocked to a stop by a gun in my face. I'm used to teeth and claws and posturing; this is the first time I've had the barrel of a handgun a mere inch from my nose.

It is somehow a thousand times more frightening, maybe because it doesn't carry the rules and restrictions of Society with it. I am Elysium's linchpin, and although I have now been outed as a Dream I still expect monsters to reconsider the consequences of my death. But this is a gun,

120

and a human wielding it, and I know enough about my own kind to know how little we think of others' lives.

Cartilage pops like breaking sticks behind me, and I risk a look back. The cat's ears are shifting further up her head and stretching to points. Her jaws snap and break, forcing the final change that gives her a snout, and her lips thin and darken to black lines. She gnashes her teeth for a few moments, helping her skin firm up around her snout, and lets out a thick hiss that rattles my spine. I quickly look away from the last awful wrenches to her spine and turn a fierce glare on the guard.

"Have a seat," he says, and presses the gun against my cheekbone in warning.

I take a cautious step away from him, then another, and back my way across the room toward the desk. I'm halfway there when he opens the door and lets himself out, and metal jangles as he locks the office from the outside. I go still where I am and look back at the cat. She's finishing up, and she hunches a little forward to let her too-long arms dangle to the ground. I calculate my best chances and find there's really only one: I can't make it to the door without getting too close to her, so my only way out of here is the window on the other side of this desk.

"Elysium," she says. "Here you are, just as they said."

"Just as who said?" I demand.

As important as the answer is, I have no plans to stick around and hear her response. It's simply a split-second distraction, and as soon as she opens her mouth to answer, I turn and bolt.

She hits my back like a ton of bricks, sending us both crashing into the desk, and our combined weight sends it skidding all the way across the room to slam into the wall. I scrabble at the window with one hand, feeling for the lock, and grab desperately for the pen holder with the other. Teeth snag in my braids as she bites around for my throat, and in my panic I almost knock all of the pens out of reach. By some luck I manage to catch hold of one, and I stab wildly behind me.

She yowls as I catch her somewhere soft and sensitive, and I slam the pen home again and again. She recoils from me, spitting and hissing displeasure, and I throw the window open so hard it almost rebounds closed. I'm halfway out before a hand clamps down on my ankle, and the first bite of claws into tender skin has me shrieking and kicking.

Falkor appears in front of me, wild-eyed and furious, and spits blue flame through the open window. The cat lets go with a ragged scream and I fall clumsily to the ground. My hip hits so hard I probably won't sit right for a week but I manage to get my arms between my face at the dirt.

121

Falkor drops down beside me and snuffles at the back of my neck.

"I'm okay," I say, because I think it's true, and stumble to my feet. Falkor ducks away from the pat I try to land on his head and takes off for the corner of the building with his funky ferret gallop. I catch up with him easily enough, but before I can get out a warning about the traitorous security guard, three bodies appear in our path.

Falkor immediately puts himself between me and them, and it is a miracle I don't trip over him and take us both down. His lashing tail is definitely leaving bruises up and down my thigh, but I can't spare the energy to tell him to stop. More half-changed werecats are melting out of the shadows to surround us. An entire pride is trapping us against the building and I don't know how many of them Falkor can fight. More than my absolute zero, for sure, but not nearly enough.

"Rose," I whisper, and pray he can hear me like I heard him in Madtown. "Rose, help me."

The cats shift apart, not to let me out but to let someone else in. I take one look at the jagged markings curling up her throat to the corners of her mouth and know I am completely screwed. Elysium played host to a Whisperer in its early days. My status as landlady protected me from his magic, but my tenants weren't so lucky. He got inside their heads within minutes and turned them on each other. When they were all dead, he moved on to new hunting grounds. After that brutal show, Elysium restructured the safety rules for its inhabitants.

I try to pull Falkor behind me, but he holds his ground like he's cemented to the earth and growls a low rumbling warning.

"Evelyn of Elysium," the Whisperer says, completely ignoring the baby dragon between us. "Formerly, I suppose I should say, because here you are so far from your post. Are you not ashamed? The Lymanczyc gave you a sacred duty, and you repaid their faith with betrayal. Abandoning Elysium is irresponsible, borderline unforgivable."

"I don't care."

"Where is your sense of obligation?"

"In the trash where it belongs."

She sighs and treats me to a slow, pitying once-over. "How human of you."

"Human?" I echo, too startled to keep my mouth shut. The gatekeepers have known what I am since I woke Rose in Georgia, and the Guard assumed I was his Dream up until I outed myself as a psychic. That no one's bothered to correct these hunters is a little unexpected. I'm not sure if it's Rose and Betty protecting me or if the gatekeepers don't want everyone to know there's another monstrous Nightmare and Dream pair in the making.

"She is ours," Falkor says, and gnashes his piranha teeth. "We will not lets you hurt her."

The Whisperer finally lowers a hooded gaze to him, and I see the telltale glow of red beneath heavy lashes that means she's about to wreck his mind. I dive at her, nearly bowling Falkor over in the process, and use all my weight to knock her back. My thumbs in her throat are enough to distract her for the moment, but she didn't come to this fight alone. I am yanked off the Whisperer by a werecat before I can do any real damage.

Falkor is on the cat before I can blink, claws and teeth ripping her face to pieces even as blue flame erupts around us. The pride screams discordant rage as they break ranks, and I go again for the only creature I have any chance of fighting. I'm stopped again by a heavy hand around my bicep, and I'm yanked back so hard I feel every vertebrae in my spine pop. Falkor immediately abandons his current victim to come to my defense, and I know as soon as he makes the leap that it's a mistake.

He's paying too much attention to me—he always pays too much attention to me—and he doesn't see the other cat until it's too late. The beast gets him by the base of his wing and spins to throw him like a shot put. Falkor hits the hotel wall with a deafening crunch and falls heavily to the ground. His back leg gives a hard spasm that sends his head lolling against the dirt, and the bond I put on him in San Francisco snaps so hard I taste blood.

A second passes, then another, as I stare at his crumpled form. I will him back to his feet, sure he's just gotten the breath knocked out of him. Three seconds. Four, five. He doesn't move.

"Falkor, get up," I say, in a voice I don't recognize. The Whisperer crouches at my side, but she is such a distant concern right now I can't even be afraid. "Falkor. *Awlyn*."

"Evelyn."

But that's not Falkor's voice. That's Rose's, rough with a hatred that is as familiar as it is dangerous. He stalks onto the battlefield like he doesn't even see what odds we're up against. I finally drag my eyes up from Falkor's translucent corpse and watch as Rose literally rips a werecat in half.

He goes through the pride like a knife through milk, not a hint of resistance or effort, and chokes the life out of the Whisperer with the slow care of one with a personal grudge. I watch her scrabble at him, counting the seconds it takes her anger to sharpen to fear and desperation. Her mouth flaps open and closed with a rigidity that's doll-like, and then she finally goes still.

"Falkor's dead," I say, in a hollow voice I barely recognize. "He's dead. Rose—"

Rose turns on me, expression black with unthinking rage. "Go to sleep, Evelyn."

The ground gives out beneath me, and it is a very long way down.

TEN

I wake to the soft patter of rainfall. I'm flat on my back, staring up at a dark gray sky and a towering skyline I don't recognize. The clouds sit so low and heavy I swear they're grazing the rooftops, and I have the inane urge to shield my face from their inevitable fall. Shifting sends cold water rushing into my ear. The street I'm sprawled in is flooded, not high enough to pose any danger but enough to chill me to the bone. I roll over and hoist my aching body to its feet.

I don't have to look to know Rose is glaring at me. "Do I want to know where we are?"

"We," Rose says with angry emphasis, "are in my head."

I glance at him and see it's true. Rose is back in his human skin. "You're the one who put me to sleep," I point out, "so cut the attitude."

Rose kicks water at me. The look on his face says he wishes he was kicking lava instead. "I told you not to call me that! I told you to never call me that name again. You forced me to choose between your death or this fraudulent bond. How dare you. If your Nightmare did not need you—if I did not need you to break Notte's shackles—I would have watched them eat you one bloody mouthful at a time."

I try not to guess if that's an exaggeration. "I'm sorry." He draws up short for just a moment, and I somehow refrain from grimacing when I say again, "I'm sorry. There were so many of them. I panicked and went with the first name to come to mind."

"Erase it. Erase it right now. It can never be the first; it should not even be the last. Just—" Rose kicks the water again, and this time he hits me with a larger splash. It's not a difference in rage, I realize, but in water level. The water is lapping at the backs of my knees now, which should be impossible considering we're standing in a city intersection. It makes me think of the first time I saw Rose's dreamscape, and I guess he's thinking the same thing too, because he demands, "Why is it always water?"

There's a sharpness in his tone that isn't entirely directed at me, something too loud and too transparent. I gape at him as he turns away and watch him set off down the flooded streets with long strides. I have no choice but to chase after him, and I raise my voice so he can hear me over our splashing.

"You're afraid of water," I accuse him. "Really, *Brimstone*? Hellfire and gatekeepers and gods, and this is what you lose your shit over? Water? I'm actually a little disappointed."

Rose rounds on me so abruptly I almost slam into him. I have to catch his shoulders to stop myself, and I can't miss the way he flinches at my touch.

"I told you I almost destroyed Pharaoh and me both when he would not agree to be my Dream," Rose says, with a vacant stare aimed past my shoulder. "Notte already knew he could not afford to lose either of us; he knew I was what he needed if he wanted to get his war off the ground. So he made sure I understood where the line was between my needs and Pharaoh's consent. He put me in a dream like this and he let me drown."

The thump in my chest is colder than the water eating up my thighs. "What?"

"For three days," Rose says, slow and biting like every word is killing him, "he let me drown. I could not die, and I could not wake up."

He opens his mouth, like there's more he could say, then snaps it shut and jerks free of my grip. I can only stare at the tense line of his back as he sets off again, my words a coil of barbed wire and thorns in my throat.

The only thing that makes it out is a soft: "You were twelve."

If he hears me, he gives no sign of it.

I have daydreamed of beating the life from Adam a hundred thousand times since he left me to die, but right now that need burns with more desperation than anger. I want him dead. I need him dead. I need to know that he can never hurt anyone else again the way he hurt us.

Rose rocks to a halt. "Stop it."

"I'm not doing anything," I say through numb lips.

"I can feel it," Rose insists, and shoots a narrow-eyed look my way. "That outrage you feel on my behalf is a waste of your energy and intrudes on Pharaoh's rights. It is his duty to protect me. It will never be yours."

"You can't tell me my husband drowned a child and then tell me not to care."

"You are not supposed to care," Rose insists.

I start his way with a disbelieving, "You're telling me you don't care about anyone except Pharaoh? Seriously? In all the world?"

"I cannot," Rose says, holding his ground until I'm standing right in front of him again. "I don't know how anymore. I register their importance to what I am doing, and I recognize the faces I can rely on and tolerate, but my ability to feel more than that evaporated when I met Pharaoh. It is the

126

same for him, and it will be the same for you. Affection for others would distract us from each other, so our bonds mute the emotion."

"What about me?" I ask. "Does me being a Dream make me an exception?"

"You are important to me," Rose says. "I will protect you until protecting you means putting Pharaoh in harm's way." He doesn't outright say he doesn't care about me; he doesn't have to. Rose waits a beat to make sure I understand, then says, "I have told you again and again: you will cease to care about everything and everyone when your Nightmare is found. Your vampire, your ghost, your dead dragons—they are all background noise. You just don't know it yet."

"What about you?"

"Perhaps you will hate me when you are reborn. If your mind recognizes that we are a threat to each other because of this," he gestures between us and I assume he means this half-formed bond I keep pressing deeper into place, "then it will respond in kind to force us apart."

"I halfway hate you already," I tell him.

"Liar," Rose says. "You don't when you should. I blame your fraudulent bond."

"I blame your age," I send back. "You're almost young enough to be my son."

"I am not your child."

He's not, but—I catch his arm when he starts to turn away and force myself to say, "Ciara."

It hurts to have this truth out in the air between us, even if the twitch of Rose's mouth means he doesn't understand yet. It is not a secret I can keep from him forever, though, and it somehow feels right to tell him now after the ugliness he just shared with me. Still, I have to lick my lips and clear my throat before I can explain.

"Adam took something from me when he left me to die. Someone," I correct myself. "I was eight months pregnant with our child when I came to Elysium."

Rose goes still as stone. "No. We can't have children."

"According to you, I can't be both a Dream and a psychic, either, but here I am."

"Then she is proof Notte never fully bonded to you," Rose says. "If you were his and he was yours, one or both of you would have terminated the child in utero. You would have recognized it as a threat and you would have disposed of it accordingly."

Rose barely manages to catch my wrists before I get my hands around

127

his throat. My heart thuds a dangerous staccato against my ribs, threatening to break me open, and my voice is terrible when I say, "Don't you dare say that to me when you've never lost a child of your own. I would never have turned on her."

"You wouldn't if you were human," Rose says, slow but firm. "You are not. You are just a shade, and you will lose what humanity is left when you choose your Nightmare. This is neither an exaggeration nor a hypothetical," he insists when I start to argue. "How many times will you make me say it before you accept it as truth? 'Evelyn' will cease to exist and there is nothing you can do about it."

"And yet you keep telling me I have to go through with this," I snap. "Maybe because you've never been anything but a Nightmare, you don't understand what you're asking, but: *fuck you.* If I was your Dream, you'd still tell me to choose you first, wouldn't you? Over Ciara, over myself, over everything else I could have loved and wanted in life. You'd tell me to throw everything away and drown down here with you."

"Without hesitation," Rose says. "Nightmares cannot survive without their Dreams and Gaia cannot survive without Her Nightmares. You trivialize and ignore the fate of the world when you refuse to look beyond your own needs. Everyone else is acceptable collateral damage."

I try to yank free and stomp away, but Rose holds tight to me. "You are right," he says, and that admission is unexpected enough that I have to face him. "Nightmares will never understand what it takes to be a Dream. As you said, we are born into this misery, and so we are always aware of our purpose. We are weapons, crafted for one singular reason: to cut out the infection that is killing our Mother. A blade can be nothing but a blade. Only the hand that picks it up knows that there was ever anything else worth holding."

I don't know if that concession is supposed to be an apology, but it's probably the closest I'm going to get. I scowl at him and give my hands another tug, and this time he lets me go. Instead of setting off once more, though, he considers me with a heavy stare.

"What are you?" he asks at last. "A Dream is only a Dream, and only compatible to one Nightmare. Yet you kept Notte alive after Meridian died and have strung yourself to me. You carry Elysium in your veins and drag ghosts in your wake. You cannot be all of this. You should not be all of this," he corrects himself, because we're past the point where denial is any sort of comfort. "It cannot bode well for us if the Nightmares and Dreams are evolving."

"It's worked out pretty well for you so far," I say. "I've saved you how

128

many times?"

"We are what She needs us to be," Rose says. "If we are changing, it is because we are not strong enough to protect Gaia as we were. If we can't—" He forgets what he's saying when his sharp gesture has him sloshing water on both of us. The water is creeping up our abdomens now. Rose opens his mouth, closes it again, and then turns away from me. "We have to find dry land."

"Hey," I say before he can take that first step. He doesn't look back, but he waits for me. I think of everything I could say, then settle for: "I can swim. I won't let you drown."

"When it comes, you won't be able to stop it," he says.

I consider his back for a moment as he wades further away from me, then kiss his nickname against my fingertips and bury it under the waves. I leave "Rose" down here with this ice-cold current and dread, and I set off after Sol as quickly as I can move through such deep water. For now the water doesn't fight back against me, but the chill slows me down almost as much as the invisible obstacles I keep stubbing my toes against. After a while I settle for half-hopping in an attempt not to break my feet open.

We've made it a block before something nips my thigh. Sol looks back at my sharp yip.

"Something bit me," I say, swatting my hand around underwater.

"Don't run," Sol says. "Whatever you do, do not run, or we will both die."

Something brushes against my calf, then the back of my knee, and presses briefly against my back. The water's too dark to see through, so I flail my hands uselessly about. Sol hisses through clenched teeth. At first I think it's a warning against all my movement, but when I look at him he's looking down at the water as well. I hurry to catch up with him and get a bite at my knee when I reach his side.

I splay my fingers out and still my hand, and it doesn't take long before something takes the bait. It takes six tries before I can twist my hand fast enough to catch the offending fish, and I pull it out of the water with every intent of crushing it. The second I lay eyes on it, I fling it as far away from me as I can. It's no fish, it's a disembodied finger and thumb barely connected by a flap of flesh. We're not being bitten; we're being pinched.

"Out of the water," I say in a tight voice. "Right now."

We set off side by side with grabbing fingers following us every step of the way. When the water reaches my breasts I fold my arms protectively across them and strain to my tiptoes. There are more fingers at it now, and

129

they get more insistent the longer we try to ignore them. The first time one bites at my throat I almost lose my cool, but then Sol grabs my elbow and cuts a new path across the water. It takes me a moment to see what he's aiming for: there's a fixed ladder going up one of the nearest buildings.

He pushes me up it ahead of him, and in my desperation to get out of the water I bang my shoulder hard against the metal cage wound around it. My limbs are half-numb from the cold, making it hard to get a grip on the rungs, but I doggedly climb as quickly as I can. I'm starting to think we'll be able to wait this flood out on the roof when I crack my head against something that isn't there. Only Sol's hand against my ass keeps me from falling, and he holds me up until I can think straight enough to get a better grip. I try and climb again, but again my head hits something that doesn't give.

"Sol?" I ask, and pry a hand off the rung to test the air over me. There's nothing there, but the open air feels as solid as stone. I press my hand flat and shove until my fingers go bloodless, but there's no give. A frantic pat around shows it's solid. Whatever's blocking the ladder off ahead of us, there's no getting past it. The cage around us is too tightly woven for us to squeeze out that way, either. I lean to one side so I can look down past my hip at Sol. "We have to go back down. There's no way up."

I bang on the air for emphasis, and Sol doesn't ask me if I'm sure. He just starts descending without a word, and I try not to slip off the now-wet rungs as we retrace our footsteps. We make it about ten steps before Sol comes to an abrupt stop. He looks down, kicks something that doesn't sound like metal, and steps off the ladder entirely to stand on empty air. The ladder's closed off at both ends.

"What's happening?" I ask.

"I told you," Sol says, in a tone I've never heard from him before but I hope I never hear again, "you can't stop this."

"Sol, find us a way out."

"Promise me you will not call me," Sol says, and slants a haunted look up at me. "You will wake up from this, so endure it. Do not call me."

Don't wake him, he means, like I woke him at Elysium and pulled him from the other realm. As soon as he says it I know I could. At this point it wouldn't even take more than a few words, because I have both his true name and the one I forced on him. Our joint fear pulls our farcical bond so tight I can almost see it, a jagged black thread that binds my heart to his. I cut my hand open as soon as I try to touch it. My blood sings with the wrongness of it, and the taste of iron makes my teeth ache.

"Evelyn," Sol says as the water ignores the invisible barrier and creeps up his calves. "Promise me."

"This is just a dream," I say.

"This is just a dream," he agrees. "We are going to wake up."

I'm not sure which one of us he's trying to reassure, but the look on his face and the jackhammer under my skin are proof his words help neither one of us. I can't promise him I won't save us both; the words stick in my throat, glued into an incoherent mess by fear.

Sol doesn't wait for me to sort it out but slowly lowers himself to his knees and hooks his arms through the nearest rung. He digs his fingers into his short hair, gripping so tight his knuckles go a silver-gray, and waits for death to reach him. I think for a moment I hear a throaty keen when the water swallows his face, and I bite bloody holes into my hand to stop myself from calling out.

The water hits my shoes a heartbeat later and climbs up my calves. I start back up the ladder, as fast as I dare when I know I'm going to run into a ceiling soon, and am stopped five rungs later. I brace myself against the cage to keep from falling and shove both hands at the air. I push and kick and cry, but the air doesn't give. I've broken three fingernails scrabbling at it when the water reaches my chin, and for a moment all I can think about is the Whisperer's gurgling death beneath Sol's fingers. That's the death that's coming for me, that too-slow suffocation.

I didn't promise him. I didn't say it. If I call him now I'm not breaking my word.

The rush of cold water covering my face almost has me screaming. I yank at the rungs, once first then twice more. My brain has his name on deafening repeat, a panicked pulse ordering me to save myself. My heartbeat starts to sound the same, clawing at my skin: *Sol, Sol, Sol.*

I keep my teeth clenched through sheer willpower alone, trying to hold onto what little breath I have left, but death is inevitable and there's only one way to avoid it. In another second, maybe two, I'm going to lose all respect I have for Sol's wishes. I'm going to forget how close I am to destroying his bond with Pharaoh and I'm going to get us out of here, and we'll have to sort the consequences out in the waking world.

With my last shred of self-control, I inhale water. I fill my lungs with death and let my thoughts short circuit. Sol disappears; there is only me and this darkness and this deadly weight in my lungs. I would break my own arms against the ladder if I still had the strength to do so, but the best I can do is yank at the rungs until my strength deserts me. My mouth moves of its own accord, sucking in water in a desperate bid for air, and I

131

lose my grip as my body gives up. I slip from the rungs and land on asphalt.

Sol's harsh coughing tells me I'm alive, but it isn't until I roll over and retch that I realize we're on dry land. I dig my fingers into the ground until I bend two fingernails back and throw up again. I'm trying to clear my body of all the water I inhaled, but since that water was all in my head all that comes up is bile. I claw at my chest like I can somehow pull that hollow ache out of me, but the best I can do is gasp and cough and shake. It is an eternity before I can look over at Sol. He hasn't bothered to get up but is lying flat on his stomach with his arms folded across the back of his head. Even from here I can see him trembling, and I don't know if it's from the cold, his coughing, or trauma.

I'm moving before I honestly trust my body not to give out on me and stretch out half on top of him. I hook an arm around his shoulder, uncaring of the asphalt that eats rivets in my knuckles, and pull him as tight against me as possible. The anxious, prickling knot in my spine is a seesawing mess between anger that he put us both through that and fear over what we survived. I don't know which side is going to win, so I bite my tongue and refuse to speak.

It takes several minutes before Sol stops shaking, but that gives me time to relearn how to breathe. Finally he shifts underneath me, and I take the hint to sit up. We don't look at each other but consider our new surroundings. The hotel is nowhere in sight, although I know we were right out front before we fell into Sol's gift. Whatever road we're stranded on, there are no houses in sight, only trees barely visible in dawn's creeping light.

"It was night a few minutes ago," I say.

"Time does not move the same in dreams," Sol says, and painstakingly gets to his feet.

Which means we've been walking down this road all night, blind to our true surroundings. I guess that explains the tired ache in my legs, but I don't get a chance to ask. Sol is offering me a hand up, and that gesture is so unexpected I forget anything else I could have said. I hesitate for just a moment before taking it, and he pulls me to my feet like I weigh no more than a sack of flour. I wonder if I imagine the brief, tight squeeze of his fingers before he lets go. Maybe it's thanks he can't say, for a promise I couldn't make but didn't break.

"Go back for the car?" I ask.

"Do you have the wallet still?"

I pat my pockets and find it safe against my ass. When I nod, Sol sets off down the road. "Then we will find a new car. We do not know how the pride tracked us to Coos Bay, so it is best to start our trail anew."

"It'll take eight years to walk to Seattle from here."

Sol doesn't answer, but the next time a car finally appears on the horizon Sol makes sure to flag it down. I'm a little surprised the driver pulls over for us, but I guess the driver's more surprised that there are two people out in the middle of nowhere on the highway. I make up some tired and see-through excuse about how our car broke down and how we just need to get to the next town so we can call our friend to collect us. It's easier to get a yes here than it was in San Francisco, and we slide into the backseat for a couple miles. We're left at a gas station in a town with no stoplights, and the driver pulls out as soon as I promise him we'll be all right.

Sol waits until we're alone before before breaking into the nearest car. He doesn't even need a pick; he just uses that creepy strength of his to break the lock on a back door. I keep an eye out as he climbs between the front seats to dick with the wires. I'd ask him where the hell he learned how to hotwire a car and how many times he's had to do this, but I'm afraid that someone will overhear me and call the police. If this scrap of a town has police, I guess, but I don't want to find out the hard way.

The ignition turns and engine starts. Sol yanks the back door closed, slides into the driver's seat, and reaches across to unlock the passenger door for me. I hurry in and close my door as quietly as I can. I can't believe we're getting away with this, but stare as I might at the gas station door, no one comes chasing us. I breathe a heavy sigh of relief as the town disappears behind us and look over at Sol.

"What if we'd gotten caught?"

Sol looks at me. "I will not let anyone stop us."

I don't think too hard about what he means by that, but lean my seat back as far as it will go and close my eyes. I fall asleep to the sound of the road, and at least in my own head I don't dream.

The tilt of gravity going sideways has me jolting awake. I slam my elbow into the door as I flail and have to claw my way upright. I look out the windshield as the car goes off the wrong side of the road into the shoulder, expecting to see gatekeepers or more werecats. There's nothing out front, and more nothing out the side, but Sol brakes so hard we skid.

As soon as the car stops moving I turn on him, twisting as far as my locked seatbelt will let me, and find him hunched over the steering wheel. He's gasping for breath like he was drowning again, and my first thought is

133

he fell asleep driving and had a nightmare.

"Sol?" I demand, and reach for him. My hand is only halfway to him before I feel the heat radiating off him. He's been ice cold since he woke up, so this new development has me recoiling against my door. "Sol!"

"Pharaoh," Sol manages. His fingers tighten and twist against the steering wheel, and leather creaks in warning. "He's hurt, but he's there. *He's there.*"

I check the glove compartment for a map and find a GPS instead. It takes a minute for it to boot up and find our signal, and then I zoom out on the map until I can see both Oregon and Washington. The scale is awkward at this distance, but I put a finger against it and measure the map in fifty-mile increments.

"I'll be damned," I say. "I think he flew into Vancouver. How'd he get over the border?"

"What human could stop him?" Sol asks.

I click the GPS off and toss it back where I found it. I've barely got the compartment shut again before Sol hits the gas and sends us careening back into our lane. I claw at my window as I'm thrown up against it and belatedly pull my seat back upright.

"If you get us killed I will come back and haunt you," I warn him.

"I can't see ghosts," Sol reminds me.

"I'll figure something out."

Sol is obviously not at all intimidated, and he doesn't even pretend to slow down. A hundred and eighty miles is a lot of ground to cover, especially when we're hugging the ocean on the world's slowest highway, but I'm assuming Pharaoh will feel that same ping against his radar and meet us halfway. For now I sit here and wonder for the first time what's going to happen when Pharaoh and I see each other again.

"Pharaoh hates me," I tell Sol. "If he wants you to hurt me, will you?"

"We need you," Sol reminds me. "I will not let him kill you."

"I said hurt," I say.

"I said kill," Sol says, and gestures from himself to me with his next words: "Blade, hand. Dreams will always have lead in bonded pairs since it is their total sacrifice that makes our existence possible. If Pharaoh is fully committed to the thought of hurting you there is only so much I can do to restrain him."

"He's committed," I say. "He faced down a flock of gatekeepers to get to me."

"You brought it on yourself."

For calling Sol "Rose" in front of Pharaoh, he means, not that I knew any better at the time. I scowl at him for his complete lack of support and say, "You said only Nightmares can recognize an unmatched Dream, so blame Pharaoh's suicide run on Adam. Pharaoh wouldn't have figured out that my nickname was a legitimate threat if Adam hadn't already warned him."

"Warned him," Rose echoes, not following.

"Adam told him I was going to take you from him," I say, "but I don't think Pharaoh realized he meant *me* until I named—"

Sol hits the brakes so hard my seatbelt snaps taut against my chest. It knocks the breath out of me and snaps my head on my neck, and I put a belated hand out to the glove compartment in front of me. I claw at the seatbelt, trying to find a little leeway, and have to actually pop it open before I can breathe again. I rub a line from shoulder to hip, wincing at the bruised feel beneath my fingertips, and turn a wary look on Sol. He is staring out the windshield, expression dangerously blank.

"Say that again," he says.

I consider lying for only a second. "Pharaoh said he didn't care what Adam wanted, that he would kill me before he let me have you."

Sol literally rips his seatbelt on his way out of the car, and he slams the door so hard behind him I'm half-sure it'll never open again. I turn in my seat, trying to keep an eye on him as he stalks down the length of the car. There are a couple cars behind us, but they give Sol a wide berth on their way by. One honks; another passenger presses against her window to see if we have car trouble. I wave them on with hurried gestures, not wanting them anywhere nearby if Sol is about to lose his temper. Sol's fuse is too short, though, and he screams wordless bloody murder at the open road.

His rage is a dry heat against my skin, like the warning sizzle that comes from sitting too close to an open fire. It has to break somewhere, I know, and the blast comes only seconds later. Sol punches the trunk so hard the front of the car comes off the ground, and as I'm thrown back against my seat I can see the massive dent he's left in the car's frame. I nearly bite my tongue off when the car falls back to its front tires, and I rub at the new ache in my neck. That outburst did nothing for Sol, judging by the twisting anger still cutting holes in my gut, but he stands very still as he tries to reel it back in.

I almost jump out of my skin when someone speaks up: "It seems we were right."

Yasmin wasn't there two seconds ago, but now she's sprawled sideways in the backseat in all her naked, disemboweled glory. She picks idly at the shorn edge of an exposed rib as she considers Sol out the back window, then lolls her head until she's looking at me. She's lost a bit more flesh since the last time I saw her, including most of her upper lip and a strip from her cheek. Her smile is the thing of nightmares, and she clacks bloody teeth at me.

"Hello again, love. Are you ready to come home with us now?"

I close my eyes and will her to disappear, but she's still there five seconds later. I consider ignoring her, then look past her to where Sol stands silent and furious.

"Right about what?" I ask.

"We told him it was no coincidence, the two of you both being at Elysium." She sits up with obvious effort and I hear the crunch of a vertebrae giving way. Blood trickles out of the corner of her mouth as she hunches forward on her misshapen spine, and she beckons for me to lean closer. I refuse, but she doesn't wait for me to comply before continuing. "We know how much the master hated our bright brother-in-law, you see."

"What did Adam have against Pharaoh?" I ask. "Besides his charming personality, I mean."

"She makes jokes," Yasmin says with what might be approval. "The master made none. Unworthy, he said. Coward. Too weak to protect our brother from those that would have used him. He put our brother to sleep every time the gods caught up to them."

"Sol said it was the only way to reset his power," I say.

"The master said a stronger Dream could find a different workaround that wouldn't set the war back so far," Yasmin says. She picks idly at her face, and as I watch she pulls the tear in her cheek a little wider. My stomach threatens to turn itself inside out, and I have to swallow hard against a blinding rush of nausea.

"He said if the bright one would not live up to his role, then he would find someone worthy of holding our brother's chain. Our brother dismissed it as a wretched but empty threat; he could not believe his master would profane something so sacred as a bond. He did not listen when we told him otherwise, but now here you are, yes? Here you are where only they should be."

Sol went to sleep willingly eighteen years ago, but he told me he wasn't put to sleep in Georgia. Notte moved him to Elysium—right after he put Pharaoh to sleep for choosing Sol over the war. It took him only a year to find me in Florida, and he brought me on a winding path to Elysium. I've always wondered why he backed us into a corner at a gate, why he took the time to break Elysium and steal Ciara but no time at all to protect me from the gatekeepers hot on our heels.

Notte left me because he never wanted me for himself. He only wanted me to find Sol and take Pharaoh's place. There's a cruel irony to all of this, that Pharaoh's desperation to stop Notte's plan is exactly what finally put it in motion. By now Pharaoh knows he failed; news would have reached him that Sol is awake and on the move with a stranger in tow. They are racing for each other knowing Notte orchestrated this sledgehammer to their bond.

"I didn't want any of this," I say, as if that changes anything. "I didn't know. How do I undo it?"

"We do not know," Yasmin says.

When I glower at her, she offers her hands palm-up to me. In one hand is a lock; in the other a key. I take them from her with unsteady hands. The key slips in without resistance, but it refuses to turn. I look at her, and she gives me another bloody smile.

"Our brother is the lock, and you are the key. You are inadequate, but you still fit. How does one change a key so it no longer slides home? Perhaps we should break you down until your teeth catch too much to pass through these pins."

"Perhaps you shouldn't," I say. "Sol says he needs me to break free of Adam's control."

"Oh?" Yasmin picks at her cheek again and I resist the urge to smack her hand away. "Such ambitious plans! We are interested to see if you can pull it off. We would like to meet our brothers without his chains on them. No?" she asks, seeing my frown. "Did he not tell you how afraid the bright one was, how hard he fought not to see us?"

"He said Pharaoh didn't want to pair," I say, but then Sol is yanking the driver's door open. I go silent as Sol throws himself into the driver's seat, but Yasmin doesn't share my discretion.

"The master is a puppeteer," she says. She is still smiling, but this time it doesn't reach her eyes, and there's more venom than mirth in her voice. "He put his claws in the bright child's power and called it protection, and he used that foothold to strangle our brother as soon as they embraced. We tried to warn him, but he did not understand. All masters can control their children, he said to us, but he stopped pretending the first time the master made them dance. We tire of the taste of poison on our teeth when it is not poison of our own choosing."

"Go home, Yasmin," Sol says, voice unsteady with rage. "Right now."

She takes the lock and key from me and buries both in the ruins of her abdomen. "We will spare you a little longer then, sister not-our-sister, and

137

see if you can live up to these expectations. It is not in our nature to be optimistic, but we are curious."

She fades from view, but the blood on the upholstery takes longer to disappear. I watch until the last hint of her is gone before turning a careful look on Sol. Yasmin's presence likely only worsened Sol's terrible mood, since she's proof the bond Notte wanted still exists between us. I steel myself for violence and am more than a little surprised when it doesn't come. A minute ticks by, then another, and finally I undo my buckle.

"I'm driving," I say. "I don't trust you at the wheel right now."

He's smart enough not to argue. We cross in front of the hood, and I'm almost past him before Sol catches my elbow in an iron grip. I look at him, but he's staring straight ahead. I wait for him to say something, anything; the look on his face says there's a world of hateful things he wants to put into words. At length he lets go of me and continues toward the passenger door. I watch him until he's slammed the door closed behind him, wondering if maybe I was the one supposed to fake reassurances. There's nothing I can say now I haven't said before, though, so I bite my tongue and head to the driver's seat.

We're four miles up the road before I opt for a different course of comfort: "If I was meeting Pharaoh for the first time today, what would you want me to know about him?" I ask. When he doesn't answer, I try a different tact: "What do you like about him?"

"Everything."

I forgo sarcasm in favor of a weary: "Sol."

"Everything," Sol says again.

This time he sounds so calm and sure I risk taking my eyes off the road to look at him. The tension's gone out of him as he considers his other half, and if I didn't know any better I'd think that was a smile tugging at the corner of his mouth. For a rare moment he looks his age, and I'm reminded that he's barely older than Ciara would be. It puts a twist in my stomach and has me tightening my grip on the wheel, and the way Sol tenses up says he can feel that protective surge in me. The moment is gone as quickly as it came.

"Evelyn," Sol says in quiet warning.

"I can't help it," I remind him. "You're—young."

"I am not your child."

"You're not my son," I agree, "but maybe I'll let you be my baby brother."

"Gaia kill me now," Sol mutters.

His dour tone startles laughter from me, and I reach out to tweak his hair. "And here I was thinking you had no sense of humor. If I'd known Pharaoh would put more than just body heat into you—wait, that sounds completely wrong. Back up. Don't say anything." I stab a finger at him in warning, then chance a sidelong look at him.

I've joked about him and Pharaoh a half-dozen times by now without any solid confirmation in return, but now I'm finally bold enough to say: "Pretty lucky, isn't it, finding a gay Dream?"

"The odds were in his favor," Sol says. "Nightmares and Dreams are born for each other; we are what we need each other to be to survive. While the majority of pairs fall into bed with each other, there are pairs that are built on different needs. Tempest are brothers, whereas Shadow needed a father figure. I'd always assumed your Nightmare would be a grown man who would be devoted to you no matter the personal risk." Sol sends me a considering look. "Now I suspect it'll be a replacement child."

It feels so much like getting gutted that I have to press a hand to my shirt. I'm surprised when my hand comes back clean. I'm more surprised that my voice is steady. "You cannot replace a child."

He looks like he might argue, but I don't want to hear about the psychosis involved in being a paired Dream. I cut the radio on and crank it up. Sol sends it a significant look like he's considering turning it off to finish this conversation. Why he lets it slide, I don't know, but there's more resentment than relief eating at me when he obediently leaves me to my own thoughts.

ELEVEN

At Raymond we abandon the coast and start curving inland. I watch 105 peel away out my window and try not to feel like we're heading into an obvious trap. I want to ask Sol to show me the GPS so I know how far inland we're heading. More than that I want to ask how far out Pharaoh still is. Although I'm hoping we're barreling toward each other with equal desperation, chances are good it's not just Pharaoh's extensive injuries slowing him down. If there's a bounty on his head and neither the vampires nor sirens were able to locate him, he's had no help getting this far.

We've gone about fifteen miles before the road starts to turn west again, but Sol aims us east. The sign at the turnoff says Olympia isn't much further, and I cut a hard look across the front seat at my companion.

"There's a gate in Olympia," I say, but he has to know that.

"More than a gate," Sol says. His head is cocked to one side like he's listening to something, but the radio's been off since he first pulled us off-course. The hard line of his mouth isn't promising, and I can only hope I'm imagining the tension in his shoulders. He presses his thumb to his forehead and gives his head a fierce shake. "The wastes are coming aground there as well."

"To hell with the wastes," I say. "Gates mean gatekeepers."

"Get us to Olympia."

It's a risk, and I want to tell him that, but I swallow my protests and do as I'm told. We're twenty miles out from Olympia before we're close enough to feel Darowel's magic, and where we can feel the gate, the gate can feel us. The sky is quick to fill with gatekeepers, and the sight of their shadows falling over the road has my blood going cold. I risk a peek up through the windshield. The gatekeepers don't have eyes, but their smooth white faces are turned downward as they track our car's movement.

"Reassure me," I say. "How many can you fight off at once?"

"Pharaoh's absence is crippling," Sol reminds me. "Without him, all I have is what the gate will let me draw from it, and I have to reach through the Lymanczyc to do even that. The further out we are, the harder it is."

"Next time just lie to me," I say.

"It does not matter," he says before I can turn the car around and dart us back to the ocean. "Lily was responsible for passing our route along to allies, and this is the only gate between Coos Bay and Canada. By now we should have allies in the area, so we will not be fighting alone."

The gatekeepers scream a warning, and I feel the first bite of their mental claws against my brain. Sol reacts in a heartbeat, snapping a hand out to catch hold of the back of my neck. His touch is hot enough to scald me and just hot enough to burn away their attack. I pray to any gods that might still be listening and crush the gas pedal to the floor. The car jumps forward with a lurch that leaves my stomach six miles behind us, and I ignore the gatekeepers in favor of watching traffic become a sickening blur.

A gatekeeper drops in front of us, but Sol throws it out of the way with a fierce swipe of his free hand. Black fire curls along the dashboard, sending spiderweb cracks up the windshield. The next gatekeeper to fall gets murdered against the hood, and I scrabble for the windshield wipers to get its blue blood off the glass. Cars honk strident warnings at us as we swerve, and I pull too hard to right us. Gravity does a sick tilt as a tire leaves the ground, and I barely manage to get us between two cars instead of up a big rig's ass.

"Cross the lake," Sol says, sounding far too calm for what we're up against.

I have to cut across two lanes of traffic to merge onto the 5, and the cacophony of crunching metal and squealing tires says I'm leaving wreckage in our wake. I look back to see how bad it is and end up swiping a cop car. The response is immediate, and for a moment he's so close to us his flashing lights are a strobe inside our car. I can barely hear his sirens over the gatekeepers' screams.

I have no idea where the gate is; all I can do is follow its magic and hope not to kill us along the way. I take an exit ramp off the interstate that by sheer dumb luck is a straight shot, but am forced to slow down as the ramp dumps us onto a downtown street. I get a glimpse of two more cop cars joining the chase. The light is turning red ahead of us, so I lean on the horn and press harder on the gas once more. Two cars careen out of our way, but a delivery truck can't turn fast enough. I clip it and stomp the brakes. Tires scream, the car tilts, and I lose control as we go sideways.

I have only a dizzying second to fear death before Sol is suddenly in my lap. The world goes ink black as he pulls his coat around both of us. We tumble, end over end, in a death trap of exploding glass and crumpling metal. We slam home against an immovable object seconds or an eternity later, and the world goes deadly still. And for some inexplicable reason, nothing hurts. The only discomfort I feel is Sol's unbearable heat. With him this close, he scorches the very air in my lungs.

A half-second later Sol is gone. He straightens away from me and kicks the driver's door clean off the car. When he's out on the sidewalk I can see what I've done to the car, and fear has my heart eating a hole through my throat. We're half inside a store front, stopped up against the wreckage of its foundation. The car is an accordion around me, crunched in on itself like a discarded soda can. There is absolutely no way either one of us could have survived, yet here we are, unharmed and unhurt.

"Oh my god," I say, as I let Sol peel me from the car. "Fuck the Nightmares' disapproval—that coat is amazing."

I am suddenly grateful that Pharaoh did not have it in Augusta, because if he'd had that shield against the gatekeepers he definitely would have murdered me. I wonder now if that's why Notte took it from him before sending him to my doorstep, if Notte was hedging his bets on Pharaoh getting himself killed along the way, but I only have a startled heartbeat to consider it. We're surrounded by a half-dozen cop cars, and the sky is full of gatekeepers. Notte's unending betrayals will have to wait until we actually survive this next bit.

Pedestrians gather in small clumps to watch this excitement, oblivious to the danger flying overhead. Two cops attempt to corral the crowd and move them back to a safer distance. A third chatters updates into the walkie strapped to his shoulder. The rest waste no time at all to draw arms on us, and it is way too soon for me to have another gun pointed my way. Sol idly reaches up to tug his hood further down into his face and I'm positive I hear every gun cock in warning.

"Get on the ground!" one cop yells, and swivels his gun between the two of us as if we needed clarification that he means us both. "Get on the ground and put your hands on your head right now!"

"I don't have a coat," I say in a low voice.

Sol slowly lowers himself to his knees. It's not the reaction I expected, but relief is a warm knot at the base of my spine. I follow his lead and risk a glance up at the hovering gatekeepers.

"All the way! Face down!"

This time Sol ignores the command, seemingly content to sit on his heels. The police shout and threaten and take a few careful strides toward us, but Sol's head is tilted to one side as he ignores them. Like me, he's more interested in the gatekeepers. Although they exist outside of Society, and therefore outside the laws GLOBE uses to keep Society hidden from the human world, there's a chance they'll wait to eat our faces until the humans are out of sight. Upheaval in the human world means significant problems for Society, and they've got enough threats to their precious stolen ley lines as-is.

One cop finally races forward, intent on wrestling Sol to the asphalt. Sol lets the man get a hold of his arm and then leaps to his feet. He takes the startled officer with him, swinging him completely off the ground before throwing him at his brothers-in-arms. He's moving before he's even let go, even as the cracking pop-pop of gunfire has me going flat against the asphalt, and he hauls me to my feet. My shoes barely scrape the ground before Sol rolls me over the top of our destroyed car, and I'm happy to stay out of sight behind the car while he goes after the cops.

He's going to kill them, I know, and I know I need to stop him. They've done nothing to deserve his wrath and retribution, same as the customers at Jinx didn't need to die to Pharaoh's outrage. But it's them or me, and I'll have to come to terms with this cruel injustice later. I want to crush my hands against my ears to drown out the panicked screams of a scattering crowd and the strident yells of the overwhelmed police, but I can't afford to block this out. The gatekeepers' magic is still a hum against my skull, barely held at bay by Sol's protection. As soon as I think it, I know I've made a mistake, because it's not my ears I need right now.

I have only a split-second of warning. When I open my eyes the gatekeepers are already inside the shop with me. Fear locks every muscle in me and I gape up at them in slack-jawed horror. Talons flash in the store's florescent lights as one tries to gut me, and I bring my hands up in an ineffectual shield. I catch hold of its toes a spare second before it can slice my face in two and shove as hard as I can.

The snap of bone is unexpected, moreso because it isn't mine. The snap in my chest is almost louder. The chill that lights up every synapse should have me freezing to stone where I stand, but instead it sears through passageways that shouldn't be open yet. I feel it come alive in me like the power I called on in Pariah, buzzing and hungry and bone-deep. I spare only a split-second to register that it is not a threat to me, and then my desire to not die to the gatekeepers washes away every other concern. I throw the gatekeeper away from me as hard as I can, sending him clear across the shop, and punch the next one in what passes as its chest.

Its body splinters and shatters around my fist like a stained glass window, and I waste a precious second to watch jagged lines spider out away from my knuckles. Shock almost costs me my life; talons come at me again in my peripheral vision and Sol dives to my rescue just in time.

The tip of one talon still manages to cut me from chin to cheekbone and I drop to a crouch to get out of the way. Sol plants his body between us and tears the gatekeeper's leg clean off. His coat saves him from being disemboweled by the one I knocked back first, and then Sol gives up on taking them on one at a time. The store goes up in black flames, and the surviving two gatekeepers vanish from sight to escape the inferno.

Sol catches hold of me, only to flinch and stare when my power snarls between us. I feel our magics grate against each other like sandpaper on asphalt. I can feel every place our powers line up—and every place they snag and bite. I think of the lock and key Yasmin showed me, the teeth of my power snagging on the pins in Sol's. The bond between us fractures a bit under the weight of that screaming wrongness, and I have to pull out of Sol's grip before the dissonance eats me alive.

"Not so compatible after all," I say. "Ouch."

"You woke your magic up," he says.

It sounds like an accusation. "Yell later, escape now."

We make a break for it, aiming for the nearest parked police car. I barely have time to slam the passenger door shut before Sol hits the gas, and we ram at least two other cars out of our way as we break free of the throng. A good Samaritan tries to cut us off when he realizes we're running, but Sol darts past him just in time. Getting free of the humans only solves one of our problems, and I plaster myself against the window to look up at the sky.

"They're coming," I say.

"We are almost to Darowel. Get ready to jump."

Buildings give way to trees. When I blink, the trees fracture and come apart like a disturbed reflection. It takes a moment for me to catch the significance: Darowel is out of sync with Earth the same way Madtown is. Even if it's just a fraction of Madtown's disconnect, it's enough that we can lose our human tail.

Sol pulls onto the shoulder and practically throws himself from the car. I leap out and run around the hood, reaching for his outstretched hand. I have to grit my teeth at the bite of our magics and follow him through the first line of trees. Roots and brush grab at my shoes, slowing me down, and I have to catch a trunk or two to keep from falling over entirely. Every stumbling step brings us closer to Darowel's embrace, and then the ground gives a short bounce beneath my feet as we step through the gaps in reality. We slow to a stop to watch the police run right past us.

"Now what?" I ask.

"Now we hope I was not wrong," Sol says, and sets off through the trees.

I smear blood off my chin and wince at the burning ache in my face.

"That's a great plan."

The gate's a half-mile from where we stand, and I spend the entire walk looking over my shoulder and trying to get a good glimpse of the sky. It worries me that the gatekeepers aren't trying to tear us open when they have to know where we're headed, and their absence suggests a possibility I am not ready to deal with yet.

Life still doesn't care what I want from it, though. When we finally step clear of the trees into a field, gatekeepers are standing shoulder to shoulder waiting for us.

I know the answer, but I have to ask: "Can you fight this many?"

"This is not our fight. Get behind me."

He's dropping even as I shift to take cover behind him, falling to his knees and punching an arm into the earth all the way up to his elbow. It's not an attack against Darowel, but the gate groans in response, and a column of black light shoots from gate to clouds. The gatekeepers shuffle a bit, stone-smooth faces tilted back as they consider this display. The way their talons grip the ground make me think they're braced for an explosion, but nothing comes. Sol isn't fighting them, I realize with a sinking sense of dread. He's sending out a beacon to the help that Lily may or may not have rallied for us.

"What if no one—" I start.

The sudden crackle on my skin is a gate yawning open. I can't see the entryway through so many gatekeepers' bodies, but the clearing is silent enough that I hear a singsong greeting. My ears tell me it's French, a language I've never even attempted to study outside of an ill-pronounced *Bonjour*, but my mind understands the words anyway:

"Twenty years dead and can't stay out of trouble, Brimstone."

Sol calls back in a different language. I can only assume that unrecognizable tangle of sounds is supposed to be Finnish. How and why I can suddenly understand him, too, is beyond me. I understand even less how they can understand each other: "I would have stayed dead if I'd known you two would be the first to answer."

Despite his words, there's no heat in his tone, and a peal of laughter is his response.

Between us the gatekeepers shift and totter, trying to turn to see both of us. More of them are looking at the gate than at Sol. They know what it takes me a minute longer to understand: the real threat isn't us anymore. I look down at Sol, but he doesn't return my questioning stare. He rises to his feet in a lithe motion and brushes soil from his arm.

A third voice—a third language, no less—joins the fray: "Oh, I cannot

145

wait until Wrath finds out we beat them here. She will be sore at us for ages, I am sure. She always did like feeling she had one up on you, yes? But speaking of ladies: is it true then that you've got one with you? We should very much like to meet our new sister. If only we could see her properly."

It doesn't sound like a threat, but in the next instant the field turns end over end. It takes my eyes a moment to realize what I'm looking at, because twisters are things out of movies and weather reports, not things that drop out of the sky a foot from my face. It is impossible for it to be here, more so for it to be this close and not have pulled both Sol and me into the gale. It has no problem at all yanking gatekeepers from the ground, and their white bodies crash into each other like fish in a barrel.

The sky around the twister goes jet black, but not from a storm. It's a swarm of bats, and they throw themselves into the storm until the twister is nothing but a funnel of dark bodies. Mist hits my face, but it isn't water. My fingers come back blue. The gatekeepers are being torn apart one tiny bite at a time.

Two men walk through the storm unharmed to stand in front of Sol. The Nightmare is gray as uncut shale with hair only marginally darker, and his Dream is a smiling Korean. The Dream nudges his Nightmare and gestures at Sol. He has to yell to be heard over the wind, and I still almost miss his words:

"Is it just me or has he gotten younger?"

Maybe it's meant to be a joke, but Sol is regarding the two like the storm has taken the wind out of him. He's been gone for eighteen years, and most of the people he's met since waking at Elysium are the ever-changing faces of the Guard. These two are the first real, visible proof that the world kept turning in his absence. They look only a few years younger than me, which means they would have been small children when Sol went to sleep. He's missed their entire lives.

The Dream must catch on that he's said something wrong, because he slants a look over at me. His smile is quick to disappear and his red eyes go wide. "Oh, but what is this? What have you done, Brimstone?"

"The gods waste no time," Sol says. "We fell through to da-Vìncún."

I take it the Dream can smell Sol's magic on me or sense the bond still knotted between us. The gods aren't why we're bonded together, but Sol told me they're the only gray area of forgiveness when it comes to Dream and Nightmare bonds. I decide not to tell these strangers the real reason Sol and I are a hot mess of tangled power. Omission is definitely the better option, because the Dream's expression relaxes immediately.

146

"Nevere has been hunting Wrath in your absence," the Nightmare says, and brushes blue blood off the shoulder of his jacket. It's hard to see the field now through the layer of glistening gatekeeper blood. "It is unknown which of them is happier to have you back."

The next blood to splatter against us is red. The Nightmare tips his head back as far as he can so he can consider his twister. "Ah, but here they come."

He might have caught the gatekeepers off-guard with his attack, but they're rallying. I can feel Darowel tremble in response, and then the twister is ripped apart. There seem to be half as many gatekeepers now than there were before, but there are still plenty to contend with. The pair don't seem a bit concerned, though, and the Dream motions for us to go on ahead.

"Find us when you find him," the Dream says. "Tempest will follow you always, even if you are still a child."

"I need one of them," Sol says with a gesture up. "Crash it at the waterfront."

"Inky pinky ponky," the Nightmare says, and a gatekeeper goes flying. "Have fun."

Sol catches me by my wrist. "Be ready."

I don't have time to ask "For what", because the gatekeepers dive en masse. The Dream is laughing like this is the most fun he's had all year as he and his Nightmare raise their hands. Sol doesn't wait to watch the attack but bolts back the way we've come. He nearly pulls my arm out of its socket before my feet get the hint we're moving, and I chase him through the woods.

"Wait! We're not going to help?"

"They are a united set," Sol says. "Do not worry about them."

That doesn't make me feel better. Nor does the screaming that starts as soon as we're out of sight. I've heard agony before, but nothing like this. I look back, but there are too many trees between us and them now, and too much underbrush to not pay attention to where I'm putting my feet.

We run until the trees thin and the lake spreads out ahead of us. There are girls wading in the shallows, and they point to the gatekeeper's crumpled form as soon as they spot us. I guess that means they aren't human, but the gatekeeper deserves more of my attention right now. Sol lets go of me and strides over to it, pushing it down with both hands before it can find its feet.

"Juluveya Maha'rhen," Sol says, and whatever language that's supposed to be doesn't translate. "I have a present for you."

147

The air shimmers, and I watch as thick scales melt into sight. A massive rope isn't long in forming, encircling us completely, and a second and third layer form atop it. I know what I'm looking at before the serpent's head finally materializes, but that doesn't make it any easier to stomach. I finally understand why mice don't run. The snake's stare is piercing, pinning me in place as effectively as spikes through my feet.

"Look at him," the snake says without moving its jaws. It tips its head to one side and flicks a tongue out lightning-quick to sniff the air near his temple. "Long time no ssssee, Brimsssstone. You ssssaid, perhapssss, a gift?"

Sol drags a hand through the gatekeeper's blood and holds his palm up for inspection.

"How ssssweet. I like you more each time I sssssee you."

"Consider this my toll, paid in advance," Sol says. "We will call on you shortly."

"One more for the infesssstation," the snake says. "Perhapsss I will let you in."

It unhinges its jaws as Sol gets up and backs out of the way. Its lower jaw drops inch by agonizing inch to the ground, and the fangs that grow longer and sharper in turn belong to no snake. If a python screwed an alligator and threw a piranha in for kicks, we might have ended up with this monstrosity. I'd hate it on sight except that it's eating a gatekeeper head first. Talons twitch and curl in protest as the gatekeeper disappears further and further into the snake's maw, but the gatekeeper is too close to death to properly fight back.

"Bring your children," Sol says. "Tempest fills a field with the dead."

The snake considers this as its jaw snaps back into place, then sets off through the woods. It is too big to fit, but it passes through the trees without disturbing a single leaf. Sol does not wait for it to disappear entirely before turning me back toward the water.

"We going to talk about this?" I ask.

"Not right now," he says, and we hurry instead toward the waiting girls.

They hold their hands out at our approach. As soon as my fingers slip into hers, the girl yanks me off my feet with unexpected strength and pulls me out from shore. She considers my face a moment, then works her jaws and dribbles something honey-gold and sticky into her palm. I tip my head back when she first tries to pat it onto my torn skin, but she gives me an insistent tug.

"This will keep the water out," she says. "Let me."

I look past her at the water and stop struggling. She slathers the warm mess into place while I try not to gag. When she's done she presses me flat against her body, winding her arms around my waist and back, and offers me a beatific smile.

"Breathe," she says.

I fill my lungs, but she leans in and covers my mouth with her own. I jerk back, but her grip is too tight for me to escape her.

"We are going to be underwater a long time," she says. "Breathe."

She slides her hand up my back to catch the back of my head and pulls me back in. This time I don't fight when she presses her mouth to mine. She gives an inhuman twist to pull us both underwater, and we're off like a shot. I hold my breath as long as I can, knowing we have to break the surface soon.

Each second drags by longer than the last with no hint that we're angling up from the depths. I can almost feel the metal rungs of a ladder beneath my hand, and the memory of drowning has me digging my fingers into her. That's not just my heart racing, though; Sol's fear is a monster barely kept at bay as we streak through the endless waves.

I start to struggle, but she gives my side a vicious pinch, and I gasp despite myself. I get a lungful of air that tastes fresh. I try to look at her, but the water is too cold and the speed too great. She relaxes her grip and keeps breathing for me, in and out as calm as you please. Her hand finds mine where I'm hanging onto her waist, and she drags my palm to her ribs. Her skin moves beneath my fingers, up and down in equidistant slats. She's got gills. I'm taking a ride on a mermaid of all things.

Knowing I'm not going to drown only helps a bit. I'm so cold I can barely feel her beneath my hands. I'm weightless and disoriented, aware only of the speed at which we're moving and the heartbeat thumping in my throat.

Just when I'm sure I'm going to panic, we break the surface. Land is a fuzzy line on the horizon, and the sun is so bright and beautiful I could claw my eyes out in supplication. There are fishing boats scattered in the distance, too far out to see their owners as more than smudges. A warning press of thumbs against me is all I get before we dive once more.

I count seconds, thinking it will keep me from going mad, and get to six hundred before I see the sky again. We're closer to land now, close enough that the mermaids carry us on their bellies at the surface. When we're near enough, they execute neat rolls to drop us, and I've never been happier to feel sand slip and slide under my feet. I wade for shore as quickly as I can go, gasping for air like I haven't been breathing this whole

149

time. I sink to my hands and knees and Sol is too happy to throw himself down on his ass beside me.

"We can rest here a moment," one of the mermaids says as she does a barrel roll in the shallows. "This is Hartstene Island. No one from Society lives here."

I've never heard of Hartstene, but I'll take her word for it.

She must see my ignorance on my face, because she lifts an arm and points. "You are forty miles from Seattle. If we take you all the way there, it will be longer, for the waters between here and there are home to too many islands. Would you ask that of us?"

"Take us to shore," Sol said. "We will figure it out from there."

"As you wish."

I rub at my arms, trying to coax warmth back into them, before realizing the long swim didn't put a dent in Sol's heat. I press against his side like I plan on burrowing inside him. Sol must be timing our break to my chattering teeth, because I have just enough time to stop trembling before he painstakingly gets to his feet.

"We have to go."

I want to argue, knowing he wants to be underwater even less than I do, but I follow him back to our unorthodox rides.

"It is not far," the mermaid promises, and pulls me into a kiss and cold darkness.

TWELVE

We come ashore in Hell.

There is no other word for the nightmare the mermaids leave us in; the moment their hands let go in the shallows outside Washington, the entire world shifts into one of Sol's ugly dreamscapes. The water is hot and choppy against me, throwing me closer to shore, and I stumble out onto a beach that's more glass and bone than sand. The tide bubbling against my feet is red, and the scent of blood is so overpowering I nearly throw up. I catch at my throat like I can somehow still my gag reflex and cut a hard look Sol's way.

Sol does not look at all surprised to be here, and there is a tired familiarity on his human face as he considers the rocky land stretching out ahead of us. The ground juts up in jagged black peaks, miniature mountains sharp enough to catch birds on. More than one body has been impaled on their surface, and they hang limp in varying stages of decay. If the wind changes and brings that smell of decomposition to me I really will lose the battle with my stomach. I focus only on Sol and where I put my feet.

"Pharaoh?" I ask as I make my way to his side.

"Close," Sol says. "That's why we are here at the core."

At the core of his power, I guess, and I shouldn't be surprised that a man called Brimstone would ground his powers in this wretched landscape. Nightmares are simply Gaia's corruption given form; Sol carries the nightmares of humanity in whatever shape his gift finds easiest. He is hellfire and damnation because too many people believe in it and fear it. Maybe too many humans fear this place, or maybe he and Pharaoh left behind religious families that struck the first blow. Sol did mention exorcisms along with shock therapy, after all.

The sky is an ugly gray-red, with roiling clouds that move fast enough to be dizzying. Lightning spiders through them almost constantly, snapping and sizzling and putting too much energy in the air. Every hair on my body is standing on end in response, and the birds that attempt to cut through the air are electrocuted and cast back to earth.

Sol leads the way, giving the craggy spikes a wide berth and stepping

151

over the dying birds. We haven't gone far before we meet a new obstacle: a river of lava cuts through the ground ahead of us. I gape at it, refusing to believe it is real. Lava is a thing of movies and science books. This is not reality, but seeing it with my own eyes is both humbling and frightening.

I look both ways for a way across, but the only path I can see is a half-sunken string of rocks from one shore to the other. That is not at all a viable option, and I doubt I have to tell such a thing to Sol, but in the next heartbeat he's jumping from one stone to the other.

"Absolutely not," I say as he makes it to the other side. He turns to look at me, and I give an emphatic shake of my head. "Absolutely not! Fuck you."

Something laughs behind me, and the weight of eyes on me puts a harder prickle on my skin than the overcharged air does. I glance back but see nothing.

"Evelyn, we have to go," Sol calls.

I take a couple steps back to get a running start. The rocks dip under my feet, not enough to sink my shoes into the lava but enough to completely throw my balance out of sorts. I pinwheel and slip and jump like a panicking rabbit, and Sol hauls me to safety as soon as I'm close enough. I cling to him and stare over my shoulder at the horror I just survived. Shadows are gathering at the far shore, and a hundred glittering yellow eyes survey us with intense interest.

"Can we run now?" I ask.

"Don't look back," Sol warns me.

I don't need to be told twice. We run for it, breaking bones and glass beneath our shoes, and I try not to guess where that new screaming is coming from. Arms burst from the ground as we pass the last jagged outcropping, and clawed hands grab at our pants. They tear through denim with no problem at all, leaving white-hot stripes of torn skin on my thighs and shins, but I don't dare slow down long enough to fight back.

Sol points, and I change course. The landscape is morphing around us, and before my eyes a mountain is slowly pushing up from the ground. It's practically a vertical cliff face by the time we reach it, but I can see a narrow ledge just out of reach. I jump for it anyway, scrabbling desperately at the rocks, and then Sol catches my leg and ass and throws me. I yelp at the unexpected help but manage to get my arms onto the ledge. I hoist myself up with a desperate lack of grace and lie flat to extend my arm to Sol. The mountain's still growing, so he misses my hand on his first jump.

"Come on!" I yell at him, and he takes a running leap. The sudden weight of him almost pulls me off, but I grab him with both hands. He hangs on just long enough to brace himself and then heaves himself to safety. He grabs my shirt as he goes, dragging me after him, and we sit backs flat to the wall to catch our breath.

"Seriously," I say. "Please take us somewhere nice sometime, because this is completely—"

"SOL!"

It takes me a second to recognize that voice. It takes Sol no time at all, and he's on his feet in a heartbeat. A hole opens up in the mountain behind us, leading clear through to the other side, and Sol races down it without stopping to consider whether or not it's a trap. I gape after him a moment, then struggle to my feet and give chase. He clears the other end a couple seconds ahead of me, and those seconds are all the time he needs. When I reach the exit, the sky has gone a too-bright blue, and the sun is so harsh and so large I have to cower back and shield my eyes.

It takes ages to blink the spots out of my eyes, and when I finally feel safe enough to lower my arms I'm staring out at a dead wheat field. Someone's smashing an uneven path straight through it as they race for the mountain, and Sol is leaving an identical mess behind him as he goes to meet our visitor. There is only one person it can be, then, and I am as relieved to see Pharaoh again as I am leery of this reunion.

By the time I catch up to them, it's impossible to tell where one ends and the other begins. They're holding each other like they'll die if they let go, Pharaoh's hands knotted in Sol's coat and Sol hanging onto Pharaoh's face in a fierce grip. I've never seen anyone kiss like they're kissing now, and that's including the sloppy drunk make-out sessions I had to break up in Jinx from time to time. Everything I ever thought I felt for Notte feels like a cheap charade when faced with this single-minded desperation and devotion.

I'm jealous, but it doesn't last long. I'm close enough to them now to realize something is extremely wrong. It takes a minute to put my finger on it, and the pieces only fall into place because my magic is wide awake now.

When I first met Pharaoh he seemed intimately familiar in a way I couldn't understand, the way a childhood scent can stop you dead in the supermarket with a pang of unmistakable nostalgia. It's not cologne or aftershave I'm picking up on, though: it's Notte's magic. Pharaoh wears it like a second skin.

Pharaoh's voice startles me from my frantic thoughts, but the words are lost as he kisses them into every inch of Sol's skin he can reach. Sol understands, at least, and works his fingers deeper into Pharaoh's ragged locks.

"I'm here," he whispers. "You're here. We're here."

Pharaoh smiles, and for a moment he looks positively radiant. That lasts only until he straightens and realizes they have an audience. His face goes bloodless so quickly it's a wonder he doesn't pass out, and he pulls Sol hard up against him. Sol half-twists in his grip, trying to follow Pharaoh's wide-eyed stare.

For a frightening moment he looks confused, like he isn't sure who I am or what I'm doing here. Kissed brainless, I guess, because recognition sets in a second later. I dredge up a mocking smile, and he answers with a weak scowl.

"Pharaoh, this is—"

"*You!*" Pharaoh tries to lunge past Sol, but Sol catches hold of him and drives him back away from me. "I should have killed you when I had the chance, you backstabbing thieving bitch! How dare you stand where we stand? How dare you touch what isn't yours to claim?"

"Jesus, it's a broken record around here," I say, like my heart isn't pounding a mile a minute at that near miss. "Why don't you do the adult thing and just let us start over, since we obviously got off on the wrong foot." I thrust my hand out, knowing there's a fifty-fifty chance he'll try to break my wrist, and force myself to use the name that's most likely to get his attention: "My name is Evelyn Notte."

Pharaoh stares. "Sol, the hell is she—"

"She's looking for Notte," Sol cuts in. "I've taken her under our protection."

"I refuse," Pharaoh spits. He tries to wrench out of Sol's grip, but Sol is too strong for him. He goes at Sol instead, slamming both hands into Sol's chest to throw him. Sol drags Pharaoh after him when he stumbles, and despite that outburst Pharaoh is quick to pull Sol back up against him. "Let me kill her. Let me kill her! I will feed her to the vultures and buy us both a good night's sleep."

"She's under our protection," Sol says again. "We need to pair her."

"Pair her," Pharaoh says, sharp with agony. "Looks like you've already started. Why is she here, Sol? What have you done? She's trying to steal you from me just like Notte said she would. I told him you'd never leave me. I told him you'd never think it. But here she is where only I should be, which means you did use her. Why didn't you wait for me?"

I'm too annoyed to suffer Sol's placating excuses, so I butt in with, "He used me because Nevere was pulling his skin off one gray scrap at a time."

154

Pharaoh goes still as the dead. "No."

"Sol was willing to die, except then Nevere said he'd use Sol's body and eat you in retaliation. It was use me to save you or let Nevere have you. He made the only call he could, so fuck you and the self-righteous horse you rode in on."

It's amazing how quickly fury can one-eighty to panic and self-loathing. Pharaoh abruptly forgets I exist and drags Sol hard up against him. Sol hadn't leaned on me back then, but he trusts Pharaoh with his naked fear. He buries his face in Pharaoh's throat and pulls so hard at Pharaoh's shirt I can hear threads snap. Neither man says anything else, but they don't have to. They absorb strength from each other, and they both slowly relax.

"Look," I say, when I think they're calm enough to not kill me. Pharaoh's dark look makes me rethink my chances, but it's too late to back out now. "I made mistakes, okay? I didn't know what a Dream or Nightmare was before Betty brought you into Jinx. I figured I was just a psychic who loved slapping nicknames on everything I had to put up with on a daily basis. I woke Sol because he was my best ticket to Adam—to Notte," I correct myself, because I know Pharaoh won't understand the first name. "I had to find out the rest of the truth from him after the fact.

"I am not here to take Sol away from you," I say with quiet and slow emphasis. "I'm just here to beat Notte to death with the biggest sledgehammer I can find."

"She hates him almost as much as we do," Sol says.

"Unlikely," Pharaoh says, but there's a little less acid in his voice now.

"She is dangerous," Sol says, "but she is not dangerous to us anymore. I believe that."

Pharaoh considers me with a long, hard look, then turns his full attention on Sol. "I trust you."

It sounds like it hurts him to say it, but Sol answers with a slow smile. Pharaoh can't be angry in the face of such a pleased expression, and he visibly relaxes. He tips his head in for another kiss, then another that lingers a little too long considering I'm standing right here. I idly wonder if I should find a safer place to wait this out, but now that Sol's gotten what he wanted I want him to hold up his end of the deal. I'm not waiting for them to screw before I find out what happened to Notte and Ciara.

"Before you get frisky, please remember that he was gutted just a couple days ago," I tell Sol.

"Russian sorcerers fixed most of the damage," Pharaoh says, but it's too late. Sol's leaning back and looking down. When he unbuttons

155

Pharaoh's shirt, it's to take in the bandages wrapped rather generously around his middle. Sol's expression goes tense, so Pharaoh presses a quick kiss to his temple. "I'm still here. Still invincible and ready to raise hell, literally and figuratively."

"You're careless," Sol accuses him in a low voice. "You always, always have been."

They stand silent, swallowing the rest of what feels like an old argument, and then Sol blessedly tugs Pharaoh's shirt closed again.

"Notte will know I have you," he says. "We have to find him."

"He went into the wastes after he woke me," Pharaoh said. "Who knows when he'll resurface?"

"I wasn't planning on waiting for him."

Pharaoh stares. "You aren't actually considering going in after him, are you? Remember what happened the last time we tried to break into the wastes?"

"I told Juluveya we were coming," Sol says.

The silence that follows is telling. It is an age before Pharaoh finds his voice. "You did what?"

"The wastes have spread as far as Darowel," Sol says, and Pharaoh sucks in a short, sharp breath through clenched teeth. "We had the opportunity to bargain for passage, so I took it."

"You bargained with Jules," Pharaoh presses. "Same Jules that promised she'd route us to the southern gate the next time we so much as stuck a toe in her territory? Sol, are you mad?"

"Maha'rhen," Sol says, "not A'fridava."

"That makes me feel so much better," Pharaoh says tightly. "Last I checked she only likes us marginally more than her sisters do."

"We have no choice but to trust her. He waited eighteen years to wake you because he wasn't ready for us. He's ready now, which means we cannot afford for him to make the first move or we will not stand a chance."

Pharaoh taps a nervous beat against Sol's lower lip. "We have only half a chance as it is. What happens when we fail, Sol? He will never forgive us."

"Then we will not fail," Sol says. "Stand with me."

"Always," Pharaoh says, and despite his grim warning there is no hesitation or fear in that promise.

Sol pulls back to shrug out of his coat. Pharaoh's mouth thins to a hard line when he understands Sol's intentions, but the look Sol gives him warns him not to argue. He eases into the coat like it might bite him and

156

holds his hands palm-up to Sol. Sol motions for me to step closer, and I am careful to stand closer to Pharaoh than I do to Sol. Sol waits until I've gone still before drawing symbols on Pharaoh's palms with his index fingers. Black fire curls over their hands and between their fingers, and blood wells up on Pharaoh's fingertips from cuts I don't see.

"Always," Sol says in quiet promise, and he clasps Pharaoh's hands.

The second their hands lock, the ground drops away. It takes Pharaoh and Sol with it. I call after them, but my voice is yanked away by the wind as a new world falls into place around me. Wheat fields and open sky are replaced by stone walls. I am alone in a tunnel, and the only light comes from scattered bits of luminescent moss.

That pinprick in the distance might be a trick of my eyes, but I'm hoping it's the way out. I put my hands out to the wall for balance and set off as carefully as I can. Within a few minutes the growing light tells me I'm going the right way, but my cautious optimism dies the second I reach the opening. Four massive snakes are waiting for me.

"Oh, she is quite sssstrange, isn't she?" one asks. "Interessssting."

"Evolution in the making," another agrees. "How unpleasant for ussss to live through it."

I risk a look down and find the ground only a short slide away. Before I can take the first step out of the tunnel, though, one of the snakes puts its giant head in my path.

"Careful, child. You do not know where you sssstep."

I look out past them, but all I see is a gray desert. "Where am I? Where is Sol?"

"You are at the wessssstern gate. Brimsssstone was routed to the north. It is their favorite."

Last I checked, snakes couldn't smile, but the looks these four give me is pretty damned close. I'm not sure if they're laughing at Sol's predicament or my misfortune, but right now I have to worry about me. I fold my arms over my chest and look from one snake to the next.

"Why did you split us up?"

"Why?" the snakes chorus, and one continues, "We did nothing. You brought thissss on yoursssself."

"I had nothing to do with this. I only halfway know what the wastes are."

"Perhapsss it was not your intention, but that does not change factssss."

"Is it sssuicide or foolishnessss? The Nightmares would bleed dry to avoid thissss gate."

"Three pairs they've lossst here already, yet you expect to ssssucceed alone?"

I swallow hard against dread. "Can't you send me to Sol and Pharaoh?"

One snake tsks. "Too late. You have already arrived."

"You cannot turn back now," the second agrees. "You can only go forward."

"You musssst go forward," the third says. "Be careful, death Dream. There are rules. Your firsssst sssstep putsssss you in play, and you cannot sssstop again until you win or die."

"You musssst not stop."

"If you do, you are lossst, and you will never find your way."

This is sounding like a worse idea by the second, but I can't see a way around it. "What did you call me?"

"We only call you what you are. Are you not pleased?"

"Not really," I say.

"Neither are we," one admits. It smacks me in the forehead with a quick dart of its tongue. "The Nightmares control sssso much already. Perhapssss it was inevitable they would come to take what is ours. We expect you will be a lessss toxic massssster than the one who came before."

"Adam," I guess. "Is Notte here?"

"Here? No. Fathom is in the catacombsssss where he does not belong. We should like him removed, if you do not mind."

I'm treated to another creepy smile. "You do not mind, do you?"

"That was the plan," I say. "I'm here to kill him."

"How bold is the Dream with no Nightmare to call her own."

"These are the wastes, right?" I ask. "Sol said Nightmares' powers are muted here."

"In the wassssstessss, yes. The catacombssss are a little lessss friendly to your kind."

"A Dream with no one to protect her will surely die."

"Thanks for the vote of support," I say, and look out at the wastes again. My nerve is threatening to fail me, so I look for the only thing that can get me moving toward a certain death: "Does he have a girl with him?"

"Oh, the girl. Isn't she beautiful?"

My heart stops. "She's alive."

"She lives," the snake says, "and cries. Any Dream raised in the catacombssss would."

It feels like Madtown all over again, a sucker punch to every nerve ending in my body. There's a deafening ringing in my ears as I slowly come back to myself again, but it takes an eternity before I can look at the snake who spoke. I dig my fingers into my shirt, trying to feel my scars through the dirty cotton. For a blinding moment I'm sure I feel the hole the gatekeepers left in me.

"You're lying."

"Ssssee for yoursssself, but you will not like what you ssssee."

I scramble down the rocks as quickly as I can go without breaking my neck and take off across the desert.

The snakes' laughter follows me for miles.

THIRTEEN

The wastes are a colorless, washed-out expanse of gray. There are no solid edges, even in the mountains that line the distant horizon. Everything is blurred just a bit, as if someone sneezed while taking a picture. More disturbing than that, though, is the complete lack of sound. There's no wind, no pat of my shoes against the ground, no distant birds or rustling creatures. The silence is oppressive, and when I clear my throat to break it I feel deafened by my own noise.

I run until the stitch in my side forces me to slow to a hurried trot, but I don't seem to make any progress. The skeleton trees in the distance draw no closer, and the horizon doesn't change. Only the absence of the snakes and the western gate behind me prove I've moved at all. I can't help but keep looking back for that reassurance, but the absence of my footprints in the sand creeps me out too much to let my stare linger. All I can do is point my eyes forward and try to keep going.

I'm afraid to speak against this quiet stillness, but the silence just makes my thoughts louder.

"She's not a Dream."

She can't be, but even as I refuse to entertain the thought I know she's the best answer to the biggest remaining questions: why Notte risked capture to steal her from me and how he's stayed alive this long with neither Meridian nor me to prop his gift up. Sol has said over and over that a Nightmare cannot have a second Dream, but Notte's attempts to get Pharaoh killed are proof he is willing to replace Dreams for the Nightmares' sake. He left me behind for Sol and took Ciara for himself.

I think about Nevere and Yasmin and the agony that fuels Sol's powers, and the thought of Notte introducing a baby to that world has me screaming myself hoarse.

"I'm going to kill him." It's a rough whisper that does nothing to make me feel any better. I shriek it at the unchanging horizon next: "I'm going to kill him!"

Minutes turn to hours that blur together in a meaningless hum. I walk until I can't feel my feet anymore, until my legs throb with every step and I have to beat a rhythm into my aching thighs. Rage fuels me when the rest of me would have given up; hate helps me put one foot in front of the other as I stay the course. I don't care how tired I am or how long it will take me to get to the catacombs from here. Notte turned that power on our newborn daughter, and I am going to kill him no matter the cost.

I walk nine hours through the wastes, then ten. Eventually soreness dims to a bone-deep exhaustion, and I do whatever I can to chase away the fog in my mind. I name every cocktail I can think of, rattling off ingredients and proportions, then list my customers and all of Elysium's tenants. I name and spell all fifty states, give a half-hearted guess at naming the capitals, and count until my tongue is too numb to continue.

The world remains unchanged.

I've been walking almost a full day when I start falling asleep standing up. At first I keep myself awake by pinching my arms, sometimes hard enough to draw blood, but a couple hours later not even that can keep my eyes open. I talk to myself again, but I'm so tired the sound of my own voice is infuriating. I just want peace and quiet and rest.

Every time that angry feeling starts to win the argument, I whisper Ciara's name. It's enough to pull me back on task, at least for now. I am sure I drift off for a minute here and there, but my body keeps moving, and that is all that matters.

My second day in the wastes, something moves. I'm running before I even realize what's happened, booking it back the way I came. Surprise offers a temporary jolt of adrenaline and wakefulness, but I'm a quarter-mile away before I realize what I'm running from. I wheel around and go back, eyes wide and searching for the anomaly.

Somewhere between me and the eternal horizon is a moving figure, and as I jog that way the shape grows larger and closer. It's a woman, pacing in circles and toeing at the ground. When she notices me in her peripheral vision she goes still and looks up to watch my approach.

"Don't stop!" I call, horrified.

She gapes, then runs to meet me halfway. I slow my pace and she falls in easily at my side. Before I can tell her the snakes' warning about stopping down here, she points an accusing finger at me and says, "You can see me. How is that possible?"

"What?"

"You're in the wastes," she says, a tad impatiently. "How did you get here?"

"Same way you did?" I guess.

"Not likely. I've been dead six years at least."

It takes my tired brain a moment to understand. "You're a ghost."

"And you're a psychic, which means you shouldn't be here."

"I came with two others, but we got separated."

"You got lost, you mean," she says, and clucks her tongue in sympathy. "Terrible way to go."

"I'm not lost. I'm still on the path."

Her smile is a tad too pitying for my tastes. "How's that trail working out for you?"

Her attitude leaves much to be desired, but I'm so desperate for company that I let it slide. "It's horrible. I've been on it for over a day and there's just—nothing." I make a wide gesture to indicate the unchanging world.

"Only a day?" she asks. She shields her eyes from a nonexistent sun and peers out at the mountains. "I followed a Dream and Nightmare once, when they made the mistake of coming into the wastes through the west. They made it three days, you know. Almost four. I tried to keep them awake, but they couldn't see or hear me. They only had each other, and in the end it wasn't enough. He carried her for a couple miles at the end, and then she made the call he couldn't. She sang them both to eternal sleep."

"Three days," I say bleakly. "No problem."

"At least you have me," she says brightly. "I can't sing half as well, though."

That's absolutely no comfort. "Which pair? The Dream and Nightmare, I mean."

"No idea. Does it matter?"

"Sol will want to know, I'm sure," I say. "I'll tell him when I catch up."

"Catch up?" she echoes. "You can't, not if you got separated. The wastes reset for every living party that passes through. He could be standing twenty feet from you and you'd never know it. The only ones with freedom between the layers are the dead."

"Fantastic. Got any good news for me while you're at it?"

"I'm dead and you're in the wastes. What do you think?"

I bite my lip so hard I taste blood. "I hate my life."

"Not for much longer." She shrugs when I glare at her, then says, "Jessica Laurell. My name," she explains. "You didn't ask for it."

"I didn't," I agree, and we continue on in silence.

I half-expect her to leave when I opt for ignoring her, but I'm probably the most interesting thing she's seen since the Dream and Nightmare died down here. She keeps pace with me, picking at her fingernails and humming to herself now and then.

Horror over my predicament has to give way to inevitable exhaustion, and within two hours I'm falling asleep standing up again. I dig my thumbnails into my tear ducts. I can risk sleepwalking again, or I can strike up another conversation with a woman who's just waiting for me to die. Neither one feels like a lesser evil right now, but Ciara matters more than any of this.

"How long is this path, anyway?" I ask.

"That depends," Jessica says. "Last time I walked from gate to gate, it took twenty-three days, but it could be longer by now. The wastes are always growing, you know?"

I almost give up on the spot, but her misunderstanding is a spark of much-needed hope. "I'm not going gate-to-gate. I'm heading to the catacombs. How far are they?"

She cuts a sharp look at me. "You can't be serious. You're going the wrong way." At my dumbfounded look, she stabs a finger at the ground. "The catacombs aren't on this layer. They're one down. The northern layer's the only direct route if you can survive the trip, and even that takes a day and a half if you're not familiar with it."

"No," I say, voice raw. "There has to be a way from here."

"If you're that keen on dying you might as well just wait up here with me. The catacombs have been a righteous mess for years now, courtesy of their half-mad king. Better to sleep in this wasteland than be eaten alive in that, don't you think?"

"I have no choice," I insist. "My daughter is down there. I have to find her."

I expect laughter or mockery, but Jessica looks stricken. She drops her gaze to her hands, and I follow her stare to the wedding ring on her finger. It's my only shot at getting out of this hellhole, so I press the advantage with a quiet but insistent, "If you were ever a mother, you know I can't stop now. Help me find my baby girl. There has to be a way down from here, a trapdoor or something the dead use to go back and forth. Let me use it."

"There's no guarantee it'll work for you."

"I'm the death Dream and a psychic," I say. "It will work."

I sound a lot more confident than I feel, but she doesn't call my bluff. She gnaws on her lower lip for a moment, then abandons the path to cut straight out into the desert. All I can do is follow after her and hope she's not leading me astray. A glance back shows the trail disappeared as soon as I left it. My stomach clenches a bit in cold fear and I jog to catch up to her.

We continue on like this for an hour, almost long enough for me to well and truly panic, and then Jessica stops and gestures for me to go ahead.

"It was fun while it lasted," she said.

I step through a patch of cold air to a world of thick, warm fog. I'm almost startled into stopping and cast my arms out to either side in an attempt to find support. I graze a thick rope with my left hand and flail around until I find its companion on my right. The ground dips and sways under every step, but I'm so disoriented and tired it takes me a minute to realize I'm on a suspension bridge. I slow to a cautious pace, not wanting to rock off the side. I can't see further than my nose, and I lose sight of my legs around my knees. It's probably for the best that I can't see whatever chasm the bridge goes over.

The air tastes so much cleaner than the stagnant death of the wastes, but the warmth here is dangerous. It lulls me to sleep despite my best efforts to stay awake. I tilt forward more than once, but each startled jolt awake does little to keep me from doing it again a few seconds later. I rake my hands over the ropes, hoping the friction burns will sting a bit of clarity back into my mind, but it's a dull annoyance my body is happy to tune out.

Muffled footsteps echoing behind me are a little more helpful, and I slow down a bit to listen. They're gaining on me, and there's definitely more than one person. I stare hard at the fog, trying to see, then set off as quickly as I dare. The only sound I hear now is the pounding of my heart in my ears and the soft click of my shoes against wooden planks. If I can just make it across the bridge, I can run for it, though god only knows where I'm supposed to go from here.

It's not a great plan, but it's all I've got, at least until my foot comes down on a plank that doesn't exist. My leg drops through to open air and I fall after it. I hit my shin blindingly hard against the planks and the rotting wood splits open beneath my weight. My arms snap taut and I cling to the rope for dear life as I fall through the bridge. I attempt to pull myself up only once before stretching my legs out in search of nearby support.

"Help! I call. "Help!"

The footsteps come again, faster this time, and then hot hands seize my wrists. I know this heat, but I only have a split-second of realization before I'm yanked back up to the relative safety of the bridge. I scrabble at the ropes for a second, reassuring myself that I've got a better grip, and then reach out blindly to the pair that's caught up to me. I can't see Sol, but I find his shoulder on the second try, and I cling to him until my legs stop shaking.

"Your timing's getting better," I say weakly.

Pharaoh speaks from further back: "Jules says she routed you through the western gate. No one survives the west. How did you get down here?"

"A ghost showed me a backdoor," I say, then cry out. "Oh! We're not moving. The snakes said we couldn't stop moving or we'd be lost. What have I done? What are we supposed to do now?"

"That rule is for the western wastes," Sol says. "You are nearly to the catacombs from the north."

Relief almost takes me off my feet. "Sol, I'm so tired."

"You cannot sleep yet," Sol says. "We are too close to stop now."

I know he's right. My head and my heart say we're past the point of no return, that I can't stop when Notte and Ciara are finally within reach. My body tries to beg and compromise, because how are we supposed to be at all effective against Notte in a fight if we're falling asleep standing up? I stare numbly at the space where my feet should be, incapable of deciding either way. For a wretched, selfish moment I'm willing to lie down and die here if it just means I can rest.

"I've got her," Pharaoh says, and then his fingers are little spots of heat on my temples. His magic lacks the violent edge Sol's has, but it feels twice as deadly as it streaks through me. There are bugs in my veins, I think, and for a split second I swear I see my skin shift over their scurrying bodies. Then my body is as it always was, and my brain comes wide awake. The world is still a dreary mess, but it feels like morning to me, and I am rested as if I spent the last day sleeping.

"How?" I ask as he drops his hands. "And why?"

"We spent six hours arguing about you yesterday," Pharaoh says. "I still don't trust you, but I believe Sol when he says we need you if we're going to survive this fight."

Sol eases past me, a brief line of scorching heat at my side, and the bridge dips a little as he checks for a way across. When his voice comes, it's further away, and his words are not as reassuring as he probably thinks they are: "The gap is short enough to jump."

"Ladies first," Pharaoh says when I balk.

I center myself with the ropes as my only guide and jump into open air. The jump feels a hundred times longer and higher than I know it really is, and landing has me falling awkwardly against Sol's waiting body. He grunts and stumbles back under my weight. I don't waste my breath apologizing but scoot around him to make room for Pharaoh. Sol calls out an okay, and the bridge gives a sharp swing as Pharaoh jumps over to us.

The fog slowly clears as we reach the other side, though the dusk we enter is only marginally easier to see through. I step off the bridge with a whole new appreciation for solid ground and look back to check on the others. Sol has gone perfectly still at the end of the bridge and is staring past me. I follow his gaze and see a freestanding door.

"Sol," Pharaoh says, and I look back to them. Sol doesn't seem to have heard his name. Pharaoh gives him another moment, then catches hold of his arm. "Sol, come back to me."

"He's destroyed them," Sol says. "Can you feel it?"

"I can feel it," Pharaoh agrees grimly. "He really did replace her, didn't he?"

"He's using Ciara," I say, very quietly. Neither one reacts, and their silence is telling. I resist the brief urge to claw Sol's eyes out. "How long have you known?"

"A Nightmare cannot survive without a Dream, and no Nightmare can survive the wastes for sixteen years," Sol says. "I suspected he had found another Dream to lean on, since he'd already proven he could use you as a stopgap for his sanity. I did not know who he'd chosen until you told me about your daughter. The timing meant it could be no one else."

"The snakes told me," I say. "Sol, she—"

Words fail me; there is nothing I can say. Sol gives me a minute to see if I figure it out, then shakes his head and motions for me to step aside.

"Wait here for us. We will come back for you when it's over."

"No."

"I have warned you about Dreams a hundred times by now," Sol says, but for once his warning lacks its spiky anger. He's being firm, not cruel, but my heart bleeds at his words anyway. "If you listened to any of it, you know why you must stay here. She will not know you."

"She is my daughter."

"Don't be stupid," Pharaoh says. "She's not your daughter anymore; she's his Dream. Notte is her entire world. You are nothing to her but an unmatched Dream who intends to slit her Nightmare's throat. You think *I* hate you? She will cut you into so many pieces people will forget you ever existed."

Their words are ice chips on glass: I hear them, but I refuse to let them sink in. I can't listen to them right now. I can't let Pharaoh's rage and Sol's endless, frantic lectures and this horrible truth become my reality, or I will go mad before I ever set eyes on Notte again. I listen to my heartbeat, to the sound of my strained breaths in and out of my too-tight lungs, and tune everything else out with sheer force of will. I lift my chin in defiance and stare down Sol, daring him to argue with me again.

Pharaoh scowls and lets go of Sol. "Let her find out the hard way, then."

"The decision is made," Sol says, and it sounds like a warning. "Notte has to die tonight. I will not let you change your mind."

"I won't."

"You'll regret this," Pharaoh says, but they give up arguing with me.

Sol leads the way to the door and opens it. The doorway yawns pitch black. I test the air with a cautious palm, then slowly poke my fingers into the darkness. I lean to one side to watch, but my hand doesn't come out the other side, and I can't see Sol or Pharaoh through the doorway. I look to the others for their opinion and regret it almost immediately. The tightness on Pharaoh's expression says he approves of this not at all.

"On three?" I ask.

Sol steps through before I have to count, and Pharaoh swears as he follows after. I hurry in behind them, afraid of being separated like we were at the gates.

Black fire snarls to life around us, then pulls apart and scatters. Stalagmites are packed so tightly together it's hard to find enough space to put our feet. Sol's fire settles on the spiked peaks like candle flames. The flames are small enough to pose no real threat to us, but the heat they give off is sweltering. I start dripping sweat almost immediately, and I have to check my forehead to make sure I'm not actually melting. My eyes are so dry they feel packed with grit. I'm impressed with Pharaoh for not chucking his coat immediately.

We make it to the bend before the catacombs respond to our presence. Stalactites fall from the ceiling, shatter to dust and shards, and pull together into stone wolves. Sol's magic hums under my skin as he and Pharaoh respond. Giant burning scorpions erupt from the ground, bringing the stalagmites with them. The scorpions rush past us, snapping their claws in warning, and the wolves bark and howl back at them. Pharaoh and Sol don't even slow but take the opening their beasts make for us, and I chase after them. A wolf nearly makes it through the fray to disembowel Sol, but a spiked tail impales it midair and drags it back into the fray.

I'm too busy watching the fight to watch my feet and trip into Pharaoh. He rights me and pushes me ahead of him, bracketing me between his and Sol's bodies. We make it safely around the bend and halfway down the hall before something hits my head. I reach up to check my hair, half-sure I'll find blood or worse, but my fingers look clean when I hold them out. I frown at my hand, mystified, and watch a drop splatter against my palm. I look ahead of me to see if Sol has noticed, but of course he has. His shoulders are hunched and tense as the ceiling starts to rain on us. Water sizzles as it hits his clothes, and he leaves a faint trail of steam behind him.

The ground rumbles beneath our feet and there's a low groan behind us. I look back and forget about the strange noise when I see Pharaoh. He's gone perfectly still several feet back and has his hands out in front of him. My first thought is he's as worried about the rain as Sol is, but the look on his face suggests a more immediate threat.

"Sol," I say.

Sol needs only a glance to know why I've called him, and he pushes past me. "Pharaoh?"

Pharaoh slowly drags his gaze up from his hands to Sol's face. His mouth moves, but no sounds come out. Instead water streams from between his lips, cascading down his throat and spilling over his coat.

Before our eyes the color melts out of him until a man-shaped body of water is standing where he once stood. It collapses on itself before I can properly grasp what I'm looking at, and Sol gives a frantic jerk of his arm—not to catch Pharaoh's liquefied body, but to extinguish the hell-hot flames that are still lighting our way. The hallway goes pitch black in an instant, and the heat is instantly replaced by a debilitating cold. Sol's hand is agonizingly hot by contrast when he seizes my elbow a second later.

"Keep going," Sol says, in a voice more animal than human.

"But Pharaoh—"

Sol shoves me, and I swallow the rest of my argument. I honestly have no idea what I'm supposed to say to him, anyway. I reach out for the wall with my free hand and set off into the darkness as fast as I dare.

The ground trembles again, and another groan echoes down the tunnel to us. It hasn't faded before there's the dull rumble of thunder. White noise fills the air, a distant annoyance at first before it gets loud enough for me to know what I'm hearing.

I twist my arm out of Sol's grip in favor of catching hold of his hand. Sol hauls me around in front of him and pulls me flat up against him. I have to shift my grip before he wrenches my arm out of my socket, and I have just caught hold of him again before water hits us like a ton of bricks.

The force of it sends us flying forward, but the water is moving fast enough to catch up with us before we hit the ground. We're swallowed by the waves and roll end over end as the current whips us along. I have the dizzying sensation of going up, and Sol's body takes the brunt of our collision with the ceiling.

We ricochet off long enough for me to smash a shoulder into the wall, and then we're tumbling through the darkness once more. The ferocity of it almost rips me from Sol's arms, but by some cruel fortune we are thrown against the wall again. It crushes me against him once more, giving us a spare half-second to tighten our hold, and we're dragged down the jagged length of the wall.

Sol's pain is a biting sting along our bond, lighting up every pathway still open between us, and I know that heat swirling around us is as much his blood as it is his natural body heat. He could evaporate this water in an instant with that fire of his, but saving us means burning Pharaoh out of existence. There is nothing he can do but ride this out with me as the water tries to tear him in two. I swing a leg toward the wall, hoping to kick us off and back to the safer center of the tunnel, but we're going too fast. I succeed only in bruising every square inch of my foot, and the stabbing pain up my calf says I nearly twisted my ankle with that impact.

My chest feels like it's expanding; my lungs are balloons under too much pressure. I grit my teeth and groan deep in my throat, fighting the need to take a breath. The last time I drowned I woke up, but this isn't a dream. This place is real, and these injuries are real, and this death will be as lasting as it is painful. I can't give in, but I have no choice. I'm breathing before I realize I've lost control, and the first rush of ice cold water down my throat sets off every alarm in my brain. I cough and convulse as my body fights back, and every instinctive gasp pulls more water in.

A hand flattens me against the ground before I realize I've stopped moving, and magic shudders through me with violent force. I puke water, then a sick mix of water and bile, and clutch at my quaking stomach. I choke on the first breath I manage, and the second, but I'm breathing air, I'm breathing air, I'm alive. Panic and relief are aching companions sending tremors through my body, and it is forever before I realize that buzzing in my ears is a voice.

"Hey, hey, hey."

I don't think I have the strength to sit up, so I sag onto my side to look. Pharaoh is back, and he's got Sol pulled up against his chest. For a blinding moment I think Sol is dead, because the limp set of his body looks horrendously unnatural, but then I hear his wet, short gasps. His fingers are hooked like claws into Pharaoh's knees and he flexes them every few seconds as if to assure himself Pharaoh is still a solid presence.

"I've got you," Pharaoh promises, low and urgent and afraid. "I've got you."

I struggle to my hands and knees, wobble a bit on limbs that feel like rubber, and crawl over to them. I try to speak, but my throat is too raw to manage it yet. I reach for Sol instead, but Pharaoh's magic is a hateful bite against my fingers when I get too close. I flinch and look his way. Pharaoh doesn't return it and doesn't even seem to realize I exist. That attack was instinctive as he puts all his focus into his injured lover.

I put my hand out slower, palm-first as I try to figure out where Pharaoh's barrier starts. It only takes a moment, but this time I shove against it instead of recoiling. It snaps and crackles in response, and Pharaoh flicks a startled look up. Sol opens his eyes at last, focusing first on Pharaoh and then on me. He attempts to sit up, then sinks back against Pharaoh with a quiet gasp.

Pharaoh's barrier gives way, but the haunted look he gives me is more effective than his magic. I reach for him instead and drag my fingers through the blood on his coat. Sol's blood, I know, because Sol gave his coat to Pharaoh before leading us into this trap.

"Always—fucking—water," Sol manages, in a voice like sandpaper. "How bad is it?"

"Three broken ribs at least," Pharaoh answers in a low voice. "One came through."

"And you?"

"I'm fine," Pharaoh says, more guilt than reassurance. Sol lets go of Pharaoh's knee with visible effort and reaches up, and Pharaoh catches his hand midair. Sol winces when Pharaoh gives his hand a squeeze, so Pharaoh tilts forward as carefully as he can to kiss Sol's knuckles. He looks positively wretched. "Sol, I'm sorry."

Sol doesn't get to answer, because a new voice speaks up: "You always have been sorry."

I know that voice. I'm not drowning anymore, but I can't breathe either.

Pharaoh shoots a look of absolute loathing over my head. "You traitorous—"

"Your Nightmare looks unwell, Pharaoh. Did you fail to protect him yet again?"

"*Fuck you.*"

Somehow I make it to my feet, and I turn on unsteady legs to face my long-lost husband. After sixteen years, Notte is finally standing within arm's reach, but this is Notte in his true form. The impractical three-piece suit is the same and he stands with the same practiced boredom I could pick out in any crowd, but his skin has gone thunderstorm gray and his eyes are two white holes in his face. His magic was always a distant hum before, a static charge that could never snap, but now it radiates from him with enough force to squeeze my bones.

His lips twitch into that honey-slow smile I remember too well. "Hello, Evelyn."

I go to slap my name off his lips, but fingers seize my wrist and haul

170

me back with inhuman strength. I have to go with it or have my arm ripped clean out of its socket. My spine screams warning, but my heart screams louder, because the young face I'm now staring up at is as unfamiliar as it is unmistakable. That's my dark skin and Notte's wide smile on a mouth Ciara got straight from her grandmother. She's at once the most beautiful person I've ever set eyes on and the most terrifying, because her eyes are as coal-red as Pharaoh's.

Sixteen years old. Sweet sixteen. She should be passing notes at school. She should be learning to drive and cheering at football games, sneaking cigarettes and lovers and beers behind her parents' back. She shouldn't be here in these wretched catacombs with Notte's two-faced cruelty and all of this hideous magic.

I reach for her with my free hand. She twists my captured arm a little further in warning, but I can't stop. I touch careful fingers to her face, feeling out the soft line of her cheek and the curve of her jaw. Her face goes in and out of focus as tears well up in my eyes, and I blink them away because I can't stand not to look at her.

"Ciara?"

Her smile twitches wider as she looks to Notte. "I do not know this one. Shall I kill her?"

Notte considers it for a moment. "Not yet, Alba. She is no threat to us yet."

"She wishes to be one," Ciara says. "I should at least chew her fingers off."

Each word is a blade sinking between my ribs. She isn't joking; she isn't making idle threats. That venom in her voice is all promise.

"Gentle," Notte says. "There will be time for that later."

Ciara hangs on a moment longer, then hauls me upright and pushes me aside. She looks to Sol and Pharaoh next, obediently acknowledging them as the larger concern. My shoulder throbs, but it's a dull ache next to the lava in my chest. I stare at Ciara while she's distracted, trying to drink in every detail. She's my height already, so I imagine she'll be nearly as tall as her father when she's done growing. She's not as thick as I am, but that has nothing to do with bone structure. I can tell by the awful way her coat hangs on her that she's at least halfway starved.

Pharaoh's coat, I realize a heartbeat later, because I've been following its twin up the west coast for nearly a week now. Notte took it from Pharaoh and gave it to Ciara to keep her safe down here. Safe from these monsters, or safe from the Brimstone retribution he had to know was coming?

"Ciara," I say again, because I need her to look at me. She is long in responding, but finally slides a bored look my way. I cradle her face in my hands and try not to think about how cold she is. "Hi, love. Do you know who I am?"

"She knows what you are," Notte says. "That is enough."

I ignore him in favor of smiling at Ciara, but my lips are trembling too much to hold the expression. "How dare you, Adam. She—"

I've made this mistake before, but I'm careless enough to make it again. Ciara's face goes slack with shock before twisting with rage, and the wrenching snap in my back is my shoulder dislocating. I scream as the world goes white and am only distantly aware of my feet scraping against the floor. Ciara uses her grip to swing me around and throw me, and I hit the wall so hard I black out for a second. Pain brings me back when I fall on my bad arm. I don't have the breath in me to scream again, so I mouth helplessly at the floor.

"What did you call him?" Ciara demands, voice shrill with fury. "I'll kill you!"

Heels snap against the floor as she strides for me, then skid to a stop, and I look back to see Notte's hand on her head. Notte's gaze is impassive as he considers me. "Really, Evelyn, you should know better by now than to name what isn't yours."

"Do not raise your hand against her," Sol says, voice still a little hoarse around the edges. "We have taken her as our charge."

Notte swivels a too-dark stare toward Sol. "You've what?"

"Why didn't you use me?" I demand, and my voice has Ciara's hateful stare snapping back my way. It breaks apart pieces of me I didn't think I still had left, and I have to close my eyes against her murderous rage. "She was just a baby, but you let her see those things. You hurt her to save yourself. Why? I was right there, and I loved you. I would have done anything for you. Why didn't you take me and spare her?"

"You are incompatible," Notte says. "I tried and failed."

"So you stole her childhood instead? Damn you."

"I did what any Nightmare would do to ensure his survival."

"Not any Nightmare," Sol insists. He attempts to sit up, but the twist at his mouth says it hurts too much. A tug at Pharaoh's knee is a silent bid for help, and Pharaoh carefully maneuvers Sol as upright as he can go. Sol waits until he's stopped swaying before continuing. "We are only allowed to have one Dream. How dare you corrupt something so sacred. You should have died when Meridian did."

Notte's expression goes impossibly cold. "A hypothetical situation for you, my self-righteous protege. If I should kill Pharaoh right here, right now, what would you do?"

Broken ribs notwithstanding, Sol is halfway to his feet before Pharaoh can stop him. Ciara strains against Notte's grip, teeth bared in a manic grin, as she readies for a fight. Notte drops his hand to the back of her neck and waits for Pharaoh to get control of Sol once more. Sol is too injured to break free of Pharaoh's tight grip, but that doesn't stop him from digging his fingernails into the backs of Pharaoh's hands.

"I would kill you," Sol spits. "I should kill you for even suggesting it."

Notte is unimpressed by Sol's anger. "But what if I did? Could you kill me without a Dream to anchor your power? You would try, certainly, but even now you know it would be hopeless. Would you commit to a futile battle and die a failure, or would you link with Evelyn to ensure my death?"

"Pharaoh is my Dream," Sol says heatedly. "I would never betray him."

"I will not share him," Pharaoh chimes in. "Not in life, not in death."

Notte slides a cool look to Pharaoh. "How selfish. You would let him join you in death just to preserve that which was no longer yours to claim? When it happens, you will be beyond knowing, so let me tell you now: I am going to make it slow. I will make it last days. I will make him beg for it just to spite your wretched memory."

Sol digs in his heels when Pharaoh tries to lunge past him. It's a weak defense at best, but his broken body can't handle Pharaoh's weight and the agonized sound he makes is more effective than a tackle at getting Pharaoh's full attention. Pharaoh comes around him instead, Notte and Ciara instantly forgotten, and catches Sol's shoulders to steady him. He whispers apologies, as afraid as he is guilty, and Sol catches his face to pull him in close.

"Stand with me," Sol reminds him, so low I almost miss it. "Please."

The desolate look on Pharaoh's face is achingly familiar. It is the haunted look of someone on the verge of losing everything, who knows there was probably something they could have done to stop things from spiraling out of control but who also understands they're long past the point to save things now.

It is the same look I saw on my bathroom mirror at Elysium every day for the first four years. Back then I still grieved Notte. I mourned his loss alongside Ciara's. I tried to figure out how I could have loved him more, what I could have said to ease his nightmares, and why I couldn't see his betrayal coming.

173

I am repulsed: by my past self, for ever accepting blame for this, and by Notte, who promises torture as easily as he once promised me the world. My hatred moves like a live wire under my skin and I cling to its energy to get to my feet.

"If you touch either one of them, I will kill you," I say.

"Try it," Ciara warns me. "I will pull you to pieces."

"Ciara? Not now, baby."

"How interesting," Notte says. He steps up alongside Ciara to give me a long look. "Looks like I was right about you after all. I knew that corruption in your power would settle in alongside his. And yet Pharaoh and Sol think they can lecture me about the sanctity of the one and only?"

"There are allowances for this atrocity," Pharaoh says without looking away from Sol.

"Convenient," Notte says.

I hold my good hand out to Ciara. "Ciara, please. Come with me. Let me take you out of here. Let me help you."

"You intend to save her from me?" Notte asks. "From me, her Nightmare? Which one of us is actually out to destroy her, Evelyn?"

"She will have to get over you."

"Don't be ignorant," Notte says. "A Dream does not revert to being human when she loses her Nightmare. She lives as a shattered remnant the rest of her life, forever aware of what she's lost. Look at your distasteful companions, would you?"

He beckons, and I can't help but follow his gesture to them. "Once Pharaoh had free will, but he destroyed it for Sol's sake. Were I to kill Sol now, Pharaoh would not rejoice in his freedom from Sol's power. He would not 'get over' Sol. He would hate me for the rest of his life—as she will hate you forever for even hinting you would hurt me."

"I'm not going to hurt you," I say. "I'm going to fucking kill you."

Notte lets go of Ciara, and she across the room faster than I can blink. She uses her body like a battering ram to throw me up against the wall again, and I scream as it jars my wrecked shoulder. Ciara catches me by the throat and hauls me back toward her, and I have only a moment to see her other fist go back for a punch. Then black fire snarls up between us and she retreats with a startled curse. I stumble, coughing for air, and look to Sol.

"Do not," Sol warns Notte again, "raise your hand against her. She is ours."

"Then she will die with you," Notte says, "just as slowly."

The catacombs shift beneath my feet. I cradle my aching arm and creep closer to Sol and Pharaoh, needing whatever protection they can offer in their battered state. The air hisses with gathering magics: hell on one side, the unforgivable ocean depths on the other. Sol called himself strongest, but everything here is stained with Notte's touch. He's had sixteen years to make the catacombs his home. More importantly, he has so much magic buried in Pharaoh that I'm surprised Pharaoh can even breathe anymore.

Notte was right—Pharaoh isn't strong enough. He feared Sol's truths enough to put his trust in Notte, and Notte in turn put a cage on Pharaoh that ensured the Brimstone pair could never fight back against him. If I don't do something, we are going to die down here. But even as I look around for a miracle option, I know there's nothing I can throw into this fight. I'm just an unmatched Dream, an untrained psychic with a ley line bound to her soul. The best weapon I have is "Rose", but if I call him that here I will destroy him and Pharaoh faster than Notte and Ciara can.

There is no chance we are walking out of here, but that doesn't stop me from reaching out to Sol. "Please, Sol. Please, don't hurt my baby."

"Shut up," Pharaoh warns me.

"Ciara," I call. "Please. *Please* come away with me."

"That is not my name," Ciara says. "Notte, are we going to kill them now?"

Notte, she calls him, as if he's not her father, as if he's never been anyone else but this hateful monster. I stare at her, then at Notte, and realization makes the world spin. It isn't Rose I need.

Notte said he tried binding with me but failed—maybe the same way I tried to bond with Sol and fell short. A key that fits but won't turn, Adelaide said. The death Dream, the snakes called me. If I am death, then it makes sense that I could steady both Sol and Notte enough to keep them alive. Death wins over everything in the end, especially in a race spawned from a dying mother. I can claim them, even if I can't keep them.

Sol asked me who named Notte Adam, and I told him the truth: Notte was Adam to my Eve. I am the only one who's ever called Notte Adam, and he is the only one who's ever called me Eve. I am Evey and Evelyn to everyone else. It is a tiny detail, insignificant in the grand scheme of things, but it is the tiny detail that matters most in this horrid new world of mine.

"Yes, Alba," Notte says, but he sounds a million miles away. "We are going to kill everyone."

I brace my feet and lift my good hand, and I trace symbols in the air as fast as I can. "I am Evelyn Notte of the fourth-tier Downey clan. Where my feet stand my territory begins. I anchor my corners on every inch of

175

Adam's skin. Any trespass across these lines is a declaration of war against me and mine. Let it be known."

I don't see anything, but I feel it. There's an ugly wrench in the air, a break in the magic boiling between Notte and Ciara, and Ciara looks positively betrayed.

"You bitch!" she shrieks. "I'll kill you first!"

Tentacles burst from the ground around my feet and grab my legs so tight I know I'm about to have them ripped off. Fire burns them away right when I start to feel a real strain in my hips, and Pharaoh redirects the flames at Notte and Ciara. Notte pulls water up in time to catch it. The fire's hot enough to evaporate the water in a heartbeat, and steam billows around the faltering Fathom pair.

Notte slowly tilts his head my way to consider me, then reaches out in front of him. He grasps open air, and before my eyes a blue cord comes to life between us. It's as jagged and brutal as the black link between Sol and myself, and my first attempt to steady its lashing has me tasting salt.

I've made a fatal mistake. By chaining Notte to me, I've chained myself to him, and he does not carry the same angry restraint Sol has practiced all this time.

"Foolish little Dream," Notte says. "Go to sleep, Eve."

I hear Sol's shouted warning, but it's already too late. The ground disappears and I fall alone into Notte's power.

I hit the ground hard enough to jar my ankles and can't keep my balance. Catching myself with both hands is instinctive, and I waste a precious second being grateful that my arm seems to be healed down here. I test the line of my shoulder, reveling in how perfectly everything fits together, and take a careful look around. This is a less dramatic scenario than Sol's dreams, and I plan on taunting Notte for his boring landscapes as soon as I figure out how to wake up again. Instead of flooding cities and the shores of hell, I am alone in a long hallway.

There's nothing to distinguish one way from another. It's just metal walls and closed doors as far as I can see in both directions, with florescent lights casting an off-white glow on everything. I go to the nearest door and test the handle, first with a cautious fingertip and then with my whole hand, but the door is locked. I try the next three with similar results, and take a minute to consider my options. Staying here is obviously out of the question, but there's no hint as to which direction I'm supposed to go from here. I check my pockets for a quarter, find the vampires' wallet, and settle for flipping a credit card.

My footsteps echo quietly down the hall as I set off in my dictated direction. I try fifteen doors before writing them off as decoration. I still can't see the end of the hall, but it's too late to turn back. For now I keep my eyes forward and revel in the temporary lack of pain.

It's a peace that can't last, I know, but it lasts long enough that I'm almost lulled to a false sense of security. When the first light flickers overhead, I don't notice it except in passing. When the next light flickers, I realize things are finally about to start changing. I glance up the buzzing light, then look back to see the hall has gone dark behind me. The overhead light goes out a few seconds later, and I pick up the pace before I'm swallowed by the darkness.

As if the hall understands my intentions, the rest of the lights go out. It's dark for a few endless heartbeats, and then those ahead of me light up crimson red. The metal halls look a hundred times more sinister as they try to reflect that ugly hue. I test the nearest wall to make sure they're not really bleeding, and in the darkness behind me there's the scrape of metal on metal. I look back, fighting to make some sense out of the inky darkness, then take off at a good trot.

Losing it will do me no good, so I hum *Sunday Morning* to keep my thoughts from spiraling out of control. It feels appropriate, somehow, to sing our wedding song here at my would-be funeral.

I'm nearly to the chorus when metal screams behind me again. My voice fails me, but it doesn't matter: somewhere in the shadows someone is singing the song back to me in a voice I don't know. It's husky and muffled to the point I can barely understand the words, but I would know that tune anywhere.

Behind me a light flicks back on, and then another, and the hall slowly comes back to life. Ten lights back is a man so tall and wide he nearly fills the hallway. He drags an ax behind him, teetering it this way and that. Every time the blade skims across the ground the metal floor squeals in warning.

My resolve to stay calm breaks. I turn and bolt, flying down the hall as fast as I can go. My arm was fine a few minutes ago, but as I run I feel the ache return, until every step I take sends pain knifing down my side. I clutch my arm to me with my good hand but refuse to slow. That thunder echoing in my ears isn't my heartbeat for once, but the stomping footsteps of the man giving chase.

A door pops open ahead of me, and I'm too close to stop. I slam into it and go wheeling into the opposite wall. Blood is hot and thick as it trails from my now-broken nose, and my tongue catches hard on the jagged edge of a front tooth. I try to blink my wits back into my scrambled brain, but by the time I think to reach for the door it has already slammed closed again. I chase after it and yank the knob, but it doesn't turn beneath my desperate pull.

Metal flashes in the corner of my eye, and I dive out of the way as the man takes a swing at me. I give up on the door and run, but now doors are opening and shutting at random ahead of me. I glance my bad shoulder off one and nearly throw up at the pain. By some dumb luck I manage to outpace one of the open doors, and I get a glimpse of stairs through the doorway. I grab the edge of the door in an attempt to pull myself back to it, but the door doesn't wait for me. It slams shut—and takes my hand with it.

I scream against the frame as my fingers are crushed. My blood looks black against the red metal, and no matter how hard I pull at the knob, I can't get the door open again. I kick at the wall, then at the man when he's close enough, but there's nowhere I can go when he takes an upward swing at me.

The edge of his ax comes up through my rib cage and slams to a stop against my collarbone. My left lung is sliced clean in two, and my crumpling ribs stab into the right one. My mouth moves—to scream, to breathe, to do anything—but my lungs are a severed mess that can't help me. The man leans in close, giving me a good look at rotted teeth, and then pulls me as hard as he can. Bones shatter and flesh shreds with a noise I hope I never hear again, and I leave my fingers behind in the doorway.

He gives a fierce flick to shake me free of his blade, and I hit the ground hard. I scrabble at my chest and abdomen, pressing ineffectual hands to the bleeding gouge he left in me. I don't want to die like this again. I can't drown again. My sanity can't handle it. I dig my fingers into my own opened chest cavity in an attempt to hold my lungs back together. My index finger touches something softer than bone and muscle, but I can't get a second finger in deep enough to get a good grip.

Ciara steps into view and crouches at my side. There is no pity to be found in her expression, just a cold rage and a colder satisfaction.

"I'm sorry," I mouth at her. "I'm sorry."

"I will not let you take him from me," she says. She pushes my hand to the floor and holds it down with a heavy heel. "Don't fight this, you useless bitch. It will all be over soon."

She presses her hands flat against the hole in my abdomen, takes a deep breath, and pulls me open.

I can't scream, but that doesn't stop me from trying. I kick and flail, but I'm in too much pain and too many pieces. All I can do is scrabble ineffectually at her shoulder as she tilts forward and buries her face in my opened middle. I feel her nose slip against my stomach and her smile against my kidneys. Inch by terrible inch she climbs inside me, and my body opens up to let her. The death I was so scared of a few minutes ago is all I wish for now, but Notte's power refuses to let me die. I can only lie there as Ciara's arms push inside of mine.

"I came with you, *Mama*," Ciara says, her voice echoing in my throat. She laughs, a wretched and gleeful sound. "Isn't that what you wanted? Aren't I a good little daughter?"

But she's not my daughter. She never was. My daughter died the moment Notte pulled her out of me in Elysium. This girl who looks too much like me and too much like him is nothing but a Dream destroyed by a Nightmare who never should have touched her. I wasn't strong enough to save her sixteen years ago; I am nowhere near strong enough to save her now. There is nothing I can do to reach her, nothing I can do to make her not hate me, and that hurts more than everything she has done to me.

I stop fighting and let myself fall.

Fingers tap an impatient beat on my face, forcing me out of sleep long before I want to be coherent again. With wakefulness comes a stabbing ache in my wrecked arm, and I groan as I force my eyes open. I'm curled up in a fetal position on bloody stone, staring at a pair of well-worn denim jeans. The air reeks of sulfur and salt, almost strong enough to turn my stomach inside out, but I've got nothing left to puke. That thought has me reaching under my shirt, and I dig my good hand into unbroken skin. It was just a dream, but that does nothing for me. My heart is so shattered it's little more than dust.

"Not going so well, I see."

I drag my stare up to see Jessica kneeling beside me. "Am I dead?" I ask, and a too-large part of me hopes the answer is yes.

"Not yet," she says.

I don't want to cry in front of her, so I look past her to the people standing at her back. "You brought friends."

"They brought themselves," she says. "The magic in the catacombs called to them, but they couldn't find a way through. I found them pacing circles outside and figured I'd show them the way. You wanted their names, right? Meet Nova."

It's the deceased Dream and Nightmare pair she followed across the wastes. Even in death the Nightmare's skin is a brilliant, untarnished silver.

"You're welcome," Jessica says. "I hate how it feels in here, so I'll wait for you at the western gate. At this rate you won't be far behind me."

I start to protest, but she's already gone.

Nova taps long fingers against her lower lip. "This is unexpected."

"Impossible, you mean," the Nova Dream says, disbelief plain on his face. "Are you a psychic or a Dream?"

"Both, unfortunately."

"What is an unmatched Dream doing alone in the catacombs?"

Alone, he says, and it finally clicks that I am not in the same room I was in before. I can feel Sol and Notte's magics still fighting, but I can't see them. Guilt over my readiness to die when they are still at Notte's mercy is enough to drive me to my feet, though I have to catch at the wall when my legs aren't ready to support me.

I blink quickly as I wait for the world to swim back into focus. It takes a moment to make sense of the magic roiling through me, but I think I can at least pinpoint the vague direction. When I set off, the Nova duo trail after me.

"Not alone," I say belatedly. "I came here with Sol and Pharaoh. The Brimstone pair," I say, when it's clear the names mean nothing to them.

Nova brightens. "So he's awake at last? We feared he'd sleep forever."

"He's awake and fighting Notte. Fathom," I add, but it's an unnecessary addition. These two know who Notte is, and they are significantly less pleased by the sound of his name.

"Impossible," the Nova Dream scoffs. "He and Meridian are long dead."

"Meridian died. Notte found a new Dream to steal."

Nova grabs for me, but her hand goes straight through me. "Do not lie to me, Dream. Nightmares cannot bond a second time. We—"

"—have a one and only," I finish for her, because I don't have time for this sanctimonious spiel right now. "Take that up with Notte when we find him. That's why we're here. Brimstone wants to execute Notte for his crimes."

"Brimstone can't take Notte in a fair fight," the Nova Dream says. "Not after that damned Dream of his—"

I don't hear the rest of the sentence, because we round the corner and find the Nightmares in question. The room has flooded, and shadow monsters chase each other through the current. Notte and Ciara stand against the far wall while Pharaoh and Sol hold the center. Sol's fire is the only thing keeping him and Pharaoh alive; it spins and burns around them so fast it evaporates the water before it can drown them.

The water is proof of Notte's ultimate betrayal, and the Nova Dream cries out in anguish. "How could he do that to Meridian?"

180

Nova laces her fingers through his and gives a fierce squeeze. "Damn him."

Tearing my eyes away from Ciara's face takes more strength than I think I have left in me. I whisper her name over and over in my head, trying to commit it to memory, trying to remember this demon as Notte's precious Alba instead of my stolen daughter. It is more agony than it is comfort, but I finally manage to face the dead pair at my side.

"Help me," I say. "Please."

"We have no power in the catacombs," Nova says. "We're dead."

"That's the point."

The dead don't dream. They don't have nightmares. Neither Brimstone nor Notte can see these ghosts, which means their power isn't a threat to them. The only one who can use these two is me.

She doesn't understand, but she looks to Notte and nods acceptance. I draw sigils on their skin and bind them to me with quiet whispers. The spell has them both flinching away from me when they realize I'm claiming them, but I refuse to look up as I add: "Let it be known this is a possession only temporarily bestowed; once they have fulfilled their promise they are free to go with no further ties to me."

It isn't much comfort, but it's too late for them to back out now. I drop my hands and face the Nova Dream. "Promise me this will save her," I say. "Promise me she'll sleep well when this is through."

He looks from me to Alba. "Her death will free her."

It is all I can ask for, and all I can do. I walk toward Sol and Pharaoh on legs that want to take me anywhere else. Snakes and sharks weave around my legs as I step right into the bubble of water. I squeeze my eyes closed and bull through the fight to the questionable safety at its center. I don't know how I'm supposed to jump through Sol's spinning fire, but I needn't have worried. He knows I'm here because his creatures know I'm here, and a dark hand plunges into the water to help pull me through to his side.

Pharaoh looks like he's seen a ghost. "How the fuck did you wake up on your own?"

I have no answers, so I just shake my head and watch the Nova pair stride past me. If I close my eyes a little too long I can see every line I've cast in here: the pale gray ties to these ghosts, the jagged black wire binding me to Sol, and the electric blue line that leads me to Notte. I seize the last in an iron grip and pull as hard as I can.

"Damn you, Adam, you're mine."

The link between him and Alba shatters a second time, and the water bubble around us bursts to flood the room to our knees. Fire spikes up to the ceiling without enough water to press against, but Sol calls it back with a quick curl of his fingers. I feel Pharaoh's heavy stare on me, but when I open my eyes I look to Nova. She reaches Notte a second later and plants both hands against his chest. For a fearful moment I think it isn't going to work, but then she shoves—and Notte crashes into the wall at his back.

She is dead, and he is no psychic, but they are both bound to me. That makes all the difference in the end. I am a linchpin; it is what Notte made me when he left me behind sixteen years ago and it is what will destroy him now.

Alba takes a quick step toward Notte, eyes wild as her connection to Notte spirals out of control a second time. "Notte? Notte!"

The Nova Dream digs his fingers into Notte's wrist, and Alba is thrown into the far wall by Notte's power. Her coat protects her from getting hurt, but she's jarred enough to fall to her knees, and she takes a second to catch her breath.

"Sol," I say. My voice threatens to fail me; my lips twist and pull in sobs I can't afford to give into yet. My mouth moves once, twice, but I can't get the words out. The best I can manage is a strangled, "Please."

"Pharaoh," Sol says.

Pharaoh is across the room in a heartbeat. He picks Alba up by her throat and slams her against the wall. Notte's magic gives a vicious roil, but I hold onto it with everything I have, and it succeeds only in tearing my fingers. I won't be able to restrain him a second time, but he'll never get that chance. Pharaoh's got his free hand inside Alba's coat, flat against her chest, and I feel the backlash of his power as he chars her heart. Alba's eyes go wide a second before her body goes horribly limp. When Pharaoh lets go of her, she falls to her knees like an abandoned puppet.

Notte's magic implodes, but Sol doesn't wait for his power to eat him. He hurls black flame at Notte's body and watches him burn alive. I smell blackening flesh and hear Notte's agonized screams. I feel the crackle of our bond breaking apart, and the quieter splintering of my bonds to the dead pair who saved us.

I should watch Notte die just to make sure it sticks this time, but I can't. I don't care. All I care about is a beautiful girl who didn't live long enough to be human. As I watch, her body slowly sags to one side. She sinks beneath the waves and comes to a slow stop against the rocky ground.

I start screaming, and I don't know if I will ever stop.

EPILOGUE

I wake to wind chimes and blue skies. Sun catchers in the window cast colorful shards of light across the bedspread. The spelled incense my mother lit last night to help me sleep is little more than a pile of pale ash on the nightstand, but the hint of spices linger in the air. I inhale as deeply as I can, trying to soak up whatever's left of that calming magic. It helps in that it keeps me from having a panic attack. It doesn't make me any less desperate to stop breathing.

The mattress shifts a little behind me, and I know what woke me up. I ease onto my back and stare up at my mother's calm face. She hasn't changed much in the last sixteen years, aside from a few more gray patches in her hair, but there is a new iron in her grip that was never there before. Consequence of an unending war, perhaps: my mother has forgotten how to be soft. She buried me sixteen years ago, only to have me return bleeding and broken to her life. A temporary resurrection, she and I both know, because I am an unmatched Dream and the war marches on.

"Did I do the right thing?" I ask, searching her face for reassurances she's given me a hundred times already. Maybe at a hundred and one I will believe her.

"Come downstairs," she says. "There's tea in the kettle and brunch on the stove."

I don't want to get up, but somehow I manage, and I follow her downstairs. We pass through the dining room, where the home's owners are hunched over a map. They glance up as we go by but say nothing to either one of us. They're too busy arguing logistics. We hold Madtown, or so my mother told me yesterday, but keeping it is another story. They want to send more of the Guard south as reinforcements. She doesn't say they want to send me and my keepers, but I can see it in every lingering glance her colleagues send my way.

Sol and Pharaoh are standing at the stove, poking warily at the contents of a frying pan. Sol hasn't bothered with a shirt yet, so I have a good view of his bandages. Healers can't snap their fingers and make everything better, but they can at least kick the process into overdrive, and having Gaia on our side is the best medicine anyone could ask for. My own injuries are little more than bruises and scabs now, but it's not those aches that are poisoning me from the inside out.

"Whose idea was it to let them cook?" Casper asks from her perch on the kitchen counter. She just got in last night, summoned straight from Madtown by the biggest circle I've ever seen my mother cast, and she wasted no time at all in making herself comfortable. "I hope you like having toast for breakfast again."

"I'm sure it's fine," my mother says, but obediently goes over to inspect the damage. Her silence is telling, and at length she says, "I'm always in the mood for jelly toast. What about you, Evey?"

I don't want toast. I don't want anything. I want to sleep a dreamless sleep and never wake up. This is not something I can or will say aloud, though, so I just open the fridge and stare numbly in at the contents. I've already forgotten what I'm looking for, or if I was looking for anything at all. I should close the fridge again and walk away, but my body doesn't move until a too-hot hand takes hold of my wrist.

"Evelyn," Sol says.

His voice grounds me the way nothing else can, and I step out of the way. "I'm not hungry."

"Evey," my mother starts.

"Evelyn," Sol says again, but now he looks past me to the closed kitchen door. "They're here."

I stare blankly back at him, but then every ward built into the house shudders in alarm. Floral curtains cover the window on the kitchen door, but I see a shadow fall across it a second before someone raps imperiously on the glass. Pharaoh is closest, but the hard curl of his lip says he's in no hurry to answer. My mother has no choice but to let our unexpected guests in, and I understand Pharaoh's reticence as soon as Mom gets the door.

The woman in the doorway is impossibly black, like the abyss has been given human form, and towers over my mother in six-inch heels. My mother gives ground to her immediately, and the stranger crosses the room toward Sol. A second woman steps through the doorway not far behind her, and her red gaze swivels straight from Pharaoh to me.

"Wrath," Sol says, with all the warmth of an iceberg.

"Brimstone," the Nightmare returns as she stops right in front of him. "How nice of you to join us again, and what quick work you've made of things. Here we thought you were too fond of Notte's shackles to ever break free of them. I would say we underestimated you, but perhaps it was only chance on your side."

"We would like to believe otherwise," her Dream says, but there's

184

more mockery in her voice than encouragement. "We cannot afford for you to be rusty. We need you now more than ever."

"And her." Wrath tips her head toward me. "We are taking her off your hands."

"She is not yours to take."

"You do not deserve her," Wrath says. She starts to turn my way, but Sol takes a careful step to stand between us. Wrath puts a warning finger to his throat and taps along to his heartbeat. "Step aside."

"I will not give her to you."

"You do not have to," Wrath says, and there is no mistaking the quiet threat in her words. "I am willing to take her from you by force. I found the Nightmare, so she comes with me."

"Let them have her, Sol," Pharaoh says. "Maybe she'll kill them too."

"Tempting," Sol returns, "but we need them alive for now."

"Ah, but you don't know yet," Pharaoh says when the Wrath Dream casts a sidelong look at him. "Did you really think we were the ones to kill Notte? All we had to do was land the finishing blow."

"Your lies are as weak as your spine," the Wrath Dream says. "An unmatched Dream is no threat to anyone."

"Her next slight against Pharaoh will be her last," Sol tells Wrath. "Muzzle her if you want to keep her."

"Do not threaten my Dream," Wrath warns him.

"I'm not," Sol says, with a cold smile that's all violent promise.

"Enough," I say, sharp enough that both Nightmares look at me. I point to Sol first, then swivel my finger to Wrath. "You: do not start a fight in this house. It's not ours, and I am not cleaning up behind you. You: shut the fuck up. I am not an object to be passed around. I am not going anywhere with you. Say what you came here to say and get out."

"You are a fool," Wrath says. "They will ruin you as surely as they ruined themselves."

My smile threatens to tear my face in two. "There is nothing left to ruin."

Wrath stares me down an endless minute, then gives in with a disgusted noise and gestures to the kitchen doorway. "Go, then, and try her on for size. If you are going to claim her, do it now. If you are not, then we will be on our way. We've got places to be and cities to conquer."

I look from her to the doorway, then back to Sol. "Do not let them take me."

"I will kill them first," Sol promises.

It's hollow comfort, but it's all that helps me cross the room. I step outside and find the pair from Olympia waiting on the lawn. They know what I'm looking for and point to the car parked at the curb. There's a small figure sitting on the trunk, rocking so hard it's a wonder she doesn't tip off and break her neck on the asphalt. Hands are knotted in hair that hasn't been brushed in a week at least, and she's mumbling a terrified prayer in Russian.

I stop in front of her but can't get a good look at her face through her hair. I reach out and take careful hold of her shoulders, and as soon as I touch her I know Wrath was right. This child belongs to me the way Sol and Notte never could. Her death-cold magic feels the same way mine does as it seeps into my skin.

Sol warned me my Nightmare would be a child, but that does not make her any easier to look at. It is too soon to have another daughter thrust on me when Alba's death still haunts my every waking moment. A part of me wants to turn around and walk away like I always said I would. A louder part is violently relieved to have this frightened child fall into my waiting arms. Sol promised I would stop caring about my human life when I found my Nightmare. Since I can't lie down and die here in Seattle, the next best thing is to stop feeling. It feels like a savage betrayal of Alba's memory, but it is the only way I know out of this suffocating darkness.

"Hey," I say. My voice hitches, and I clear my throat. "It's going to be all right now."

It tastes like a lie even as I say it, because how the hell is any of this supposed to be all right? I'm a Dream who communes with the dead, and she's a child who's a Nightmare. We are children of a dying god and foot soldiers in a war we didn't ask for. But then she finally tips her head to look at me, and the world gives a sharp tilt out of focus. The only thing I see, the only thing that matters, is the upturned face before me.

My life ends with haunted blue eyes and small hands reaching out for something to hang onto.

My life has just begun.

Acknowledgments

More people have helped me hold onto this project than there are stars in the sky, from the tightknit WK circle to the Courting Madness lovelies. Mad props to Jyn, Jill, and Z for trying to make something legible of it, and to my sister who read it and threw it at me with alarming aim. A million thanks to KM Smith for taking the world's vaguest description and creating a cover so beautiful I can't believe it's mine.

24119372R00114